RETURN TO WILLOW FALLS

MATT BANNISTER WESTERN 7

KEN PRATT

Published in the United States by Wolfpack Publishing, Las Vegas

CKN Christian Publishing
An Imprint of Wolfpack Publishing
6032 Wheat Penny Avenue
Las Vegas, NV 89122

christiankindlenews.com

Paperback ISBN: 978-1-64734-162-6
eBook ISBN: 978-1-64734-161-9
Library of Congress Control Number: 2020932886

RETURN TO WILLOW FALLS

Prologue

Prologue
Portland, Oregon
1883

Floyd Bannister looked at his reflection in the mirror and squeezed his lips together as a thin layer of moisture covered his tired, blue eyes. His hair had turned silver over the years, and his well-groomed goatee had long before his hair did. The lines on his face seemed to double in the past year or two. He was no longer the handsome young man with a golden future that he used to be. It was strange how fast life could pass a person by one day at a time, year by year without realizing how much time had slipped by. One day he was a young newlywed just starting his life out as the heir to a dynasty his father had built over in Jessup County. He had one of the largest cattle ranches in Oregon handed over to him free and clear. He was the heir to various properties his father had bought, and other investments in the county that had made his father a wealthy man. Floyd, at one time, owned it all and had a beautiful young wife as well. She was a halfbreed Indian and more beautiful than any sunset he had ever seen. Her name was Ruth Fasana, and they were happy, in love, and their future promised to be one of ease and comfort. Floyd had employees who ran the day to day business of the ranch, and all he had to do was make the decisions and enjoy the life they were blessed to have. He had it all, and he let it all slip away.

Drinking and gambling had become a favored pastime at first, but it ended up costing him far more than his inheritance. There was nothing left of what Floyd's father had built in his lifetime. Floyd wasn't a stupid man, but he had a weakness that took over, and it had become a lifestyle that he hated on the one hand and too weak to give up on the other. He had it all; everything that a man could dream of was in his hands. A beautiful wife pregnant with their sixth child, five healthy sons, a beautiful home, wealth, and a thriving ranch to keep going for generations. He could have given his children an inheritance and a legacy to be proud of. He could have if he made better decisions and been a stronger man.

He had no reason to be an angry young man, but he was. Hindsight was a cruel monster when it comes in focus. Regret is such a heavy burden that it becomes a killer of the soul, an anvil tied to the past that exhausts a person over time and leaves them an empty shell of who they once were. Floyd looked in the mirror and still looked distinguished after all these years with his silver hair combed straight back and groomed goatee on his handsome oblong face. The burden of his past weighed heavily upon his brow. A man can smile, but it doesn't hide the sadness revealed in a man's eyes. The combination of regret and shame mixed together like lead bricks and made a man's path burdensome to travel.

He had many regrets during his younger years, but one Floyd had never been able to come to terms with was when he took his five sons and new infant daughter to his sisters-in-law's house and abandoned them there. It was a long time ago and far away, but the memory still haunted him. Floyd had never been a strong man nor all too responsible. Ruth was his backbone that held him together, and when she was gone, he packed up his children and hauled them out to the Big Z Ranch and left them for Ruth's sister Mary and her husband, Charlie Ziegler to raise. Floyd sold what was left of his property and left Jessup County for good in search of a new territory where no one knew who he was. He wanted to get lost in a world of self-pity and alcohol abuse to cover the pain and be able to laugh. He found an abundance of all he wanted in Portland, a city where he could drink and gamble all night and day if he wanted to. He lived off the money from his property sales, and when the money ran out, he then got a job at a small tavern. Keeping a job was a hard thing to do when he was drunk a good portion of the time, but there was always another tavern, bar or saloon that would hire him.

Now, twenty-eight years later, saloons had become his life. He had worked his way to a manager position at The Silver Casterlin Saloon in downtown Portland near the waterfront of the Willamette River. It was one of the largest saloons in Portland. It was on the ground floor of a four-story apartment building. As luck would have it, the owner of the building hired Floyd's second wife, Rhoda, to manage the apartments while Floyd managed the saloon. They lived in a nice two-bedroom apartment on the fourth floor of the building where they could keep watch over the tenants and the saloon.

Floyd washed his aging face with water from a bowl below the mirror and combed his silver hair straight back. He sighed deeply and wiped his eyes as he grabbed a dingy cloth towel to dry his face. The thought occurred to him how disappointed his mother would be in him if she could see him now. His father would shake his head in disgust and shame. Floyd squeezed his lips together and forced the thought away from him. Despite his success as a manager, he knew he was a failure. He tossed the towel down and stepped over to their davenport and sat down heavily.

Rhoda looked at him curiously. "What's wrong with you?"

"Nothing. It's Ruth's birthday," he said softly.

Rhoda frowned. "Well, that was a long time ago. You shouldn't be thinking of her anyway, what you should be thinking about is what you failed to get me for my birthday. It's been three months, and you still haven't got me that necklace I wanted."

Floyd smirked slightly. "I'm thinking about maybe going back to Jessup County to see my kids and grandchildren..."

"No way! The last time you went over there, you were gone for nearly a month on some wild goose chase to see Matt, and I won't let you lose this job because of that. We finally have a decent place to live and some money hidden away. I won't let you waste it to go see your son you probably won't find anyway!" Rhoda was in her late fifties and overweight. She had dark brown hair with heavy streaks of gray held up in a bun on top of her round face. She had a narrow nose above her full lips and large blue eyes that had hardened over time. At one time, she worked the saloons as a prostitute but found a way out of the profession by becoming a bartender before meeting Floyd. "Floyd, I don't mean to be rude, but if your kids wanted to see you, they'd take the time to write a quick note at least, but they don't. They don't want to see you. You left them, Floyd. Leave it at that. Besides, now you have my kids, Robert and Maggie."

If she had been paying attention, she would have seen the layer of moisture that filled his eyes as she spoke. He looked away towards a window and their view of the river. He tried to force the moisture away. "Matt's in Branson now. He has a Marshal's Office in Branson," he said quietly.

"He does?" she asked with interest and a touch of excitement in her voice. "You should have said so! We can save up to make that trip, Floyd, but I'm going with you this time. I've always wanted to meet your family. It's about time we get to know them. We just can't afford for you to go looking for him again. How old is Matt?"

Floyd's eyebrows narrowed with a bit. "Oh, I don't know, probably around thirty-five maybe. He was seven when I left. So yeah, thirty-five years old. My gosh, I haven't seen him since he was seven. No, nine. I visited the kids when Matt was about nine. I went back to visit with my children about eighteen years ago when Matt was around seventeen or so but didn't get to talk to him. I was drunk and he didn't want to talk to me. He went back inside the house after a few words, and I was run off the Big Z Ranch by my former brother-in-law. I don't count that one." The sadness showed on his face as he thought about how many years had slipped past. "So, it's been twenty-six years since I've seen my son. Maybe you're right, Rhoda. Maybe I should leave them well enough alone."

"No, I think we should go. I want to meet your family and especially Matt. And we'll take Maggie with us. Wouldn't it be wonderful if those two fell in love right away like we did?" She chuckled slightly. "Do you think Matt will find her attractive?"

Floyd shrugged. "I couldn't tell you. I don't know him, Rhoda."

"It's about time you get to know him then. Hey Maggie," she yelled towards a back room where Maggie was getting dressed. "We're going to take a trip over to Branson to meet Floyd's family, including Matt Bannister, the Marshal. And you're going with us and don't argue with me about that! When do you think we should plan on going? We have to save up because it's going to cost a lot to travel there. I'm sure Floyd's kids will let us stay with them."

The bedroom door opened, and a slim, dark-haired lady stepped out wearing brown canvas pants and a thick flannel shirt. She worked at a butcher shop and was told not to wear a dress to work due to the nature of the business. The owners didn't think a lady should get blood on her dress. Maggie had her dark brown hair tied in a ponytail, her green eyes looked at Floyd with surprise. Her face was triangular shaped with a nice smile. "Are you really going to see your family?"

"Thinking about it," he answered.

"You should."

"Of course, he is! And we're going with him. I want to know when we should go, though. What do you think, Maggie?"

She shrugged. "I don't know. I didn't know I was going."

"You are! We're going to introduce you to Matt and watch the love grow." She laughed. "You're the same age as him."

"Oh, Ma. I doubt he would be interested in me. Anyway, I have to get to work. I have a bunch of sausages to make this morning. I'll bring some home tonight."

"When should we go, Maggie?" Rhoda pressed.

Maggie looked at Floyd. "How many years has it been since you've had all your kids around you at once?"

His eyes widened as he thought back. "Close to thirty years. The day I dropped them off at their Aunt and Uncles, twenty-eight years ago," he said shamefully.

"Well, it's now September. It will take some time to save up enough money to go, so maybe Thanksgiving? Families usually get together for Thanksgiving, don't they? You should write to them and plan it. I have to go. Bye."

Rhoda smiled. "Thanksgiving. Yes, that will work great. Matt will fall in love with Maggie when he tastes her turkey and for sure, when he tries her mincemeat pie."

"Ma, don't even think about it!" Maggie warned as she left the apartment and closed the door behind her.

Floyd took a deep breath anxiously. "Thanksgiving, huh? Think they'll mind us being there?"

"Of course not! When Matt sees Maggie, he's going to fall in love, and that's all I care about."

1

Albert Bannister wore gray canvas jeans and a patched up blue flannel shirt under his brown wool coat. He was a big man with broad shoulders with a short thick neck with a well-manicured beard on his square-shaped face and had dark bushy hair that fell below his ears. Albert was older than Matt and owned the largest blacksmith shop in Jessup County and had contracts with the silver mine and the timber mill for various services. He scratched his forehead with a questionable smile as he said, "Mellissa's a little mad at me because we were going to butcher the turkey for Thanksgiving, but my new dog got a hold of it and killed our turkey. I had to bury it this morning. I guess we're not having that fat turkey for dinner on Thanksgiving, after all."

"So, why's Mellissa mad at you about that? It's not your fault, is it?" Matt Bannister asked. He was sitting behind his desk in his private office at the U.S. Marshal's Office. Like his brother, Matt kept a well groomed beard, but had long dark hair that he kept in a ponytail most of the time. He was a bit taller and had the same broad chest and muscular build, but was leaner than Albert.

"Well," Albert explained slowly, "I didn't exactly tell her I got a new dog to begin with. It was expensive for a dog." He frowned and seemed hesitant to continue. "It's a Red Tick Hound dog. It's not mean, but it sure howled like a bat out of hell last night and mauled the turkey this morning. I wouldn't have minded the rooster getting mauled as much, because about the time the dog stopped, the rooster started in. Anyway, Mellissa found out about it last night, and by this morning, she was furious and... Do you want a dog?"

Matt laughed. "No, I don't want a dog!"

"I'm sure my neighbors don't either."

"I bet not. A dollar says Steven will take it," Matt said of their younger brother Steven, who lived in Willow Falls. "I don't think he could say no."

"I don't think his wife will let him keep it. Adam's my best bet if I can't find anyone else to take it. I'll have to bring the thing inside tonight to keep it quiet, but then Mellissa's going to be upset because she doesn't want a dog in the house. It's used to sleeping inside, apparently."

Matt smiled. "Whatever happened to the 'it's easier to ask for forgiveness from your wife than permission' philosophy you told me about?"

Albert frowned. "There are apparently some exceptions to that rule, and this is one. The first exception is never expect good results when it comes to a dog; your wife doesn't know about."

Matt laughed. "Albert, my jail is nearly sound-proof. If you want to, you can put your dog in there tonight to save your marriage. But by tomorrow you'll have to find it a new home. I can't let the town know that I'm holding dogs for noise control, or I'll become known as the local dog stable when there's a noise complaint. And trust me, if that got out, there would be many complaints about noisy dogs all of a sudden."

"I'd appreciate it. And Mellissa will appreciate it too."

"Thanksgiving is Thursday. You are going to the Big Z, right?"

"Yeah, we were bringing the turkey this year. That's why Mellissa was so upset about it being killed. It was supposed to be butchered out at the Big Z. Now, we'll have to buy one somewhere to take out there, but it won't be as big as the one we raised."

The front door opened abruptly by the sound of the cowbell ringing loudly. Robert Fasana stepped into the office visibly upset. "Matt!" he yelled, "Where's Matt?" he asked the deputy Phillip For-rester who sat behind his desk near the door.

"Can I help you?" Phillip asked, standing quickly to stop the man from walking through the gate of the partition separating the front from the interior of the office. Phillip Forrester was a medium height young man with light brown neatly combed short hair. He kept his oblong face cleanly shaved and had a friendly smile that greeted people when they entered the Marshal's Office.

"Where's Matt?" Robert asked forcefully.

Matt stepped out of his office. "It's okay, Phillip, he's my cousin. Come on back, Robert. What's the matter?"

"Sheriff Wright arrested three of my men for the murder of that guy hanging over our quarry, remember him? He arrested three of my men for that!"

"What?" Matt asked with surprise. "Who did he arrest?"

"Ah See, my lead china-man. Chee Yik and Kot-Kho-Not. They were the first ones to find that man hanging on our derrick that morning and are now in jail for murdering him! They didn't touch that man, they found him and came and got me, and I went and got you. I need those men at the quarry. They're all fine stonemasons and we're already behind schedule. Can you get them out of jail for me? The Sheriff refused to let me get them out of there."

Matt stared at his cousin with a growing agitation on his face. He knew the three quarry employees were innocent, and he knew the Sheriff, Tim Wright, knew that as well. The Sperry-Helms Gang had hung Pick Lawson on the derrick and left him hanging over the quarry with a note nailed into his chest that had been written in Chinese. Tim Wright had lied on his final report to stay on the outlaw gang's good side. Matt nodded. "Yeah, I'll speak to the Sheriff right now. Those guys didn't hang Pick, and Tim knows it."

"Yeah, well, you know how little people think of

Chinese folks, and I'm afraid they'll be lynched for it. Then we're out three skilled stonemasons. I need them, Matt. I can't communicate with our Chinese without Ah See." Robert wore a clean blue suit, though it was old and seen better days. He was the son of Joel Fasana and had worked in the granite quarry all of his life. Robert Fasana knew every aspect of the business and was now the manager of the Fasana Granite Quarry. Their uncle Luther was the only person Robert couldn't tell what to do and could override him now that Joel had retired. Their uncle Luther continued to work as a stonemason only because he wanted to. Robert had taken control of the company and spent his days behind a desk overseeing the whole operation. He was the exact opposite of his brother, William. Robert had a dedicated drive to do the job mentality while William hated physical labor. They didn't even look alike. William had long blonde hair and a goatee while Robert looked like a businessman with short light brown hair combed neatly and kept a clean-shaven face. Unlike William, Robert was far more serious-minded and direct.

"I'll take care of it," Matt said with a slight shake of his head.

The Branson City Sheriff, Tim Wright, wasn't surprised to see the U.S. Marshal, Matt Bannister, step into his office. He knew Robert Fasana had run to his cousin for help when he had left the Sheriff's Office. "Hello, Matt. What can I do for you?" Tim asked in a friendly manner, though underneath of his tone was a hint of his bitterness towards the Marshal.

Matt sat down in the chair across the desk from him. "What do you think you're doing?"

Tim looked at two of his deputies who were in the office and said, "Boys, go patrol the town so I can talk with Marshal Bannister alone for a bit." He waited for his deputies to step outside. He looked at Matt and spoke sarcastically, "I don't understand."

"Really? We both know those three men didn't do anything. You have no reason to hold them here." He nodded to the three Chinese locked up in one of the two jail cells in the main office.

Tim took a deep breath and raised his hands innocently as he explained, "The evidence points to them. They were the only Chinese around Pick's body, and we have the note written in Chinese. We know Pick crossed the leader of one of those Chinese groups that run Chinatown. , I don't know much about the Chinese, but I hear they identify that group as a Tong, , whatever that is. . Anyway, they hung him for it, and these three china men did the hanging for them. Normally, I wouldn't care what the Chinese do to each other, but they hung a white man, and that makes all the difference."

Matt glared at Tim harshly. "You're willing to see three innocent men hang or sentenced to prison because you're afraid of the Sperry-Helms Gang?"

"Chinese, not men."

"They are men!" Matt shouted. "It doesn't matter if they're Chinese, Japanese, Black, Brown, Red, or Pink! Let those men go and leave them alone. I won't let you get away with framing innocent men to cover your cowardice. If you want to lie and say Pick escaped on his own, fine. But I will not allow you to harm these three men. Now let them go."

"What are you, Matt, a Chinese lover?"

Matt stood up quickly and leaned over Tim's desk. "One more snide remark, and I'll knock that grin right off your face! I told you before the corruption is ending in this town. If that's too hard for you, then step down and let someone who dares to do the job take over. Because quite frankly, I think you're weak, a liar, and a coward. Now, to save your pretty face from embarrassment, I suggest you let them go and say you made a mistaken identity before the truth comes out. And it will because I'll tell the truth."

"Matt, you don't understand. If I don't arrest someone, it's going to be an unsolved murder, and I can't have that. But like I told you before, I'm not going to tangle with the Sperry-Helms Gang. I'm not going to die because they hung one of their gang members. What do I care? But I have to arrest someone."

Matt grimaced. "How many innocent men have you framed?"

"None!"

"I don't believe that. We should be working together more often than not, but it seems like I'm always fighting you. That tells me everything I need to know about you. I would love to go to the city council and get you fired, but I know it won't do any good. You all have a tight little club going on here until the next election anyway. Trust me; I'll be petitioning to get you all out of office. But for now, unlock that door and let those men go!"

Tim stared at Matt momentarily and then opened his top drawer and pulled out the key to the jail door. He walked over and opened the door. "Get out of here," he said irritably.

Ah See bowed towards Matt and thanked him in English before leaving the building.

"There," Tim said. "Are you happy? You know you talk about cleaning up the so-called corruption, but you're the one who just blackmailed me. I suppose that makes you a bit of a corrupted hypocrite, doesn't it?"

Matt shook his head and chuckled softly. "Corruption never does what's right, Tim. Leave those men alone," he warned and walked out of the door.

2

Floyd Bannister arrived in Branson and stepped out of the stagecoach. It had been a long trip in a crowded compartment with his wife Rhoda, step-daughter Maggie, and three others who were traveling further eastward. Floyd stretched his back and bent his knees to get his joints moving after the long uncomfortable ride. They had been able to save up enough money to travel by steamboat from Portland to Walla Walla, Washington, and rode a stagecoach for three and a half days to reach Branson. He looked to the west towards the mountains with a faraway look in his eyes.

Maggie noticed and asked, "So does this feel like home, Floyd?" They had passed by the old Bannister Ranch homestead, and after talking about it, he had grown quite sad as the stagecoach drove through the valley.

He nodded his head slowly. "It was much smaller when I lived over here. The mountains are the same, though. Do you see that peak standing up like a thumb way over there? That's Pillar Rock and right down below it, is Lake Jessup. We had a beautiful cabin up there on the lake. I sold it to my friend Clyde Waltz when I left here. I wish I would've kept it, though. It was beautiful in the summertime."

"I bet," Maggie said, looking at the mountains. "So, where's this hotel we're staying at? I've been freezing this whole trip. A bath, some good food, and a comfortable bed would be great."

"My son, Lee, owns the hotel. We'll go check-in, and then I'll introduce you to my boys."

When they arrived at the four-story granite block building with red decorative brick arches around all the windows and doorways, the doors had brass handles and kick plates with large glass windows. Inside the walls, support posts and grand stairway were all paneled mahogany. The Oak floors were clean and waxed to a fine shine that reflected the light from the crystal chandeliers. There was a restaurant that offered the delicious scent of fresh-baked bread mixed with apple pie, and maybe a hint of pork chops mixing in the air like a salad of pleasing aromas. It filled their senses and caused their stomachs to grumble for a filling meal. Rhoda gasped at the beauty of the entrance hall, which was stunning to her. "Your son owns this?"

Floyd smiled slightly like a proud father. "Lee does, yeah. Well, let's get checked in, and then we can get something to eat."

Rhoda looked at the lunch special advertised on a paper on the door. "I don't think we can afford to eat here, Floyd."

He approached a curved reception desk where a woman in her forties stood in an attractive dress and a waiting smile. "Can I help you?" she asked.

"Yeah, I'm here to check-in. My name is Floyd Bannister. I'm Lee's father."

"Oh! Very good," she said with a friendly smile. "Well, Mister Bannister, would you like one or two rooms? We do have rooms with two beds, and some with two bedrooms?"

"Yeah, that's what I want. One with two bedrooms. Also, we'll need three baths, and do you still offer laundry services?"

"We do. Well, Mister Bannister, that will be twenty-six dollars. Twenty for the room for one night, and six for the baths. Laundry services are another three dollars per person if you want your laundry done. And I applied the twenty-five percent family and friend discount."

Floyd shook his head. "No, Lee told me I could stay here for free anytime I came to town. Meals and laundry are free too."

The lady grimaced. "Um...I applied the discount we have, and unless Lee says so, I can't give you a free room or meal tickets."

Floyd smiled patiently. "Young lady, we're tired, dirty, and hungry. We just got here from Portland, and I'd appreciate a room so we can get cleaned up. Certainly, Lee can clear this up later today."

She shook her head. "I'm sorry. I'm taking your word that you're who you say you are, so I gave you the discount. Aside from that, I can't give you one of our better rooms for free. I'm sorry."

Rhoda glared at the lady. "This is Lee's father! Now give us a room before I get you fired! I'm Lee's step-mother, and I will not stand here and be treated like this in my son's own hotel!" she spoke loudly.

"I'm sorry. But if you're going to yell, I'm going to ask you to leave."

"I'm not leaving!" Rhoda yelled. "Now, give us our room!"

"Ma'am. I'll call security…"

"Rhoda…" Floyd said softly to calm her down.

"Call them!" Roda shouted. "And why you're at it have them go fetch my son so I can have my room! And we're staying through Thanksgiving, not just one night," she spat out bitterly with her eyes glaring at the lady behind the desk.

"I'm sorry, ma'am, I can't give you a room without my manager's approval." She reached behind her and pulled a string that rang a bell that they could hear slightly.

"Are you calling your manager? Where's your manager?" Rhoda shouted.

"Rhoda, it's okay. We'll get it straightened out. She's just doing her job," Floyd said easily.

"You're making a scene, Ma," Maggie said, sounding embarrassed.

A door opened behind them, and William Fasana stepped into the entry with a serious expression on his face. "What's going on?" he asked. His gun belt was around his waist even though he wore a new gray suit and looked like a businessman except for his long wavy blonde hair falling onto his shoulders and goatee.

"This couple wants a free double room for a..."

His brow creased when he saw Floyd. "Uncle Floyd?"

"I don't...Willy?" Floyd asked with a surprised smile.

William laughed. "I go by William nowadays. How the heck are you?" he asked and went to shake Floyd's hand and then hugged him quickly. "I haven't seen you since I was a kid. What are you doing here?"

"Um, trying to get a room for a few days. We're here for Thanksgiving."

"Of course. Pamela, there's no charge. Put them on the second floor in a double room and whatever else they want. This is Lee's father, my uncle, Floyd. Do your boys know you're here?"

Floyd shook his head. "No. I was hoping to talk to Matthew. Do you know where I could find him?"

"Of course. He's probably at his office. It's just down the street a few blocks."

"I'm your aunt Rhoda," she said bluntly and put her hand out to shake his. "Who are you, and how are we related?"

William stared at her awkwardly. "Well, that is a good question! Who are you, and how are we related?" He looked at Floyd. "Your wife?"

"Of course, I'm his wife! You're Willy?" Rhoda asked irritably.

"No, it's William. William Fasana. I'm Floyd's nephew. He was married to my Aunt Ruth before she passed away. She was really nice, to say the

21

least. Well, nice to meet you, Rhoda. And who's this?" he nodded at Maggie.

"That would be my daughter, Maggie. We're going to introduce her to Matt. I think he'll take to her like a bee to honey, don't you?" Rhoda asked with a smile.

William raised his eyebrows noticeably. "A love connection, huh? Well, we're a metropolitan community, you know? Kind of like a city."

A puzzled expression formed on Rhoda's face.

William continued, "The whole family thing. I've heard of it in rural areas, and I even met a young man real recently who I thought might be the product of it. But I don't know..."

Floyd chuckled quietly.

"What?" Rhoda asked with a slightly bitter taste in her tone.

William waved his hands in the air in front of her face to erase his previous words. "I'll make this simple for you. I don't think it's a good idea to try to make a love connection between Matt and his new sister. People talk, you know?" William said seriously with a slight glimmer in his eye.

"They're not related!" she burst out.

"Dear Aunt Rhoda, you said it, not me."

"I said nothing of the sort!" she protested with a healthy dose of hostility.

"Aunt Rhoda, you did. You said you were my aunt Rhoda, right? That would make Maggie, my cousin, and that would make her Matt's sister... wait, are you from Prairieville?"

"I don't know what you're talking about! But you

are getting on my nerves, and I've heard enough. Give me the key to my room! Floyd, let's go," she said, taking the key from the lady behind the counter. "Where's the room?" she asked rudely.

Upstairs on the second floor to your right," Pamela answered.

"Good day!" she said to William and began walking towards the grand staircase.

"William, I'll talk to you soon, I hope," Floyd said as he carried their travel case towards the stairs.

"I'll get that for you, Uncle Floyd. I want to talk to Aunt Rhoda some more," he said loudly.

"No. I don't want to talk to you!" she sneered.

William laughed. "I'm sorry Uncle Floyd, I couldn't help it. She's just too much fun."

"You're funny," Maggie said as she passed by him.

"Thank you, cousin Maggie. Since you're in town, we might as well go for a wagon ride or something, right? I haven't seen you in forever. We should catch up."

She smiled slightly. "Maybe."

"Watch out, William, she's a butcher," Floyd offered.

"You must be good with knives, then?"

She paused on the stairs and leaned against the rail to look down at him. "Pretty good."

"Well, I'm not too bad with my guns either, so between us, we shouldn't have to worry about meeting any highwaymen along the way. Let Aunt Rhoda know that in case she worries. I'll go rent a carriage and show you around, what do you say?"

"Are you serious?" she asked skeptically.

He spoke loudly to be heard by Rhoda as she reached the second-floor hallway, "You've known me forever, cousin Maggie. Of course, I am serious." He smirked in anticipation.

"She's not your cousin! Geez, Floyd, what is wrong with your relatives?" she asked irritably.

"So, you're not serious?" Maggie asked to clarify.

"No, I am serious. Let's say in an hour?"

"Make it two hours. It's been a long trip."

"Deal." He watched her walk up the stairs and turned to face the lady named Pamela, who was smiling at him. "What did I just do?" he asked quietly.

She snickered. "You opened your mouth. I appreciate it, though. That old woman was rude."

"Hmm. I guess, I should keep my mouth shut sometimes. Well, a buggy ride never hurt anyone, did it?"

Pamela shook her head. "No, chances are you won't get run over by a stampeding elk herd."

William nodded with a smile. "We should be alright then."

3

Tim Wright walked down Main Street tipping his hat and smiling at the ladies as he made his way to the Slater Mining Company Office. He said hello to the secretary and moved down a hallway to the office of his friend, Josh Slater. He opened the door and greeted his friend with a handshake and took a seat in a soft leather back chair across the desk from Josh.

Josh spoke, "What's on your mind, Tim, you look irritated."

Tim took a deep breath. "Matt. He's threatening to have his deputy Truet run for sheriff in the next election against me. I overheard him say so the morning the Sperry-Helms Gang hung Pick. I arrested those three Chinese as we talked about, but Matt came in like a knight in shining armor and blackmailed me into dropping the charges and letting them go." He paused. "I can't afford to lose the next election because of Matt. What would I do, Josh? Work for you in the mine?"

Josh sighed. "Matt is such a... You know when we brought him in here, we hoped to have a mutually beneficial relationship with him. He doesn't seem to want to play the game with us. I wish we could get him out of here as easily as we got him in here. Oh, don't worry about the election, we can take care of that. Debra is in charge of counting the votes, and we can handle everything else. We need you right where you are, and we'll keep you there."

"I appreciate it, thanks. But you know I sure would like to get rid of him. I looked forward to Matt being here too, but we don't see eye to eye on anything. He's going to drag our names through the mud, your name too."

"Then we need to ruin him. How? I don't know yet, but he needs to know who runs this place, and it sure isn't him. He's got some support from the city planning commission and the county commissioners, but I'm sure we can ruin his reputation and blacklist him at some point. I know I want to get even for what he did to us in the hotel room that night when Christine was supposed to show up. I haven't forgotten about that, have you?"

Tim pointed at his crooked nose. "How can I? I got the worst of it. I just wanted you to know he's making threats about the election and ruining my reputation as a law officer."

"Tim, you're the Sheriff, and you will remain the sheriff. Nobody is going to vote you out or anyone else we don't want to be removed. We may not own the town, but we sure have control over it. I think the Sperry's might have done us a favor by leaving a Chinese note on that man's chest because the Chinese aren't liked around here anyway. If word gets out that Matt's protecting those Chinese murderers, that might not sit well with the general public. Right?"

Tim grinned slowly. "No, I don't think it would."

"Leave it to me. I know a few fella's who dislike him anyway, and if they got hold of that information, it would spread around town fast. He's a half breed anyway, and if word gets out that he favors Chinese and other mixed-bloods over whites, he might be run out of town by the men and women of this town. Either way, it will pit them against him and inadvertently build loyalty to you as the sheriff. We want to get even with him, and physical pain hurts for a moment, but if we hit him where it really hurts, his career and his reputation, it will leave a lasting sting. And if I know anyone who hates him as much as we do, it's the Thorn brothers, Joe and Ritchie. I'll speak with their supervisor and tell him what I know. Watch, it won't take long for the gossip to get around. I'll make a trip out to the mine to inquire about the progress of the new tunnel and let it slip out."

Tim nodded agreeably. "Excellent idea. I can't wait to see what happens."

Josh smirked. "No matter what happens, you just stand back and watch. I may not hurt people physically, but I can find a way to hurt them where it leaves a lasting scar so deep they're never quite the same again. And that's what I want to do with Matt." He paused and lowered his voice. "My bladder was full when he kicked me; that's why I urinated my pants. He didn't scare me so bad that I wet myself. That's what he told Lee and Albert and others. Now it's my turn to get even." He referred to the night Tim, Travis McKnight, and himself had rented a room in the Monarch Hotel and blackmailed Christine Knapp to come to the room or face being charged with the murder of Kyle Lenning. At precisely the time she was supposed to arrive, Matt knocked on the door and attacked them with his rifle. Tim ended up with a broken nose, Travis was given a deep gash on his head, and Josh had wet himself before Matt left the room.

"Maybe you should tell your sister about Matt favoring the Chinese. I hate to say it, but she's known for being a gossip in the higher society. That would get around in upper society too."

Josh shook his head slowly. "No, Debra is interested in Matt. I don't know that she'd say anything negative about him right now."

"Where is she anyway? I didn't see her in her office."

"The old man took her to lunch. I have too much work to do to go."

Tim stood. "Then I'll let you get back to it. I wanted to let you know what he's planning anyway."

"Don't worry about him. We'll set him up for a fall and watch him pack up and go."

Tim hesitated by the door. "Why don't you put a good word in for me with Debra."

Josh scoffed. "Tim, I could, but she's got her eyes

on Matt. And if you know her at all, she isn't one to give up easily."

"Matt's courting Christine. I just saw them going to lunch again. They spent a lot of time together since that night. He even got caught cheating with her by his lady from the Idaho Territory somewhere, and she dropped him like a rock or so I hear."

Josh shrugged. "We need to get Christine to drop him too. We'll work on that as well. Once Matt's gone, we can indict her for murder as we planned. I'll go to the mine this afternoon and spread some gossip around. We'll know how fast it gets around soon enough."

4

Matt sat at a table in Regory's Italian Restaurant with Christine Knapp eating a plate of spaghetti and meatballs. He was listening to her talk about the Thanksgiving event Bella's Dance Hall was planning for Thanksgiving night. She was excited because the night's plans included several songs she would sing. She enjoyed singing and playing the piano far more than dancing. "You're not upset with me for not going to your family's for Thanksgiving, are you?"

Matt wrinkled his nose and shook his head slightly. "Not at all."

"Honest? I told you I was, but then Bella told me she wanted me to sing. If it were just one or two songs, I would go with you. But it's a lot of them," she explained.

"Honest. It's not a big deal at all to go to my family's for Thanksgiving. Maybe next time, though. Annie and especially Tiffany, have told my Aunt Mary all about you. She wants to meet you."

Christine smiled fondly. "I liked Tiffany. When I took her shopping for clothes, she was so sweet but so skittish at first to admit if she liked something or not. And then, she was so concerned about the cost of everything. I told her not to worry about that, but she was so uneasy about the cost. But those horrible clothes you brought her back from Prairieville in had to be thrown into the burn pile as soon as possible. Those were horrible!" she laughed. She held up a palm towards Matt. "And again, you're not reimbursing me. It was my pleasure to get those for her. How is she liking living with Annie anyway?"

Matt smiled slowly. "She's happy there. They're getting along well, and she seems to be fitting right in with the ranch."

"Oh, I'm glad. She's had it so hard; I'm thankful to hear she has a happy place to call home, now."

"Me too."

Christine tilted her head and asked, sincerely, "Have you heard from Felisha?"

"No. I don't think I ever will. It's not her way to reach out to someone she left behind. I don't understand how things can go bad so suddenly, but it did."

Christine frowned empathetically. "I think I had a lot to do with it, Matt. But I didn't mean to."

"Do you think if I had married her, I would have been dealing with that jealousy forever?"

Christine nodded sadly. "I do. I don't think you could have continued to be a marshal if you had married her. She would want you home by suppertime and always be suspicious of where you were or if you were faithful when you weren't around. I hate to say it, but you are probably better off that she left you."

Matt nodded sadly. "Well, it hurts a bit. I honestly felt like she might be the one. We've discussed it before, but as you know, I wasn't planning on asking her to marry me right away anyway. She was right, though; I am a violent man. When I was in Prairieville, violence was happening all around me and of course, William and I had to fight for our lives to get out of there." He looked at Christine. "I don't think Felisha would handle hearing things like that too well."

"Nope. I think you're right. However, she was confusing your career with who you are. And it's too bad because I'm sure she's a very nice and good woman beyond the jealousy and her fear of violence. However, I appreciate your willingness to be violent because it's saved me a couple of times now!" she laughed.

Matt smiled slightly. "Sometimes you have to put your foot in the other person's pair of shoes to understand their point of view. I don't think that's a bad policy to begin with anyway."

Christine looked at him as she took a sip of her cup of tea. "Maybe that's part of the reason we get along so well, we both tend to do that, so we compromise pretty easily."

"Probably so. But I think there may be a little respect for each other in there somewhere too. You know things like that make a difference too."

"They do," she said with a smirk. "Well, I should

get back to the dance hall."

"I'll walk you back. Are you going to sing the song you wrote for me on Thanksgiving night?" he asked while standing up and pulling out his wallet.

"Ah..." she laughed slightly. "I wasn't going to, no. That one's personal to you, I don't think anyone else would understand it or how much it means to me."

Matt grinned. "Then you better save it for me, but I would like to hear it again sometime. Let's get you back home."

"I need to go back to your office. I left my bag in your office."

They stepped inside the Marshal's Office, and Matt said, "Excuse us," as he stepped around an old man in a suit with his back turned towards Matt. The old man was unarmed and looked to be content being helped by Phillip Forrester. Matt shot a quick glance at the man before putting his attention back on Christine while he held the gate open for her to follow him back to his private office.

She continued with their conversation, "As far back as I can remember, my grandmother sat me down at the piano to sing hymns with her. I have always loved to sing. I know God gives us all gifts and talents, my gift is serving, I like to help people. But my talent is singing. The thing I'm struggling with is, am I appropriately using God's given talent? I'm singing songs that the men will like and can dance to, but is that what God gave me the talent to sing for? We're supposed to use our talents for His purposes, not for my reputation or pride. Does that make sense? What do you think?" She paused to look at him outside of his private office.

He frowned in thought. "First of all, I'm excited for you to have the chance to sing. But if you're feeling conflicted about it, then sing some hymns too. The Lord knows that place is filled with lost and desperate men seeking answers in a dark world. Maybe some ray of light through a hymn will open their eyes and let them see what's missing in their lives. If they know you're a Christian, maybe one or two will ask you why and you can tell them about the hope you have in Jesus."

"Do you think Bella will let me?" she asked sincerely.

"It wouldn't hurt to ask her."

"It wouldn't hurt to ask, but she also says the dance hall isn't church. We're supposed to get the men to buy drinks, not preach to them. She's told me that before."

He smirked. "I don't think Bella is going to fire you for it."

She slapped his arm affectionately. "No, she's not. But inside, it's bothering me more. I've always dreamed of singing for a living, and this is about as close as I'll ever get to it. And yet, it's exciting, yes, but it feels like it's empty of substance somehow."

"Hmm. Well..."

"Hey Matt," Phillip Forrester said, interrupting them.

"What?" he answered, sounding irritated about

being interrupted.

"This gentleman would like to see you."

Matt looked at the man standing inside the door in the eyes for the first time. His eyes narrowed and then widened just a bit as he recognized the older man with slicked-back silver hair and a neatly trimmed short goatee. He wore a dark suit and held a black derby hat in his hand. His face had aged quite a bit, and his eyes were about the saddest eyes Matt had ever seen on a man. There was no question as to who the man was, despite the many years since he last saw his father, Floyd Bannister.

Floyd spoke nervously. "Hello, Son."

Matt stared at him, wordlessly with a growing cold expression.

Christine asked, "Is that your father?"

Matt nodded slowly, still staring at Floyd bitterly. "Yeah," he answered Christine. "Hello," he said to his father.

Floyd smiled awkwardly. He spoke nervously, "You've come a long way since I saw you last. I always thought you'd become a doctor or a mortician because I know you used to like to gut salamanders and frogs and things when you were a kid to see what was inside them."

"I don't remember that," Matt said with an edge to his voice. He had not taken a step towards his father. He just stared at him with an unfriendly glare. "It's been a long time since I was a kid."

"I know. It's been too long, Son. I came to see you a few years back in Wyoming, but you weren't home."

Matt replied dryly, "I know."

There was a bit of awkward silence in the room when Floyd said, "Well, I'm here to see if you'd like to join your brothers and me for dinner at the Monarch Restaurant tonight? Lee's arranging a family dinner in a private section of the restaurant so we can catch up, and I'd like to introduce you boys to your stepmother. You may know I got remarried?"

"I heard. I have other plans this evening. I won't be making it. Now, if you'll excuse me, I have a lot of work to do."

"Oh," Floyd said, obviously hurt by the rejection. "Well, I'd sure like to talk to you sometime. We're here for Thanksgiving and then going back home. Maybe we can talk before I go home?"

Matt shook his head slightly. "I don't know that I have anything to say. How about we leave it at that?"

Floyd's eyes went downcast as a flood of emotions went through him. He had not been invited beyond the partition that Matt had held open for the lady that was with him. There was no handshake, no hug; not even a kind word had been spoken to him. Floyd nodded sadly. "Okay. Well, if nothing else, I want you to know I'm proud of you and I love you, Son. I won't bother you again."

Matt nodded and remained silent as he watched his father turn towards the door.

"Mister Bannister," Christine said suddenly. She waited for Floyd to turn to look at her. "Matt and I will be glad to meet you for dinner tonight. What time should we be there?"

"No, we're not," Matt said heatedly.

Christine turned to Matt. "Yes! We are."

"No, we're not! I'm not going to..."

"Shut up!" Christine stated sharply, glaring at Matt with a hardened expression. She turned towards Floyd. "What time is dinner?"

He smirked slightly. "Six. And thank you, young lady."

"We will be there."

Floyd nodded and left the office.

Matt was angry. "I'm not going tonight, so you just made yourself out to be a liar!"

"Yes, you are going because you're taking me there. What could it hurt, Matt? He's your father!"

"My father?" he questioned bitterly. "That man abandoned me. He didn't raise me. He has no reason to be proud of me, either. He had nothing to do with me! Why would I want anything to do with him? You stepped way over of your boundaries by telling him we'd be there tonight. You know nothing about him, Christine!"

Christine looked at Matt irritably. "Tell me about him then. Why not have dinner with your brothers and him? What could it hurt?"

"I haven't seen him in almost twenty years. He doesn't know me, and I don't owe him a damn thing! And I don't want to spend a single moment with him," Matt said bitterly.

"What have you got to lose?"

"What have I got to gain is a better question."

"Your father," she answered simply.

Matt looked around the office and seen Phillip

listening in with interest. "Come here," he said and led her to the jail and pulled the steel door open for her to walk through. He closed the steel door behind him to be alone in the granite block walls of the jail. There were no windows, and two empty jail cells separated by a granite block wall. The jail was lit by lanterns hanging from the ceiling. He turned one up so he could see her in the darkened jail.

He spoke heatedly, "My father is a drunken wife-beater who abandoned us! He used to beat my mother black and blue. He broke her ribs, her nose. God only knows what else he broke in her and more than likely, she died from damage done by his beating on her! I'd be woken up in the middle of the night to hear her screaming and the sound of his fist hitting her! His voice, so nice and gentle just now, was fierce and blood-chilling when I was a kid!" Matt pointed at her. "You might think he's a charming, gentle sounding man, but I know what he's like! Do you know that I can watch two men scream at each other and start fighting, and I'll kick back and watch. I'll even place a bet on the winner! It doesn't bother me." His voice grew softer, "But if you get a man yelling at a woman, I get skittish, even now. Christine, I am a U.S. Marshal with a nasty reputation for being tough, and I've had hardened men on their knees begging for their lives, and I've kicked their teeth out instead of killing them. I've killed a lot of men, and it doesn't bother me. But seeing a woman crying breaks my heart. And when a man hits a woman, I want to hurt him, and I mean hurt him! All of that comes from that man!" he yelled as he pointed towards the front of the office. "And you want me to go sit down across the table from him and act like it's all okay? It's not okay!" Matt's eyes filled with tears from ages past and he bit his lip as he fought his tears.

He continued in a softer voice through thickening tears, "When my mother died, he left us with my aunt and uncle and disappeared from my life. There was no explanation or reason that I understood. We were just left behind just like that. Oh, he came back when I was nine years old and gave me a newborn blind calf with scours! Who in their right mind gives a blind calf to their nine-year-old son as a present? It had scours so severely that maggots were starting to eat its hind end, Christine. Does that sound like a present anyone with a brain would give to a child? Why not just give me a dead decomposing squirrel in a box to pet and watch over? I was a kid; I loved the calf anyway. My uncle Charlie was so mad at my father for giving me that calf. My father owned a ranch; he knew that calf was going to die when he gave it to me. Uncle Charlie explained to me that the calf was going to die, but he let me feed it for a day before he shot it. I remember crying as I waited for the sound of the shot to come. That was my gift from my father, a dying blind calf. I don't have many good memories of him. I was raised by uncle Charlie, not him. Oh, then he showed up drunk as hell when I was a teenager and uncle Charlie ran him off the ranch as soon as he got there. It embarrassed the hell out of me because my friends were there, and he couldn't speak without slurring his words. I'm ashamed of him, so what right does my father have to be proud of me? He had nothing to do with me at all! He's a stranger that I'd rather never see again. What gift do you think he brought me this time? A hand me down belt that he whipped my mother with?" He shook his head. "I don't want to talk to him. I wish you wouldn't have said anything to him." He sat down on a chair in front of the jail and ran his hand over his hair.

She grabbed another chair and moved it next to him and sat down. "Matt, I'm sorry. I suppose I stepped over my boundaries, but I don't see what harm it could do having dinner with him. Your brothers will be there. It will be fine. I'm more than willing to go with you," she said, placing her hand on his. "Let's go meet your family for dinner."

"You know Regina is going to be there, right?"

She smiled. "Yeah, but so will your other sister-in-law, Mellissa. I liked her. Matt, give your father a chance, okay?"

"Hell no, I'm not giving him a chance! I'll go to dinner because you asked me to, but that's all I can promise. As far as I'm concerned, he has no right to even come to my office. And he sure as hell doesn't have the right to call me, son!"

Christine held his hand comfortingly. "Did you name that calf?"

Matt shook his head. "I don't remember. I only had it for the day. It was shot that evening."

"Were you with your uncle when he shot it?"

40

"No. He wouldn't let me go. I stayed out by the barn waiting for the shot to come."

"Were you sad?"

He nodded slowly. "I was very sad. It was my calf, given to me by my father. I loved it. And I wanted my father too. I didn't know why I was left behind again. I felt lost, and like I couldn't keep anything that I loved. My mother was gone, my father, and my calf." He smiled sadly and sniffled. "I was abandoned and just felt like I was unwanted. And then the shot came, and I just wanted to cry, but I was a man, and men don't cry." He looked at her with his eyes filled with tears.

A tear slipped out of Christine's eyes, and her lips squeezed together tightly as she squeezed his hand. "I'm sorry. You were just a boy, Matt, not a man."

"You couldn't have convinced me of that. At some point, I realized I wasn't important to him, or he would've been there. He would've written a letter, came to see us, or something. He just abandoned us. I saw him when I was nine, and he brought the calf. When I was a teenager, he came out to the ranch drunk as I told you, and just now. Those are the only times I have ever seen him since I was seven years old." He took a deep breath. "Anyway, I'm glad I was out of town when he showed up in Cheyenne. I would've hurt him, I think. Believe it or not, I'm nicer now than I was before coming back home. I'm not as angry and have more to lose now that I have my family back." He paused and looked at her. "I suppose I better get you back to the dance hall."

"Matt," she said softly. "I've told you before, but I'll never abandon you. I want you to know that."

"That's because I'm the only one that keeps you safe around here." He grinned as she laughed.

"That's true, but that's not the only reason." She finished with a tight smile and shook her head, still humored from his statement.

The steel door opened unexpectedly, and Albert Bannister backed into the jail, pulling a rope with a defiant dog with braced legs on the other end through the door. Albert looked at Matt and Christine oddly. "This seems like an odd place for a romantic talk. And this is my new troublemaking dog. The owners named it Beasley or Digsby, something like that. I've been calling it a lot of foul names, myself."

"Ohh, how cute! Come here, Pup," Christine said and called the dog to her. It came to her with its tail tucked between its legs and sat down in front of her with a nervous look back up towards Albert.

"It acts like I've been beating it, but I haven't," Albert said. "I wanted to."

Phillip stepped into the doorway and looked nervously at Matt. "I tried to stop him, but he just brought the dog back here."

Matt shook his head and shrugged. "Big brothers, what can I say? It's fine, Phillip."

"She's a good girl," Christine said as she pet the dog with both of her hands.

Albert raised his eyebrows with sarcasm. "Yeah, she is. If you want her, you can have her."

Matt reached into his pants pocket and pulled

a ring with a few keys on it. "Here. Lock her up. I hope you brought her some food and water. And I forgot to mention earlier; you're cleaning up her messes. That means mopping the jail cell."

"Uh!" Christine scoffed with an incredulous look at Matt and then at Albert. "You're locking her in jail?"

Matt nodded as he pet the dog. "For the destruction of personal property and disorderly conduct, yes. Very serious crimes around here. Especially in Albert's neighborhood. Albert, this is Christine. This is my brother, Albert."

He shook her hand, looking at her awkwardly. "Ma'am."

Christine shook his hand. "We've met before. I was with Kyle at the play of Romeo and Juliet. You and your wife were the only ones nice to me when Kyle introduced us."

"Oh! Yes, I remember. Yeah, that was an odd night."

"I liked your wife, Mellissa. She was so nice."

Albert took a deep breath. "She wasn't so nice this morning. But that's why the dog's here. It's a long story," he explained.

Christine laughed lightly as she put her face close to the dog's nose. "Did you cause a ruckus, pretty lady?"

Matt scowled. "I wouldn't say she's pretty. That's the most blotched up looking dog I've ever seen." It was a Red Tick Hound Dog and had solid red spots around its ears and on its sides, and the rest of it was a blotchy mixture of red and white. "It's more of a red roan, wouldn't you say?" Matt asked Albert.

Albert nodded. "Hey, did our Pa come by?"

Matt stared at Albert with cold eyes and nodded slowly one time. "He did."

"Are you going to the dinner tonight?" he asked Matt curiously.

"I wasn't going to. But I am."

"How'd it go seeing him again?"

Matt took a deep breath. "I didn't have anything to say to him. I still don't. But I'll go to dinner and sit through it. I'm taking Christine with me."

Christine volunteered, "Yeah, he wasn't going to go, but I talked him into it."

Albert looked at Matt. "He is our father. He may not have done much, but without him, we wouldn't be here. I guess we ought to be there."

"I don't owe him anything. Not even the least bit of respect."

"No, you don't owe him anything, and you don't have to respect him either, but it would be nice if you were there. Do you think Lee and I have a great time visiting with him? No, we don't. But he's our father, so we go visit and say, 'hi.' It would be nice to see you there too."

"I said I was going, but I'm not promising to stay long."

"Trust me, I understand. And thanks for holding the dog here for me. I appreciate it."

Matt nodded. "My pleasure."

They put the dog in a cell, and it began howling and barking to get out as they left the jail cells. Matt closed the heavy steel door behind him and locked it. He could still hear the dog howling and looked at Albert irritably. "Seriously?"

Albert scoffed. "Yeah, all night long! Now you know why it's here. It's the worst ten dollars I ever spent."

"I wish I could take her," Christine said sadly. "I love dogs, but I don't want the fleas."

"I never thought about that, Albert. Is your dog infested with fleas?"

Albert put up his hands up innocently. "It's more than possible, but just think, the next outlaw you arrest will never want to be arrested again if he's eaten alive by fleas in your jail. This is benefitting both of us, wait and see. Arrest someone tonight, and you'll have a law-abiding citizen by morning." He smiled. "I'll see you tonight."

5

William Fasana had kept his word and rented a one-horse buggy with a folding top to keep the light rain off the seat. However, there wasn't much of a side cover, so the rain soaked the seat anyway. He parked in front of the Monarch Hotel and was met by Maggie, who was waiting inside the main entrance doors. She stepped out of the hotel and paused in front of William.

He furrowed his brow as he looked at her. She was dressed in bib overalls over a green sweater under a brown wool coat. On her head, she wore a blue knitted stocking cap with white stripes. Her black hair hung straight down to her shoulders. She was dressed more like a man, and it took William by surprise. "I would like to say you look nice, but you look like one of my Pa's quarry workers. All you need to do is hold a sledgehammer over your shoulder, and he'd hire you at top pay."

She smiled lightly at the slight insult and held her palms upwards. "It's raining as you can plainly see. If you think I'm going to wear a dress and flowered hat to go for a ride in the rain and cold, you're crazier than I think you might be. I'm sorry if you're disappointed, but you can take me or leave me. I don't really care which."

William nodded with a slight grin. "What can you expect from a woman butcher, huh? Hop on and let's go see the waterfall or something. I brought a blanket in case you got too cold. Tell me, Maggie, when you dress like this, do you ever call yourself Burt or Leo or something like that?" he laughed as she stepped up onto the seat beside her.

She nodded with a slight smirk on her lips. "No. I still go by Maggie even when I'm slicing a pig's throat," she emphasized while looking at him evenly. "I carry a knife by the way, so if you act like a pig, you might get sliced."

He laughed lightly. "I'll try not to be a pig."

"Well, William, you're not off to a good start. So tell me about yourself. You are obviously not married. By your two guns with fake ivory handles, I assume you're either a gambler with a big bluff or a gunfighter of some small sort. Have you ever used them for anything other than decoration?"

"Oh, it's real ivory," he laughed. "You are funnier than a fella in a dress, though! Well, I am a gambler, but I work as hotel security and I help manage the place when Roger, the manager, is gone. And no, I've never been married. I don't think I ever will be either. Some men aren't the marrying kind, and I'm

47

one of them."

"I've met a few men like you back in Portland. You know, homosexuals."

"Whoa!" William pulled the reigns of the buggy and stopped it in the middle of the road. He glared at her angrily. "I'm not a homosexual! For crying out loud, no! I meant some men just aren't the marrying kind. I love women; I'm not a homosexual!"

Maggie burst out laughing and stomped her feet quickly on the floor of the buggy as she laughed hysterically. "I know what you meant," she laughed. "I got you good!"

William shook his head slowly, without any humor on his face. "You're lucky I didn't shove you out of the buggy." He gave the horse some reins and started driving through town. "I'm not a homosexual. What is wrong with you?" he asked with disgust on his face.

"Oh, are you turning sour now?" she chided. "Well, you sure like to give others a bad time, you just can't take it, huh?" she laughed.

"I was trying to be forthcoming and honest, and you insult me like that? Well, that was good. You have a sense of humor. Kind of."

"I have to have a sense of humor because that's all I have. If it's too much for you, let me know."

"How old are you?" he asked suddenly.

"I'm thirty-six. You?"

"Thirty-seven. You know, why don't you tell me about yourself so I can drive without being insulted for a while."

"Boy, there's not much to say, really."

"Have you ever been married?" he asked.

She nodded with a weight that showed in her expression. "Yes."

William frowned. "Are you still? I'm not going to have a jealous husband come running out of the hotel to gun me down, am I?"

"Well, if so, you can pull one of those fancy guns and pretend you know how to use it."

"I will too. So, what's your wife's name, Leo?" he asked loudly as he drove past a couple of men he knew from the Monarch Lounge.

She shook her head with a slight chuckle. She spoke sincerely, "I'm not married anymore, William. My husband's name was Marvin Farrell, and he left me high and dry after our children died. A diphtheria outbreak took them three years ago. Marvin blamed me because I was their mother, and I was supposed to protect them from it somehow, I guess. Anyway, he's gone and not coming back."

William frowned. "I am so sorry to hear that."

She nodded. "Well, not near as sorry as I was and still am. I never dreamed of being a butcher. I was alone, heartbroken, and had nothing left, so I went back home. Floyd introduced me to his friend and got me a job at the butcher shop. I moved in with my mother and Floyd, and that's why I'm here. I'm just floating on a river like a leaf trying to stay afloat. Humor helps me get through the day. So, if I'm too much for your liking, you can take me back. I like to laugh."

William shook his head. "No, I enjoy a good laugh and sarcasm is right up my alley. I'm heartbroken for you, that's a…crushing. So, if your husband Marvin comes running after me in a jealous rage, I'll go ahead and shoot him for you. No charge necessary."

"Well, that's good, because I probably couldn't pay you for it anyway. I make enough to survive, and that's about it."

"How does my Uncle Floyd treat you, if I may ask? He wasn't too kind to my Aunt Ruth way back when. I never saw him be mean, but I know he was. He was my favorite uncle back then. He was always nice to me."

"I don't know what he was like when he was younger. All I can tell you is he is the best thing that ever came into my mother's life. I understand he was once quite wealthy, but you would never know it now. We live in a free apartment above the saloon he manages, and my Ma manages the apartment building we live in. But he's never been mean to either one of us if that's what you're asking."

"Good. Is he still drinking? I know he used to drink a lot. That's when he was meanest, I understand."

"No, he doesn't and hasn't in years. He's an old man now, you know. That's why we came here, so he could see his children and grandchildren before too much more time passes by. The journey getting here was hard on him and my Ma. I don't think they'll be coming back over again. This will probably be the last chance you will get to see your uncle Floyd. He's getting weaker in his old age," she said sadly. "And I hope his kids take the opportunity to get to know him. That's all he wants, you know."

William took a deep breath as he turned onto another street. "The only one he'll have a problem with is Matt. I have never heard Matt say too much about his father, except that he doesn't matter. Matt's a tough egg to crack, and if you go about it the wrong way, you'll never get close enough to get another shot at it. He's a pretty guarded man and says little unless you get to know him. He'll go out of his way to help you, but that doesn't mean you're friends. You know what I mean?"

"I look forward to meeting him. Do you think I need to put on a dress at dinner tonight?"

William frowned. "What dinner?"

"The one Floyd set up with his boys and their families. Matt's coming with some lady, Floyd said."

William chuckled. "Well, I have several siblings myself, but they're all a bit too snooty for me. I am more at home with the Bannisters, so I better come along. I don't need to be invited, because I'm family. Right?"

"Absolutely. So, is there somewhere where we can go dancing? I feel like dancing."

William grimaced. "Not with you dressed as a man, we aren't going dancing!" he said with a slight laugh.

She smirked. "Come on, the worst that will happen is they'll think you're a homosexual."

He looked at her with an odd grin. "You're such a... I don't even know. Do you want to ride out of town a few miles?"

"No, I need to get back and get ready for dinner. I

51

need to pretty myself up and put on my best dress. I hear Matt is single and quite handsome. I wouldn't know that by his relatives I've met so far, but that's what I hear. I don't want him to mistake me for a man."

William asked, "You're not captivated by me yet, huh?"

"Um...no. You're a bad tour guide for starters. And you're not much of a romantic, either, William."

"I hear that's what makes me unique, though. All the ladies I've ever courted say the same thing, 'you're so wonderfully unique.' Yep, they've all said that."

"Oh?" she asked with raised eyebrows. "I'd like to meet some of those ladies you courted. Are any of them still living?"

William grimaced with a slight laugh. "Of course! What does that mean?" he chuckled.

She shrugged innocently. "Well, our eyesight gets worse the older we get, so I'm assuming they were all quite elderly women."

William laughed. "Yeah, old widow Perkins is still alive for a few more days, I think." He shook his head with laughter. "I'm going to hate taking you back to the hotel; you're kind of fun for a girl."

She smiled. "Thank you. I kind of like to think of myself as a woman now that I'm in my thirties, but obviously, your eyesight isn't so good either. No, it's been fun, William. Thank you. But you probably didn't consider I've been in a crowded and cramped stagecoach for three days when you asked if I wanted to go on a buggy ride. It's been fun, it really has. Thank you for asking me to go with you."

William stopped the buggy in front of the hotel. "Your welcome. Well, Mister, Oh! I mean Miss Farrell, how about I meet you at dinner?"

"I'll see you then. And William, I don't care what everyone here says about you, it was nice to meet you," she said with a teasing smile. "I'll see you tonight."

6

Christine stopped outside of the Monarch Hotel to look at Matt. "How do I look?" Her brown eyes appeared to show a bit of nervousness. Her long dark hair was artistically weaved into a fancy bun behind her head and she wore a small green hat with fine ornate flowers pinned into her hair. She was wearing a green long sleeved dress that buttoned around her neck. It was a casual dinner dress, not too formal, but just enough to be appropriate for a casual dinner out of the home.

Matt smiled slightly as his eyes looked at her warmly. "You look beautiful."

"Not too formal? I don't want to be overdressed."

"Nope, not too formal, just beautiful," he said and went to open the door for her. She grabbed his hand.

"Before we go in, are you doing okay with seeing your father?" Her sincerity warmed his heart.

"Honestly, I'm looking forward to leaving already. But, I'll make an appearance and visit with my brothers if nothing else."

"Will you be nice for me? No matter what's said, be nice, okay?"

Matt smiled. "I'll try." He opened the door, and she stepped inside out of the cold. Matt opened the second set of doors, and they entered the main lobby of the hotel. The restaurant was full of people eating, and the smell of fresh bread mixed with the scent of fish baking hung in the air. The sound of forks and spoons tapping fine china and a dozen conversations came from the restaurant doorway.

William Fasana stood in front of the main hotel reception desk. He wore a black suit with a red shirt under his black vest. His gold pocket watch chain hung boldly over the vest pocket. William seldom ever had his long blonde hair in a ponytail, but on this evening, his hair was brushed and pulled back into a ponytail. His weathered face was freshly shaved, except for his goatee. Oddly, he wasn't wearing his gun belt. He smiled when he saw Matt step inside with Christine.

"It's about time you showed up. I didn't want to seem too anxious to get in there."

"Are you eating with us?" Matt asked.

William grimaced exaggeratedly. "Of course! Uncle Floyd wouldn't have dinner without inviting his favorite nephew." He drew close and spoke softly, "Besides, it's my self-proclaimed duty to keep you safe. So, I am stepping in to save you from your new stepsister, Maggie, and your new mother." He nodded emphatically.

"What?" Matt asked with a sour scowl. It irritated him to hear someone other than his mother referred to as his mother.

William chuckled. "Your new mother brought her daughter for you to start courting. Hey, I told her inbreeding isn't too common around here, but..."

Matt's eyes hardened, and he interrupted abruptly, "Don't call her my mother!"

Christine spoke softly, "Matt, let's go in and sit down."

They walked through the restaurant and into a closed-off large room with multiple tables and chairs, but everyone was sitting at one long table in the middle of the room covered by tan tablecloths. An array of dishes with salads, chicken, baked potatoes, and other foods were sitting on the table. Matt was greeted with excitement from his nieces and nephews as he and Christine entered. He smiled as he hugged the ones who came to him and greeted his brothers, Lee and Albert, and their wives, Regina and Mellissa, with a warm smile. "You all remember my friend, Christine?" he asked as he introduced her to his brothers and sister-in-laws. Mellissa Bannister was as warm and friendly as ever and gave Christine a welcoming hug. Regina smiled slightly at Christine but left it at a cold reception at best.

Floyd stood up from the table. "Son, this is your step-mother, Rhoda. This is my fourth-born son, Matthew. Or as they know him nowadays, Matt."

A short and heavy lady in a lime green dress of

lesser value stood up and stepped towards Matt with a smile. Her face was round with a touch of rouge on her cheeks, a slim nose, and her long graying, dark brown hair was braided down her back. Her perfume was heavy and could choke a hearty mule. She hugged him tightly. "Matthew, I have waited so long to meet you! My name's Rhoda, but I would be honored if you called me Ma, Mama, Mom, or Mother. I am your stepmother, after all." She chuckled a good-natured laugh. "And this is my beautiful daughter, Maggie. Isn't she a catch?"

Maggie stood up in a plain brown dress and shook Matt's hand. "Nice to meet you," she said, slightly embarrassed by her mother's introduction. Maggie had shoulder-length dark brown hair that fell straight to her shoulders. She was an attractive lady with lively large green eyes on a triangular shaped face. Her nose was long and narrow, and she had thin lips that easily smiled.

Matt shook her hand. "Nice to meet you. This is..."

Rhoda interrupted him, "Why don't you have a seat by Maggie so you can talk to your father and us?"

"Mother, stop it," Maggie said, embarrassed.

Matt answered, "No, Ma'am, I'm going to sit down over there beside little Clarissa and my friend, Christine. This is Christine, by the way. Christine, this is Rhoda and her daughter, Maggie. And you already met my father, Floyd."

"Hello, everyone," she said, putting her hand out to shake Rhoda's and Maggie's. Rhoda shook her hand without much interest, but Maggie was polite and friendly.

William shuffled past Matt and Christine pressing himself against the wall to get to the empty chair beside Maggie. He smiled at Rhoda as he did. "Excuse me, Aunt Rhoda." He sat down and scooted his chair up to the table. "Well," he said as Rhoda went back to her seat beside Floyd, who sat at the head of the table. "Maggie and I went for a buggy ride already today, and I showed her around town. And while we were out there, she asked for my hand in marriage, Aunt Rhoda. Did she tell you about that? I might be calling you Ma real soon, too."

Maggie smirked and hid her face from her mother, trying not to laugh.

Rhoda's sneer showed her disdain for William. "My daughter would not ask you to marry her. She has better taste than that!"

William looked hurt. "Ma, really, it'll be okay. I'll be moving in with you all and gambling in Portland. I'm planning on escorting you down the aisle like in a fancy wedding, but ours will be a lot cheaper. I understand you don't make a lot of money and I know it's the bride's parent's responsibility to pay for the wedding. The good news is I like nice events and have a ton of friends to feed, so I'll pay for the ring. I already have one in mind." He cupped his mouth and whispered to Rhoda, "I won it in a poker game."

"There's no chance in hell I'll let you step into my home," she said irritably. "I know your type; you're all the same. And I'd slap my daughter silly before she took up with you!"

William laughed.

"Matt, how's business?" Lee asked with a bit of a smile from William's jesting.

"Busy. You wouldn't think a quiet county like this would be so busy, but a lot is going on around here."

"Anything I should know about?"

"Probably, but not right now."

"Have you made any arrests?"

"One." He looked at Albert. "Disorderly conduct and a public nuisance."

"Oh," Regina asked, "What did he do?"

"A little bit of late-night howling and Turkey slaughtering."

"What?" she asked.

Mellissa offered, "Oh, Albert brought a horrible dog home without me knowing about it, and it howled all night! And it killed our Thanksgiving turkey we were supposed to take to the Big Z. Now, I must buy one! Matt was good enough to arrest that dog until we can get rid of it."

A good round of laughter filled the table, and as it calmed down, Floyd asked, "So are you all going to the Big Z for Thanksgiving? We were kind of hoping all of you kids were going to Lee's or Albert's for Thanksgiving."

Albert answered, "No, it's always at the Big Z. Aunt Mary is too old to travel that far in the cold now days. I'm sure they wouldn't mind you all coming out there, though."

Floyd smirked questionably. "I don't know. The

last couple of times I was there; it didn't go too well. I doubt I'd be welcomed there."

Rhoda asked, "Doesn't your daughter live there?"

He nodded.

"Then we're going," she stated pointedly. "I'm her stepmother, dang it." She chuckled and looked around the table victoriously. "It's nice to see you all and all these grandchildren of ours! You just don't know how good it is to see you all!"

"Thank you, Ma," William said. It brought an expression of annoyance from Rhoda.

Floyd asked, "Is Clyde Waltz still around Willow Falls, or has he moved on? Do any of you remember him?"

Lee answered, "He was killed last Christmas in a jailbreak. He was the deputy in Willow Falls and was stabbed to death."

Floyd frowned. "Oh." He looked sad to hear the news. "That's too bad. Did he ever get married?"

"Nope. Nothing in Willow Falls has changed that much since you left."

"No, a lot has changed," Floyd said more to himself.

Maggie asked, "Isn't he the guy you said you sold that cabin to?"

He nodded and took a bite of his dinner.

Lee spoke, "I bought his estate after he died. So that cabin belongs to me now."

Floyd looked at his son sadly. "At least it's back in the family."

Lee nodded. "That's what I thought."

An awkward quietness came over the table.

Christine asked, "Mister Bannister, forgive me for asking, but what do you do for a living?"

He seemed appreciative of some conversation. "I manage the Silver Casterlin Saloon in Portland. It's one of the largest saloons in Portland, and pretty close to the waterfront, so we stay pretty busy. It's a four-story apartment building as well. Rhoda and I manage the whole thing. I've been there for about five years now. I managed other saloons before that. But this one's the best in Portland."

Rhoda spoke to Matt, "You haven't said much tonight, Matt."

Matt looked at her and then spoke for the first time to his father, "I heard some shady things are going on over there in the saloons. Are you aware of any shanghaiing going on there? Not in your saloon, I'd hope." There was no friendliness in his voice.

Floyd frowned as he swallowed his food. "It happens, but not in my saloon."

Rhoda spoke quickly, "It may happen in saloons, but we aren't a part of it or is anyone we know that we're aware of anyway. Most of the shanghaiing is done on the streets. However, I do suspect one of our tenants was shanghaied. He up and disappeared one night."

Matt looked at her squarely. "I'd hope you wouldn't want to be a part of that. Anyone who can kidnap another person and sell them in that labor trade or any other such as prostitution, which I also hear is happening over there, is someone I would have no problem..." he paused and looked at the children at the table. He continued, "Anyone who is that morally corrupt to do something like that to another human being has no conscience and needs put out of society's misery altogether. No matter who they are." His cold eyes went to his father and then back to Rhoda.

"Well, we don't know anyone like that," Rhoda said uncomfortably under his gaze.

"I'm not accusing you. I am…"

Floyd wiped his mouth with his napkin and set it down. "It sounds like you are." He interrupted Matt. "We don't have anything to hide."

"I wasn't accusing you. But I have heard about it, read about it and I would love to go over there and end it. Having one of the biggest saloons near the waterfront, as you said, I'm guessing you've been approached at least to take part in that?"

Floyd frowned and looked at his son evenly. "I've been approached, and I told them to go to hell. I've made mistakes for most of my life, Matt, but I would never hurt someone like that. I can tell you that I'm innocent of that, at least. I don't know what kind of a person you think I am, but I'm not a monster." He finished with a drink of water from his glass.

Matt nodded, seemingly satisfied, and took another bite of his food with an irritable expression on his face.

William raised his eyebrows as the room had filled with unspoken tension. "Well, this dinner has taken a sinister turn. How about we lighten the mood just a bit and…"

Floyd cut him off. "Excuse me, William, but I

want to say something." He looked at Matt. "I came here to see all of you. I'm getting older, and I know that I won't live forever. I've made more mistakes than a man with my education should ever be allowed to make, but I made them. I came here to see all of you and spend some time with you all because Lord knows, my time's running out to make up for the years I lost with all of you. But I'd like to try, and that's why I'm here. I made..." He paused to shake his head in shame. "I'm not the man I used to be. I know I wasn't around for most of your lives, and I'm sorry. You'll never know how sorry I am."

Matt looked at him, coldly. "Were you ever around? Most of my memories were of you beating the hell out of Mom."

"Oh! Excuse me," Mellissa Bannister said, standing up quickly. "I'm taking the children out of here. Come along, children, let's go out into the restaurant and get some cake or cookies or something. Come along, all of you." She began ushering the children out of the room.

Regina stood up to leave as well. "I will help you."

Floyd stared down at the table sadly as the two women departed with the children. "We're trying to have a nice dinner, Matt."

Matt tossed a cloth napkin onto his plate. "And it was nice. But you'll excuse me if I am not thrilled to sit here and pretend to enjoy myself and talk about butterflies and warthogs when I have absolutely nothing to say to you! Not a thing! What's there to say? Hey Father, I missed you? I haven't! You abandoned that role, and uncle Charlie and my brothers filled it. I haven't missed a thing! Am I supposed to cry and say, I'm sorry that your feeling sorry twenty-eight years later? I don't care!"

Floyd's lips turned downwards in a deep frown. "That's fair."

"Fair?" Matt asked bitterly with his eyes widening in anger. "It's not fair; it's just a simple fact. Look, you can visit with everyone else, and they're fine with that, but I'd appreciate it if you left me alone. I don't want to see you and I don't want anything to do with you either. My father gave me up years ago and never came back!" he shouted as he stood up. "Keep it that way!" He turned to Christine and was taken back by the tears that slipped out of her eyes. "Are you ready to go?"

She wiped her eyes and nodded. "Yes," she said softly.

Matt looked back at his father, who was resting his chin on his folded hands on the table with his eyes downcast. "Have a good trip back home."

Rhoda spoke, "Matt, will you please stay?"

"No, Ma'am. It was nice meeting you two, but I have nothing more to say."

Floyd's eyes roamed from the table up to Matt. He took a deep breath. "You're right. I was a horrible father to all of you. I drank and I...beat your mother." His lips tightened emotionally. "I wish I could take all that back and relive those days and be the man my father wanted me to be. But I can't. I know it might be a long haul, but I hope someday you can forgive me, son. Maybe I shouldn't have come back here expecting to be welcomed, but I had to try. Maybe we won't ever have the chance to talk again, so for what it's worth, I love you, Matthew. And I'm proud of the man you've become."

Matt grimaced with disgust. "So, you've said. Goodnight." He led Christine out of the room to leave the building.

Floyd looked at Albert and then Lee. "Do you boys feel the same way?"

Lee sighed with frustration. "No, Dad. We've already had this conversation a few years ago. I'm sorry, this was supposed to be a nice dinner. I apologize for Matt and his outburst."

"Well, I'm not very impressed with him!" Rhoda said with a bitter scowl.

William sighed loudly and stretched back and put his arm around Rhoda's shoulders. "I'm not so bad after all now, am I, Ma?"

She grimaced with disgust and backhanded his chest as hard as she could. "You are an obnoxious ass! Get your arm off of me!"

William was the only one laughing.

7

"I'm sorry if I embarrassed you, Christine. It couldn't have been comfortable hearing that." Matt was walking her back towards the dance hall in a light rain.

"No, it wasn't," she sounded irritated. She stopped walking and turned to face him. "What in the heck got into you? You didn't say one nice thing! You may not have been accusing them of shangril-hai or whatever you called it, but it sure sounded like you were. You sounded so cold! I have never heard you speak to anyone like that. Can you explain that? I asked you to be nice as we went inside, but you weren't at all."

"Shanghaiing. It's happening in the Oregon shipping ports of Astoria and Portland. Men are drugged, kidnapped, and taken when they're drunk and put aboard outgoing ships to work or be thrown overboard at sea. Women too, but they're forced into prostitution. It's an ugly world we live in, and that's just a part of it."

"And you thought your father could be a part of that?" she asked, horrified.

"I asked," he shrugged. "I haven't seen him in twenty-eight years, what do I know? He could be in charge of all of it as far as I know."

"Matt, do you have any idea how offended they could be by that? I would be!"

"I don't particularly care if they were offended. I was inquiring about a simple fact. It's happening all around them and they're right in the middle of it running a business that's known for it. How could I not ask them about it? And if they did know anyone who is or were involved themselves, now they know what I think of them and people like that."

"Yeah, I know. Do you think you could have been any colder to your father? He came a long way to see you, and you made him look like a horrible person in there. People change Matt, don't you think he can too? You should have given him a chance." Her eyes showed her disappointment in him.

Matt could feel his anger rising within him as she turned away from him and began walking. He stood still for a second or two as the rain ran down his face. "No. I don't think I should give him a chance! Where was he for all of my life? He was the adult; I was a child. He had every opportunity to come back for us, but he was too much of a coward to face responsibility and gave us up! Why in the blazing furnaces of Hell would I feel like I have to make it all right nearly thirty years later? If he's changed, great! But this bridge is burned and has been since I was nine years old. Even when he showed up drunker than hell when I was a teenager, the bridge was already burned. I have nothing to say to him, Christine. Nothing at all."

She paused to look at him. "Maybe he didn't want you to say anything anyway! Maybe he wanted you to listen, Matt. Maybe that's all he wanted, just for you to listen to him."

"I did. And it's the same jargon I heard the last time he left. I love you, son. Proud of you." He paused. "I've heard it before."

"You don't believe him?"

"Let's say I have no reason to believe him. Love's a word that everyone says, but does he? I haven't seen any evidence of it, have you? He came to town, big deal! He also brought his wife, who wants me to call her, 'Mother'?" he spat out with disgust. "I just assume not to see them again."

"What if your father died? Would it bother you?" she asked.

"No. Would it bother you?"

She sighed with frustration. "I don't know him!" she snapped.

"I don't either! That's my point."

"Do you hate your father, Matt?" she paused to look into his eyes.

Matt frowned. "I wouldn't say I hate him. But I sure don't care to see him."

"Well, I hope you'll at least try to listen to him before he goes back home. This may the only time you ever get the chance to."

"There is nothing he can say, Christine. What's

done is done, and it can't be changed. My memories will never change, and the damage he did to our family, to my mother and me will never change. Saying he's sorry isn't going to change any of that! So what's the point? I apologize for putting you in an uncomfortable situation, and I hate to see you so disappointed in me, but I couldn't help it. It just came out and I meant every word of it. He may be my father, but only by blood. I don't know him. And it's too late for him to want to get to know me. The damage is done. So, let's just let it be." He took a deep breath and exhaled. "I don't want to waste any more time talking about him."

"What would you like to talk about?" she asked shortly, as they walked along the boardwalk.

"Anything except for him. I'm up for talking about puppy breath to cleaning pig pens; it just doesn't matter. I don't want to talk about him, and I know you want to. I already know you're dying inside to fix that relationship. Christine," he paused and stopped in the rain to look at her. When she turned to face him, he said, "You can't. So please don't try."

She grimaced. "Do you know why I want you to try to establish a relationship with your father?"

He laughed bitterly. "No, I don't!"

"For you to become whole. That damage to your family you talked about is like a fire long past; oh, the flame may be out, but the soot is caked to the chimney, and that soot is part of you, and it's ugly. Look what happened in there, that soot caught fire by the mere spark of seeing your father again. Get rid of that soot Matt, and you'll be a man free of your past, instead of a man who carries a soot-covered heart under the clean exterior of his suit. The only thing keeping that soot in the chimney of your soul is you. Do something about it, please. I care too much about you to see you incinerate into a bitter man every time his name is mentioned, or lord forbid you happen to see him. You deserve better than that."

Matt smiled slightly. "And just how am I supposed to sweep my chimney clean?"

"You forgive him."

"I already did."

"No, you didn't. If you had, we wouldn't be having this conversation. You might've thought you had, but you haven't. You need to go home and really think about if you have or not. I know you have a good heart, and I know you'll do the right thing. But you're wrong in how you're treating your father. Have you ever thought that maybe he loved you kids enough to know your aunt and uncle would be able to give you a safe and loving home that he couldn't provide without his wife? Did it ever occur to you that it was love and not selfishness that led him to make that choice? And from what I've heard of your uncle Charlie, if he told you not to come back, would you?" Her eyes burned into his. "Go home, and put yourself in your father's shoes, what would you have done? It's easy to be judgmental and cast stones of hurt and fury at someone we hold responsible, but maybe, there's another part of the story you don't know. And maybe, just maybe, that's what he came here to talk about, but you'll never know because you won't give him a chance. Your soot is too thick, and it's blinding you from the truth that without forgiving him, you'll never be free of that blind and dying calf!"

Matt's eyes squinted in thought. "Maggie."

"What?" Christine asked perplexed. "What about her?"

"No," he explained softly. "The calf's name. I named it Maggie."

"Oh, that's fitting because your father brought another gift for you named Maggie, too, apparently." She laughed quietly at the absurdity of it. "Matt, go home and pray about it. Maybe the soot will loosen if you don't throw a bunch of green wood in the fire, okay? I love you too much to see you self-destruct now."

He looked at her, stunned to hear her say she loved him.

She raised her finger. "Not like that! I love you as a friend," she clarified quickly.

"Yeah, me too."

"Go home, and I'll see you tomorrow."

Matt walked back up Main Street deep in thought and walked past the Monarch Hotel, knowing he was out of sight of the backroom where his family had been eating in. He didn't know if they were still in there or not, but he wasn't going back in to see. He wanted to be alone and knew his deputy Truet Davis was at the house. Matt walked to his

Marshal's Office and stopped as he neared the door. On one of the large bay windows painted in yellow paint were the words, Loves china men, hates whites painted under that were the words, Leave town Half Bread! On the other big bay window were the words, Supports yella men, niggers, red heathens and brownies over whites.

Matt snickered at the mis-spelling of breed and looked around the street and touched the paint to see how dry it was. It was still damp. He wiped the paint off his finger onto the glass. Someone had to have seen someone painting his windows. He could've taken a rag and washed the paint off the windows easily enough, but he decided to leave it on there. He went inside and could hear Albert's dog barking. He went to the jail and went inside to pet the dog for a while.

He had taken the dog outside for twenty minutes or so and found it eating a large pile of vomit around the corner of the next block. Disgusted, he took the dog back to the jail and locked it in a cell before closing the steel door to quiet the dog's howling.

Wanting to wind down and relax a bit in solitude, he went to his office and sat down at his desk. He pulled a small leather bound Bible out the desk drawer and kicked his feet up on the desk and began to read. There is no other book in the world that is harder to find the desire to pick up and read than a closed Bible. However, there is no other book on earth more inviting, soothing, encouraging and life changing than an opened Bible.

8

The next morning, Matt stood on the edge of the Fasana Quarry pit with his cousin Robert Fasana, Truet Davis, and a line of other men looking down into the pit where men were pulling the bodies of two dead Chinese men out of the quarry. They had been thrown over the edge by unknown assailants when they came to work. Robert identified the two dead men as Chee Yik and Kot-Kho-Not, two of the three men who had been arrested for the hanging of Pick Lawson. The third Chinese man who had been arrested, and the only one who spoke English well enough to be understood named, Ah See, had been found tied to a wagon's wheel stripped naked and whipped to a bloody pulp. He was alive when Luther Fasana took him to town to see the doctor. To the best information available by Robert, the three men had come to work early like they always did and were confronted at the quarry. Two were thrown over the quarry edge onto the granite down below, and Ah See had been tortured. He was left alive, but whether that was intentional, or the attackers were interrupted before they could finish the job, no one knew. Nor did anyone know who had committed the crime.

Matt and Truet rode into town and went to see the doctor at his office where they expected to find Luther with Ah See. They walked into the procedure room, where Ah See was lying on a table. His back was riddled with torn flesh, which looked like a bloody mess.

"Dear Lord," Matt said, shocked by the brutality on display before him. "How is he?" he asked Doctor Bruce Ambrose. He was a middle-aged man with a good head of brown hair cut short and a long mustache that he curled upwards at the ends. Doctor Ambrose was a heavy man and a member of the higher society, but he seldom ever turned down a patient or hesitated when he was called.

Doctor Ambrose shook his head as he moved his bloody hands to suture up a wide area of ripped flesh. "I've never seen anything quite like this. Luther, hand him that container." He nodded towards a white ceramic container.

Luther handed it to Matt. "This is the crap he pulled out of his back. Find who did this to my friend," Luther said, strenuously trying to contain his anger.

"What's all this?" Matt asked while taking the container and looking inside. Inside of the container were little bits of rock, metal, and what looked to be an incisor tooth from a small animal.

Doctor Ambrose looked at him through his

spectacles. "The works of the devil."

"What?"

The Doctor nodded quietly. "You know Jesus was scourged, right? Well, so was our friend here. Whoever did this, used a single bullwhip by the markings, but added metal, bits of thin slate, and Raccoon's teeth to his whip. Those pieces were stuck in this man's back. I figure he was struck a good twenty-five times or so. They hit him across the buttocks and legs too, but not as seriously as his back. And to add to the pain, they threw salt into the wounds."

"Oh, Lord," Matt said empathetically. "Does anyone know who did this?"

"No," the Doctor said, "I had to sedate our friend to keep him still. He wasn't in good shape, and the blood loss is very concerning. He's got a long road ahead if he makes it at all. I have cleaned the wounds the best I could and am doing my best to suture the worst wounds. But he's going to be in some serious pain for a while."

"So, he could still die?" Matt asked, verifying what he had heard.

Doctor Ambrose nodded and said pointedly, "Oh, yes. He's lost a tremendous amount of blood. Even if he survives that, the risk of infection is still quite high. As I said, he has a very long road ahead."

Truet asked with a disgusted expression on his face, "He didn't give any names or say what happened?" he asked Luther.

Luther shook his head. His expression was one of wanting to tear someone's head off with his bare hands. "He couldn't talk. But I will," he looked at Matt. "Go out there and offer a hundred-dollars of my own paper money as a reward right now to anyone with information about who did this to my friends. I want them found, arrested, and then, Matthew, I want you to give me five minutes alone with them in your jail cell, so they can't run away! You hear me?"

Matt smirked at his uncle. "Loud and clear. I'll get on that, but I can't let you hurt them once they're in jail. It wouldn't be right."

Luther grew outraged. "Is this?" he yelled at his nephew while pointing at Ah See. "You know damn well that no one around here is going to be punished for this! No one cares about Chinese men. Letting me in there for five minutes is the only justice Ah See will get for what they've done to him and his friends! Chee Yik was married with children back in China. He was planning on going back to them in June. Kot-Kho-Not was working his butt off to save money to go back to China and marry the love of his life. These were men just like you and me with plans of their own and dreams of a better future. Where's the justice for their murders? No jury is going to convict a white man for this, not around here! Matthew, I'm asking you to let me in that jail cell when you find who did this."

Doctor Ambrose spoke, "Luther, you're not a young man anymore. You may feel it, but you're not. I don't think it would do you any good to put yourself in that position. One of those men might be tougher than you."

"No one asked you, did they?" he replied sharply.

Matt asked the doctor. "How long until he can talk, do you think?"

"I don't know. I'll do what I can for him and mostly let him rest. I'll be keeping him on morphine for the first few days to keep the pain at bay, and he'll be in and out of consciousness for a while."

Matt nodded. "Okay. Truet, let's you and I go pay a visit to the Sheriff."

"He's about as much help as piss on a fire, Matt!" Luther exclaimed. "He isn't going to help you none! He arrested them for crying out loud!" he shouted as he pointed at Ah See.

Matt looked at his uncle. "I know. But we have to start somewhere, so why not start at the beginning."

"Your uncle's mad," Truet said as they left. "I'd fear he'd kill whoever did this if you let him in the jail for five minutes. And I don't think we'd be able to pull him off after five minutes anyway. He'd kill someone in there."

"I have no doubts about that," Matt agreed.

Matt stepped into the Sheriff Tim Wright's office, followed by Truet. Both men looked like they wanted to talk business. Sheriff Wright was at his desk, talking to two young ladies about a neighbor boy breaking their windows by throwing rocks. The landlord refused to replace the windows, and the ladies, both dressed poorly, were asking Tim to help convince the landlord of their small home to replace the windows before they froze to death.

"Ladies," Tim said, looking up at Matt nervously. "I know your landlord pretty well. I will talk to him today and see what I can do. Okay? Now, if you'll excuse me, it looks like the Marshal might need my help." He stood up to be polite as the ladies stood up to leave. "Marshal, how can I help you today?" Tim asked as he sat back down.

"I need you to come with me for a minute. If you would?" Matt asked nicely.

"To where?" he asked skeptically.

"The doctor's office."

Tim waved a hand. "No. I've heard about the chinamen. It's not the kind of news I wanted to hear this morning."

Matt's eyes hardened, and his voice rose, "What did you expect? You arrested three innocent men, and now two are dead, and one's been flogged like he's Jesus himself! Tell me who did it!" he demanded.

"I don't know who did it. Honestly, I don't. I have nothing to do with that!"

"Who does?"

"I don't know. I let them go, remember? You're the one who said to let them go before a trial. If anyone's to blame, it's you," he accused nervously.

"Who painted my windows for me? Certainly, you know who did that. It was done early enough; someone must have seen it."

Tim shrugged. "Well, if they have, they haven't told me about it. What did they paint on your windows?"

Matt looked at Tim evenly. "That doesn't matter;

they couldn't spell anything right anyway. Luther Fasana is offering one hundred dollars today to anyone who can identify who was involved in the attack of those three men. You know as well as I do that someone will come forward and squeal out names like a poked pig for that money. If you know anything, I suggest you tell me now. Because when I find out who it is, I'm not going to be nice."

Tim appeared to grow nervous under Matt's hardened gaze. "Matt, I'm telling you, I don't know who did it. I have nothing to do with any part of it. All I know is you forced me to let them go. So, I did."

"You never should've arrested them, to begin with. That's why they're dead, Tim. To cover up your own cowardice. Well, the truth will come out today, most likely. A hundred dollars is more than most folks make in months. I hope it doesn't come back to you, but if it does, that won't surprise me much either."

"Matt, you must think I'm the dirtiest rat in town?" he questioned more than stated.

"That's a very close call, yeah. Have a good day, Tim."

"I assure you I'm not. I do a fine job keeping the peace in this city as you can tell, we're not a wild and lawless community. I think I have something to do with that, don't you? This is my city, and I care about the safety of it, and it's citizens as much as you do. And I am sick of you accusing me of not having the backbone to do my job!"

Matt paused and looked back at Tim. "Then tell

the truth about Pick's escape. These men would still be alive and working if you'd just done that from the beginning."

"The Sperry-Helms Gang would kill us both, Matt."

"No. They'd kill me maybe, or I'd kill them. Either way, you'd be safely tucked away in your little office here. How about you show me how serious you are and do what's right for once. And talking to those lady's landlord about fixing their window is a nice start. Don't forget to do that. It's cold out. Good day."

9

Maggie Farrell had watched Floyd Bannister go from being excited to see his sons at dinner, to sorrowful and quiet for the rest of the night. She feared he'd go down to the Monarch Lounge and drink his sorrow away, but he had remained in the hotel room all evening staring at the floor with a hint of moisture in his eyes that normally wasn't there. Floyd had always had a certain sadness to him from the day she first met him, but the sorrow that filled his eyes now was from down deep in his soul. He was hired to manage the tavern where her mother worked as a bartender. Rhoda was a single mother, divorced from her abusive husband, and found herself working in a saloon as a prostitute for a while to make ends meet and keep a shabby roof over her daughter's head. The entertainment industry was competitive in Portland with all of the taverns, bars, and saloons competing for the men's business and looking for a different gimmick to bring business into their small tavern; The tavern manager put the attractive, witty and fun-loving Rhoda behind the bar to keep the men coming in. Rhoda couldn't say she was proud of her conduct back then, but by bringing some sexuality behind the bar, it did keep the regular customer's coming in but failed to increase the profits. Floyd was an experienced manager with a solid reputation and was hired to turn the tavern around and make a profit. He came in with an iron fist and within a year, had turned the tavern around and pulled it out of debt and making a profit. He had also begun to fall for his only female employee. In Maggie's opinion, it was more than luck that Floyd took a liking to Rhoda. Floyd was the best thing that had ever happened to her mother and her. He seldom laughed, and he seldom spoke of the past, but when he finally did, it was the story of a man who had a kingdom in his hands and let it all slip away because of the very product he sold to others to follow his lead.

Maggie was a teenager then and was on the dead-end road toward prostitution if it wasn't for Floyd marrying her mother and giving her some boundaries. Their house wasn't a beautiful home, but it was safe and could be warmed easily enough. Floyd insisted that Maggie continue in school and seek a higher quality of life than in a saloon. Maggie met her husband, Marvin, at school, and they married and moved out of Portland to begin a life in the rural countryside of the Willamette Valley, where Marvin worked on a farm. They had two children and were making a home for themselves when Diphtheria struck their community. During the outbreak, she lost both of her children within a week. Marvin was a heartbroken father, and in his anger, he blamed Maggie for not protecting her children more carefully when they knew Diphtheria was spreading around the community. Marvin threw her out of their house and never wanted to see her again. Devastated, she moved back home to Floyd and Rhoda's place. Floyd never once made her feel like a burden, and he always cared for her well being. He let her mourn, and when she was ready to find work, Floyd found her a job with the local butcher shop to keep her in a respectable profession and earning a living while keeping her out of the gritty saloon side of living for her own good.

Maggie knew about Floyd's past and knew his sons and daughter were a missing part of his life. Floyd had wanted to go back and see his family knowing well that they had grown up, and may not want to see him. He was terrified of being rejected by them, and it was Maggie who finally convinced him to go back to Branson a few years ago and see his grown children. He had made the extra trip back to Wyoming to try to find Matt, but it ended up being a waste of time. He had made a few more trips back to Branson in the years since and reconnected with his children, all except for Matthew. This trip was a special one because he hoped to have all six of his children around him at once. He hoped to reconnect with Matthew and finally have his family back together again and become a part of his children's life.

Unfortunately, the dinner didn't go as planned, and Floyd had been devastated by Matt's harsh words. Maggie knew her mother could be blunt and rough, but her heart was primarily a good one. Rhoda had been offended by Matt and no longer had any use for him. She encouraged Floyd to disown the disrespectful piece of rubbish and move on. But Floyd wasn't as offended as he was hurt. Maggie could tell Floyd just wanted to be alone and left with his thoughts for most of the night. She could not imagine how he felt because she had already known it was his biggest fear, and it cut deep into his soul. Floyd wasn't always a strict Bible reader, but she had caught him reading the Bible the night before for whatever comfort it may have brought him. She had tried to talk to him, but he was in no mood to talk about the hurt he was experiencing.

Maggie dressed in blue jeans and put on one of her flannel shirts and a knit stocking cap. She pulled on her brown coat. "I'll be back later," she said.

"Where do you think you're going?" Rhoda asked sharply.

"Hmm, to go see William."

"Ugh," Rhoda grunted. "Can't you do better than that gutter rat?"

She laughed lightly. "Oh, he's kind of sweet, in a gutter rat kind of way. I'll be back."

Floyd was sitting on the rooms red velvet davenport, looking as miserable as he might've felt. "Be careful, sweetheart, I don't know what kind of people are out there now days."

She chuckled lightly. "Floyd, it can't be worse than Portland. Don't worry; I'll be fine."

She left and went down the two flights of the grand stairway and into the lobby of the hotel. She became the focus of people eating in the restaurant who seldom saw a woman in blue jeans and a flannel shirt. "Hello," she said to the staring eyes and grabbed a fresh cinnamon roll before going outside. She walked up Main Street a few blocks to the U.S. Marshal's Office, eating the dessert for breakfast. She stood outside to read the painted yellow words on the big bay windows, Leave Half Bread. She snickered as there was a half loaf of bread put on the backside of the window and painted in black paint were the words, Come in and get it, you idiot. On the other bay window were the yellow words accusing Matt of preferring other races to whites. Underneath in black paint was a scale evenly weighted with the words, Yes, justice is blind to color in this office.

She couldn't help laughing as she entered the Marshal's Office.

A young, medium height, light brown haired man greeted her in a friendly manner.

"Hi. I want to talk to Matt Bannister if he's in."

"He is. Can I ask your name?"

"Maggie Farrell."

The young deputy marshal went back to a private office and knocked on the door before opening it. Matt Bannister stepped out of the office, looking as unfriendly as he had left the restaurant the night before.

"Can I help you?" he asked.

She pulled the stocking cap off her head. "Hi. I'm Maggie from last night. I hope you recognize me," she said with a slight giggle to her voice.

Matt nodded. "I do. So how can I help you?"

She frowned. She was slightly taken back by his rudeness. "I was hoping I could talk to you for a moment. Maybe back there in private?" she asked in a polite voice pointing at his office.

Matt frowned noticeably. "Maggie, I have a lot going on today. I don't have time to talk."

"Please? It won't take long, I promise." She paused and added quickly before Matt could respond, "If not, I'll bring William back with me. He says you always take time for him. Please, Matt?" She exaggerated her sad expression, which was cute enough to make Matt smirk a touch.

He sighed. "Let her in, Phillip. Come on back,"

She took a seat across from his desk as he closed his door. "Okay, now how can I help you?" he asked formally.

"First, I want to say I like your windows. Very witty. I like that."

Matt faked a tight lip smile. "Thank you. So, why are you here, Maggie?"

She frowned and grew serious. She was uneasy, and it showed in her fidgeting. "I wanted to talk about Floyd..."

"I'm afraid that's not something I want to talk about. Listen, I appreciate you coming in here, but I have a lot of work to do." He began to stand to escort her out of his office.

"Can I say one thing? Please, just listen to me for a minute. I mean, I came down here; the least you could do is listen to me for a minute, right?"

He sat down unpleased. "Fine."

"Okay," she said and seemed to rethink her words. "I won't waste your time trying to tell you why you should apologize to your father, because I know you won't. I can see that in your actions already. Look, here's what I came here to say. If it weren't for Floyd, I'd probably be a prostitute on the Portland streets. Your father is a good man. I don't know what you think he's like, but he's never hit my mother or me. He's always been kind, sweet and yet if you look into his eyes, they are always sad. It isn't because my mother's overbearing or unreasonable at times, it's because he knows he made mistakes and can't forgive himself for them…"

"As well, he shouldn't," Matt interrupted. "Look, I'm glad he has you all to fill that emptiness he has, but I'm me, and I have nothing to say. I don't know him, and I don't want to get to know him. So, please…" he stood up and motioned his hand towards the door.

Maggie grimaced and stood up slowly. "You're an ass." She shook her head slightly. "You hold that much hatred towards your father, and you don't even know him? Why I'd say, that's foolish!"

"Well, I see it differently."

"Maybe you could enlighten me a little bit then because I think you're missing out on a pretty great man." She sat down. "Last night you mentioned he used to beat up your mother, so what? My father did too. Do you think you're the only person who has memories like that? What makes you so special, Matt? Get over it and get to know your father! For crying out loud, he's trying to make things right between you two. I didn't know that was such a crime! I suppose you never made any mistakes, have you? You're my age, and I'm guessing you have, because I know I have. Coming here to see you isn't one of them, though. Your father wasn't much older than you when he left here. He made some mistakes, we all have, have we not?"

Matt opened the door hinting for to leave. "Maggie, I think I've made myself clear. But if not, you're wasting your breath. Okay? I want nothing to do with him, period. Isn't that clear enough?"

"And what if his dying wish was to make things right with you?" she asked with her restrained anger revealing itself on her face.

Matt pointed upwards. "He could wish upon the stars as far as I'm concerned. Look, he already said he loved me and was proud of me. Great. I'm glad to hear it. He said all he needed to say, now he can feel better and be proud of himself or whatever. I have my own life to live, and he's not a part of it. Now, if you'll excuse me, I had two men murdered last night, and for the third time, I really do have a lot of work to do." He waved his hand through the opened office door and waited for her to stand up and exit his office.

Maggie stood up and put her stocking cap back on. "Yeah, you are an ass. I don't know what that beautiful lady you were with last night sees in you."

Matt shrugged. "You'd have to ask her. Have a good day, Maggie."

"Is she the one who vandalized your windows?"

Matt smiled slightly. "No, I'd hope not."

"I thought she seemed smart enough to spell half breed correctly." She looked at him sadly and put out her hand to shake. "It was nice meeting you, Matt. Maybe we'll see you again before we leave."

He shook her hand. "Maybe, but I doubt it. Nice meeting you regardless."

"Matt," Phillip spoke from the front of the office. "This lady is here to talk to you." A middle-aged woman dressed poorly in a large green men's coat and a droopy old leather hat to keep the rain off her head.

"Well, I guess you are busy," Maggie said as she departed.

Matt nodded. "I am. Nice talking to you, Maggie." He walked over to the partition gate and held it open for Maggie. When she departed, he looked at the woman waiting for him. "Hello, Ma'am, how can I help you?"

"Hi," she looked nervous. "Is it true that there's a hundred dollar reward for naming the man who murdered two Chinese men last night?"

Matt nodded. "Yes, it is. Do you know who did it?"

"Yes. My husband, Jake Willingham." There was anger in her eyes that revealed a long since broken spirit.

"Did he tell you what happened?"

"No," she said with a higher pitch to her voice. "He just came home last night and said he killed a couple of China men. But he did it!"

"And what time was that, do you think?"

Her eyes rolled to the right as she thought about it. "I'd say about midnight."

Matt narrowed his eyes with interest. "One of the men was stabbed with a pocket knife. The knife had the initials A.S. carved in the handle. It was found at the scene. Does your husband own a knife fitting that description?"

"Yes, it's his knife."

"What's the A.S. stand for if his name's Jake, if I may ask?"

"It was…my father's knife. Alfred Smith was his name."

"Hmm," Matt said with interest. "Did he sleep all night after he got home, or was he troubled about it? Usually, if it was intentional, they'll sleep like a baby."

"He slept all night. I know because I couldn't sleep knowing he killed two China men. He never woke up once."

"You're sure about that?"

"Yes, sir."

"Okay, I'll check your husband out. Be sure to give Phillip your address for me. And Ma'am, I know it's kind of silly, but my deputy and I have a bet going, and we're asking everyone who comes in here today, does your husband own a bullwhip?"

She smiled a relieved smile. "No. We don't even own a horse."

"Okay, well, that's another one for you, Phillip. Ma'am, thanks for coming in. I'll come around later today to investigate your husband."

"And the money? When will I get that?"

"As soon as I make an arrest." Matt put his finger to his lips. "For your own safety, keep it quiet, huh? And I wouldn't count on the money until an arrest is made, which takes proof."

"Well, you have my father's knife. Good day, Marshal."

When the lady left the office, Matt looked at Phillip. "Anytime there is a cash reward like this, you'll have people coming in accusing their husbands, friends, enemies, anyone they don't like to get the money. From here on out, ask them questions like I did and write their answers down. If anyone seems credible, send them back to me. The other's tell them we'll get back to them and to keep it quiet for their own safety. That lady's husband didn't do it."

"I didn't know anything about the knife," Phillip said with interest.

"We don't have a knife and none of those men were stabbed; I lied. And now you know how I know her husband is innocent."

10

Gertie Haywood lived in a world of grief and fear. Her husband, Leroy Haywood, was a crew leader in the stamp mill at the Slater Silver Mine. He had worked there for eight years, and they still lived in the squalor of the Slater's Mile. It was a company housing community for Slater Mine employees a mile from the main mine and stamp mill. Slater's Mile was about two miles outside of Branson. There was no law in the housing community, and there were no rules; it was a free for all. On most weekends, the frequent cries and screaming of domestic fights could be heard along with the cries of frightened children who lived out there. Most were under the influence of alcohol, which was a common element to the community of the Slater Mine laborers. Other men didn't need it to lay into their wives or anyone else who angered them. A slight disagreement at work could escalate into a full-blown fight on any given night between two men settling their differences. Some men had shown their grit long before, and no one would challenge them now. Leroy Haywood was one of them. His small cabin was left alone, and his word was the only rule as it was in the Slater Mile. He had a nasty reputation for being cold, mean and hateful. To get on his bad side, most men understood was a bad idea because he could get them fired easily if not simply beaten up out at Slater's mile, which he had arranged many times. It didn't take more than a bad meal or a dirty fork to get Gertie beaten by a man most men feared.

Gertie was forty-eight years old, but already her gray hair was taking over, and the lines on her face grew deeper with every somber day she lived. She had three sons who had left home after she married Leroy, because of his abuse towards them. She had no idea where the two oldest boys were now, but the youngest was in the Willamette Valley, working as a carpenter. There were few things a mother could do when her husband controlled the money and every other part of her life with a firm hand. She had tried to protect her boys, but a big man's hand and hateful eyes have a way of paralyzing every muscle that wants to fight back. When her boys ran away one after another, she stood aside and let them go, too afraid of Leroy to say a word. A million tears later, she still stood quietly by as he ordered her around like a trained dog and continually reminded her of what a horrible wife she was. How ugly and how disgusted he is by the sight of her. It was true, her spirit had been broken many years before, and there wasn't much left of the lady she used to be. If her face wasn't bruised, it was only a matter of time until it would be again.

Chances come when least expected, and the news of the Marshal offering a hundred dollars for the arrest of the man or men who murdered the two Chinese men was an opportunity to escape the hell she had been living in for thirteen years. She would never marry again, she knew, but a hundred dollars and what was in Leroy's hidden Arbuckles coffee can could get her away from Leroy and into a new life with her son in the valley.

Fear was like an invisible wall of glass that seemed impenetrable. If one were to break it, the sound of it shattering could wake up the monster that created the fear in the first place. The walls of glass can keep one trapped in a world of suffering and anxiety, never knowing when the next blow, threat, or moment of torture would come. It made life a living hell, and sometimes it takes another person to open one's eyes to the fact that glass isn't concrete, and freedom is just on the other side. It was Gertie's neighbor, Lucille Barton, who walked with her two sons, five-year-old Michael and three-year-old Ray, the two miles into Branson in the rain with Gertie to see the U.S. Marshal Matt Bannister.

"Matt," Truet Davis said, opening Matt's office door, "I think we have a winner out here. Do you want to come on out?"

Matt walked out of his office and seen the two little boys soaking wet from the long walk in the rain.

"Hi, you might remember me from a few weeks ago? My name's Lucille Barton, my husband Lawrence and I met you and Truet out at our place at Slater's Mile?" She was a very attractive young lady with shoulder-length curly dark hair that was wet and dripping from the rain. She wore a coat that soaked up the rain, and her dress was wet as well. She shivered just a bit with the cold that was working its way through her body.

Matt smiled at the pretty lady. "Yes, of course. We were looking for Christine Knapp. She was found unharmed; you might've heard. So, how can I help you? By the way, did your husband ever go apply at the lumber mill or granite quarry?"

She grimaced and shook her head. "No, he has no time to. I'm afraid the silver mine is kind of a trap that's hard to get out of. Anyway, this is my neighbor, Gertie Haywood, and she has something to show you."

Matt recognized Gertie as the older woman who came out of the privy who tried to hide her beaten up face when he and Truet rode out to the mining community looking for Christine a few weeks before. "Miss," he nodded.

Gertie lifted a burlap sack to set it on Truet's desk and reached in and pulled out a leather bullwhip. The last two feet of the wound leather whip had been fitted with fine pieces of slate, metal shavings, fine-tipped bone, and one incisor from a smaller animal.

"Ma'am, where did you get this?" Matt asked quickly. He took it from her so he and Truet could look at it closer. Bloodstains were clearly visibly changing the color of the leather. "Good heavens," Matt said quietly.

"It belongs to my husband; he took it with him last night."

"Here, sit down and tell me about it. Phillip, get some blankets for those children. Misses Barton, why don't you strip your wee one's down and dry their clothes on the stove there. You can cover them with blankets. And if you want, we have a dog in the jail the kids can play with. You can dry your clothes as well if you want to. Phillip will get you a blanket. You all can change in the jail." He watched Phillip invite Lucille and her children into the jail to get them some blankets. He turned back to the older lady who wore an oilskin canvas with a hole cut out to poke her head through. "Now, tell me what happened, Misses Haywood."

She explained how Leroy and his two friends, Oscar Belding and Roger Lavigne, came into town and painted Matt's windows and then went to a saloon to wait to intercept the three Chinese men at the quarry when they went to work. They knew what time the men would be going to work because Josh Slater told Leroy, himself. They were given the day off, and Leroy and his friends had drunk all night and into the morning. Leroy was still sleeping and would for awhile most likely. It was obvious to them all that Gertie was terrified of her husband and feared going home and finding him awake.

Matt sighed. "Are you sure it was Josh Slater who told him to kill those men?"

"I never said he told them to kill them. He just told them when they went to work, and they were getting away with hanging a white man." She paused, "Leroy hates Chinese, and everyone out at the mill knows it. He doesn't like you either."

"I've never met your husband, Ma'am."

She looked at Matt squarely. "You don't have to meet him for him not to like you."

"He's sleeping now?"

"He should be. I don't want to go there and find he isn't. He'll near kill me for being gone. He would kill me if he knew I was here."

"Don't worry about that, Ma'am. Truet and I are going out there right now. Who are his two friends again, and where do they live?" He looked at Phillip who was listening, "Go get our horses saddled, yours too, and bring them on up here with three more for our new guests." He looked at Gertie. "Your husband is going to jail today, and he'll be in jail until a jury either indicts him or lets him go. That's up to them. But until then, he'll be here, and so will his friends." Matt paused. "You haven't asked about the reward. Before you leave here, I will give you a hundred dollars of my uncle Luther's money. What you do with it is up to you, but I recommend leaving town. I wish I could, but I can't promise the jury picked will indict him for killing Chinese men. So just in case, move elsewhere and leave that bag of crap behind. Okay?"

"I plan to. If they don't convict him, you better watch yourself."

Matt shrugged. "I'll be alright." He looked at Lucille Barton as she dried her son's clothes by laying them on the hot surface of the woodstove. She was wrapped in a blanket but still wore her wet clothes. "I'll get you all a ride in a buggy back home. I don't want those boys or you getting sick."

She smiled. "Thank you so much, Marshal."

"Matt. Call me, Matt. How's Lawrence doing? He has never come by so I could introduce him to my uncle Luther. If he wants a job there, tell him to come in. It'll get him out of the silver mine."

"If he doesn't work, he'll be fired, and then we'd lose our home. So it's hard for him to get away from work to come to town in the day time. He's working from sun up until after sundown six days a week right now."

"He isn't the only one complaining about the hours. That's why it surprises me that Josh Slater would give three men the day off to harass some Chinese men if he didn't tell them to do more than that." He asked Gertie, "Does your husband talk with Josh very often? I thought Josh stayed in the office here in town, mostly?"

Gertie shook her head. "Josh summoned him to his office here in town. Leroy got to pick two men, and for their reward, they got today off paid."

"Well, I think we will go wake him up and reward him a bit more. You ladies go ahead and warm up; I'll have Old Pete drive you back home when we get back."

His attention went to the front window, where three Chinese men were standing, looking at the writing and the drawn scales painted on the window. They moved to the next window, and the oldest of them in his sixties moved his lips and the other two smiled slightly.

They stepped into the Marshal's Office and nodded politely to Matt. The old man spoke, "You are the Marshal?" His voice had a heavy Chinese accent, but he spoke English.

Matt nodded as he stepped over towards the men. The older man looked to be important despite being dressed in common loose-fitting black clothing just as the two younger men with him wore. The younger men stood on each side of him like protective guardians. They had no noticeable weapons, but their faces were harsh and unintimidated, unlike most of the Chinese laborers who moved around town during the daytime.

Matt answered, "I am. How can I help you?"

The older man spoke in his heavy accent, "The doctor told me to come ask you if I can take my countryman to our doctors instead of yours. Our doctors are better, and Ah See will heal quicker and better in our care. May I have your permission to take him to my home?"

Matt frowned a bit perplexed. "Why do you need my permission? He's the doctor's patient, not mine."

"Yes. I said the same. The investigation. That is why."

"Oh, I see. And you think your medicine can help him more, than ours?"

"Yes."

"Well, if you can help him heal faster and better, then sure take him back with you. May I ask what your name is?"

"Wu-Pen Tseng," he said with a nod.

"You speak English well, Wu-Pen Tseng."

"Thank you. I've been here for a long time. Have you found the men responsible?"

Matt nodded. "We're on our way to arrest them now. Ah See's boss, my uncle Luther offered a hundred dollars of his money as a reward for their arrest, and it worked. We know who did it."

Wu-Pen spoke in Chinese to his two friends translating what Matt had said. They nodded with a stern expression on their faces. Wu-Pen looked at Matt. "Thank you."

"You're welcome," he said as the men left the office to get their friend from Doctor Ambrose.

"Who is he?" Truet asked.

Matt shrugged unknowingly. "Wu-Pen Tseng."

"I know, but he seems important somehow. I wonder what he does for a living?"

Matt shook his head. "I don't know. But right now, let's go collect a debt owed by Leroy Haywood, Oscar Belding, and Roger Lavigne."

11

Gabriel Smith was in his last year of school. Many communities offered public school up to eighth grade and then sent the young men and women who made it that far out into the world with a basic education. In Willow Falls, Reverend Abraham Ash and the school board agreed to push the grades to graduation up to tenth grade. The last two years would be more focused on higher learning and helping the teacher by tutoring the younger students. Reverend Ash knew labor jobs on the farms and ranches would always be available, but he wanted his grandchildren, and all the children of Willow Falls to be educated enough to either continue their education in college or come out of school more educated than many other schools provided. He believed the basic foundations of building a solid life were based upon knowing the bible and having a good education. It was the least the community of Willow Falls could do to prepare their children for a cruel and tough world. Many of Gabriel's friends had already quit school and were working for their family or elsewhere, but for him, school was the only option he had until he graduated. He was excited to graduate in the Spring. He had no idea what he wanted to do with his life, but he had always been told he could do anything he wanted, but to set his goals higher than a local farm or ranch laborer. Some of his friends didn't have that opportunity as their family farm was now their biggest priority. He liked school, though, and he liked it even more now that a very pretty new blonde-haired girl named Tiffany Foster had started school. It was interesting to Gabriel that Tiffany lived on the Big Z Ranch with Annie Lenning and had been brought there by Matt Bannister. The news had come to town about Matt and his cousin William Fasana getting into a gunfight in Prairieville with a crooked sheriff. Tiffany's father had been one of the people the Sheriff killed, and she had nowhere to go, so Matt brought her to Annie's. It was the same with Evan Gray, though. Evan was Gabriel's friend and new brother, as his parents had legally adopted Evan after Matt rescued him and Gabriel's mother from the Moskin Gang last Christmas. Gabriel and Evan had always gotten along well, but most recently, there had been a bit of tension between them. It could have been because they both wanted privacy and shared a small room, or it was the fact that they both were infatuated with Tiffany Foster. She was a little bit younger at fourteen, and in Seventh Grade, but she was still the prettiest girl in school. Tiffany had long curly blonde hair like Gabriel's mother's, but she had green eyes that reminded him of jewels of great value when she smiled. Her face was reminiscent of some of the great angelic paintings of the sixteenth century, at least Gabriel thought so. To Gabriel, she was stunningly beautiful.

Gabriel closed the book he was reading and glanced over to see Tiffany struggling to find the answer to an arithmetic problem on her slate. He would go over and help her in a second, but what he really wanted to do was to walk her home after school and have the opportunity for them to talk alone. He was smitten sure enough, but he wasn't the only one. Evan had his head down on his desk, staring at her like a puppy desperate for attention. The day was almost over, and Gabriel's anticipation was churning in his stomach. If he could, he would spend all his time talking to her. He was shy of calling it love, because he'd only known her for about a week, but he had never felt this way about any other girl.

After school, Evan and Gabriel both walked with Tiffany towards the Big Z Ranch. The ground was wet from the rain, and the clouds were threatening to start raining again. Gabriel had tried to persuade Evan to leave them alone, but Evan was persistent to walk her home as well. "You do realize that none of us have ever seen the ocean, right? I think we should make a pact to go see it together when Tiffany graduates," Evan suggested.

"That sounds nice, but I don't know if Annie

will let me. That's a long way from here," Tiffany answered.

Gabriel spoke quickly to get his words in, "You'll be seventeen when you graduate. Certainly, she'll let you make some choices of your own. What do you plan to do anyway? I mean, people come to America every day seeking to reach their dream. So, what's your dream, or do you not have one?"

"I want to be a doctor," Evan interrupted quickly.

"I think I'd like to be a teacher, but I can barely do my arithmetic and get it right," she answered. "What about you, Gabriel? What are you going to do after you get out of school? Go to work for Annie full time?"

"At first, maybe. But my grandfather and parents want me to go to college and do something more businesslike. I can help you with your arithmetic. It's not that hard once you get the hang of it."

"For me it is," she said with a hint of frustration.

"I can help you, too," Evan volunteered. "Gabriel is good at it, but it doesn't come as naturally to him as it does me. I had to help him a few times already. I guess that's why I want to be a doctor because I have the brains for it."

Gabriel frowned. Evan was normally a fairly quiet person, but all of a sudden, when they were around Tiffany, he spoke non-stop. "Yeah, Evan's good at arithmetic."

Evan continued, "Wait and see, Tiffany, when I'm a doctor, I'm going to own the biggest house in town. And my wife, whoever she is, is going to be the luckiest woman in town because I'm going to buy her whatever she wants."

"She sounds very lucky whoever she is. But, there are not too many people with a lot of money around here. You might have better luck living in Portland or San Francisco if you want to be rich. Me? I'm new here, but I like Annie and Uncle Charlie and Aunt Mary. I could live here and work on the ranch forever."

"They're not your aunt and uncle, you know," Evan stated before Gabriel could speak.

Tiffany stopped walking and turned to face Evan with a hurtful expression on her furrowed brow. "I don't have any relatives anymore, Evan. These people have taken me in just like Gabriel's family took you in. And I'm willing to bet uncle Charlie would smack you if he heard you say that! They are all the family I have, and I don't need to be reminded of that. Okay?"

"Sorry," he said quietly.

"You should be!" She began walking again. "I feel more welcome and at home here than I have anywhere since I was a child. I don't care what you say; they're my aunt and uncle. And I'll be meeting more of the family this Thursday when they all come for Thanksgiving. You guys should come over."

"We're not family, besides we have our dinner to go to," Evan said.

Tiffany looked at Gabriel and could clearly see the similarities he had to Matt. The dark hair, though Gabriel's had more of a curl in it than Matt's did. The square Bannister face with brown eyes and strong cheekbones. He was tall with broad shoulders and had many of Matt's small mannerisms, such as the cute little smirk that would come to his lips before trying to make a joke. "Gabriel is," she said as a fact.

"No, I'm not," Gabriel said. "Evan and I just work there. I don't think we'd be that welcomed," Gabriel said with a slight smile as he looked at Tiffany appreciatively.

"I think you would be," she answered and kept walking. They descended the hill overlooking the ranch and neared the large barn when they saw Charlie Ziegler riding his horse out of the barn to ride out onto the ranch. His rifle was in his scabbard.

"Are you going hunting, Mister Ziegler?" Evan asked his summer employer.

Charlie looked at the three teenagers and shook his head. "No. I'm just riding out and checking on the place. What are you boys doing here?"

Gabriel seemed to choke nervously on his words, not knowing if he was going to get in trouble or not, "Um, we walked Tiffany home."

Charlie smirked slightly. "I figured. Well, you three have a good day. And Tiff, I don't want you agreeing to be courted until one of those boys has the spine to ask me. Understood?"

She giggled slightly as her face turned red. "Okay, uncle Charlie. You can go on now."

Evan asked Charlie quickly, "Mister Ziegler, if you were riding out and saw some thieves stealing your cattle, what would you do?"

He frowned. "I'd shoot them."

"You wouldn't go get Tom? My Pa, I mean?" It had almost been a year since he had lived with the Smith family, but he still had a hard time referring to Tom and Elizabeth as his parents. They had legally adopted him and tried to make him feel at home, but he still felt like an outsider that didn't belong in the family.

Charlie shook his head. "Not until they were dead. Why? Are you thinking about becoming a rustler?"

"No!" Evan exclaimed awkwardly. "I was just asking."

Charlie's green eyes penetrated into Evan. "Well, that's one thing I wouldn't tolerate and would shoot someone for. I think everyone around here knows that, and they know I'll track them down if they did. We've never had a problem with that, and that's probably why. Anyway, boys don't stay too long, it's going to be dark soon, and it's a long walk home."

Gabriel watched Charlie ride out towards the ranch and said, "I used to be so afraid of him. I always thought he'd shoot me if I touched his property or even spoke to him."

"Uncle Charlie?" Tiffany asked, surprised.

"Yeah. I was always told he was dangerous. My grandfather always told me to stay away from him and his family. I always liked Steven, though."

Tiffany lowered her brow. "I've never been afraid of uncle Charlie. He's a very nice man. He wouldn't hurt a fly unless it was stealing cattle." She smiled.

"Or shooting at him," Evan said sadly. "He shot my brother last year."

"What?" she asked slowly.

Gabriel spoke, "When the Moskin Gang took my mother, they also held Evan at gunpoint and forced his brother Rodney down the mountain to ambush Matt, my father, and Mister Ziegler. I was with them too. Rodney shot my father, and Charlie shot Rodney. He had no choice. If Charlie hadn't, Matt would've had to. or we'd all be dead. Anyway, Charlie took my father back to town, and Matt and I went up the mountain to get my mother and Evan too. He's been with us ever since."

She looked at Evan softly. "I'm sorry, Evan. Uncle Charlie never would have done that if he didn't have to."

Evan nodded. "I know. It wasn't his fault. I wish Rodney would've asked for their help and not try to shoot them. I don't know what he was thinking."

"It was pretty scary," Gabriel stated.

"And your father, is Tom?" she asked Gabriel.

Gabriel nodded. "Yeah, he was shot in the shoulder. He's lucky he can still use his arm. It bothers him sometimes, but he still has it. Matt was amazing, though. It makes me wonder how different I'd be if I was raised by Charlie too. Those Bannister's are all tough as nails, and I don't know if I could ever be as brave as Matt was that day."

"Let's go in the barn and get out of the cold," Tiffany said and led the way into the barn. She looked troubled as she asked, "If you knew something about a friend that they didn't know, would you tell them?"

Evan answered quickly, "Not if it was better left,

unsaid." His eyes looked nervously at her.

Gabriel spoke thoughtfully, "I think so. If I knew something about you that you didn't know, I'd tell you. That's what friends do. And I consider you a friend of mine." A small smirk touched the corners of his lips. "Why, are you going to tell Evan about the booger hanging out of his nose?"

Evan wiped his nose quickly and looked at his fingers to be met with Gabriel's laughter.

"I'm just teasing," he laughed.

Tiffany looked preoccupied with her thoughts. It was obvious she wanted to say something but was hesitant.

"What?" Gabriel asked with a smile. "Is Charlie firing me?" he joked.

She shook her head decidedly. "I can't tell you. I promised not to."

Gabriel's smile faded with concern. "You can't do that to me. Come on, what is it?"

"I can't tell you." She turned away from him.

"Friends should be able to share anything, right? So, what can't you tell me? I promise I won't say anything."

He looked over to Evan suspiciously. "What?" he asked, feeling a pressure growing in his chest. He found it hard to breathe as the question came to mind. "What? Are you two courting or something?" The thought of it angered him.

"No!" she gasped and turned back towards him. "It has nothing to do with Evan."

Gabriel looked at her. "But he knows too? And I don't?"

"Yes," she answered softly.

"I don't know what she's talking about," Evan replied quickly.

"Yes, you do," she accused. "Matt told me he told you."

Evan stood motionless and shook his head, "Don't," he said softly.

"Don't what? What is it?" Gabriel asked, growing irritated by the anxiousness he was feeling.

She looked at him sincerely. "Gabriel, do you ever wonder why your brothers and sisters have blonde hair, and you have dark hair?"

He shook his head with a shrug. "No, they just do."

"You never wondered why your face isn't round while theirs are?"

He shook his head. "No. Why? What is it?" he asked with a nervous laugh.

She took a deep breath. "The next time you see Matt, you should go look in the mirror."

He laughed. "Do you think I look like Matt? He has long hair and a beard; I don't."

Evan spoke to Tiffany plainly, "Just tell him if you're going to."

"Tell me what?" he shouted.

Tiffany looked at Gabriel, sincerely. "Gabriel, Tom's not your father, Matt, is."

Gabriel laughed. "Yeah, right!"

"I'm not teasing. He told me so himself, but I wasn't supposed to tell you. I can't keep it a secret, though; it just isn't right to keep it from you. Ask Evan, he knows."

Gabriel's expression changed to one of disbelief. He looked at Evan.

Evan nodded. "It's true. Matt didn't want you to know. No one wanted you to know."

"Wait, are you serious? Tell me you're teasing." His chest began to expand with deep breaths. A sense of panic was beginning to take hold of him. "Tell me the truth right now, Evan!"

"I am. Matt's your real father. Why do you think you look like him and not Tom? Think about it, Gabriel," Evan said nervously.

"Go ask Annie if you don't believe me," Tiffany suggested.

"Please tell me you're playing around?" He felt like he had been kicked in the gut by a horse.

She shook her head. "Go ask Annie."

Gabriel walked past them out of the barn and walked to Annie's house. Evan and Tiffany followed him. He knocked on Annie's door and stepped inside, "Annie?" he yelled. "Are you home?"

Rory Jackson answered from the kitchen where she was making dinner for Annie and her family. "She's out on the ranch somewhere. You'll probably find her building the new bunkhouse," she answered. Rory was a very attractive black lady in her late mid to late twenties, who grew up on the ranch and was Annie's best friend. She was the daughter of Charlie Ziegler's best friend, Darius Jackson.

"Miss Jackson, you'll know. Is Matt, my father?"

Rory hesitated as her smile became a compassionate frown. She answered in a soft voice, "Sweetheart, that's a question best answered by your mother, not me, Annie, or anyone else."

"So, it's true?" he asked as his young body began to breathe heavily like the weight of the truth was more than he could bear.

Rory watched him with caring eyes. "You'll have to ask your mother."

Gabriel nodded and turned around to face his friends. "I gotta go," he said and stepped out the door quickly. He began running and never looked back when Evan and Tiffany tried to call him back. Evan went after him, and Tiffany stepped back into the house.

Rory shook her head sadly and then looked sternly at Tiffany. "How'd he hear that?"

Tiffany looked downward and admitted, "I told him. I had to Rory; it only seemed right."

Rory sighed heavily. "Oh, Tiffany. Sometimes what seems right just isn't right at the time, Honey."

12

Elizabeth Smith danced playfully with her long curly yellowish-blonde hair twirling in the air as she spun around and weaved her head back and forth with the sound of the music she danced to. Her five-year-old daughter Alexis sat on the floor of their family room singing while beating on the bottom of an overturned cook pot. Elizabeth laughed and said, "You're a wonderful singer, Alexis. But Mommy's got to get busy making dinner for Daddy when he gets home."

"No, dance with me," she pleaded to her mother.

"Okay," Elizabeth said with her smiling dark brown eyes. "One more song."

With a satisfied smile and a new touch of excitement, Alexis began drumming on the pot and, with a loud voice, began singing a song she made up along the way. It was a song declaring her love for their dog, Bear. Through the innocence of the music sung by her daughter, Elizabeth smiled, laughed, and danced herself across the room and back again.

The front door opened, and Tom Smith stepped into his home with a growing grin. "What's this? It sounds like the Branson Quartet has come to my house to play!" He hung up his hat revealing his thinning short brown hair, large blue eyes, and a round face. He hung up his coat and quickly un-buckled his gun belt and hung it up beside the door. He was below average height, broad and thick, but his eyes were kind as he said, "Well, don't stop playing, Alexis. I just got home, and I want to dance with my wife to that beautiful song." He slipped his muddy boots off and walked to Elizabeth. "My dear, may I have this dance?"

She bowed her head as she curtsied and held out her hand for him to take. "You may, indeed, Sheriff Smith."

Tom took her in her arms and danced with her in their family room. Alexis stopped drumming to watch with a pleased smile beaming on her face. Tom lowered his eyebrows at her and whispered, "Well, don't stop! I just got her in my arms." Alexis giggled and started pounding on the bottom of the pot again with more energy than she had before as she watched her parents twirling around. The sound of her mother's laughter filled Alexis's heart with joy. Her eyes didn't miss a thing, nor did her ears as her mother told her father she loved him. Alexis weaved her head from side to side as she sang a pleasant song. She didn't have to wait to hear her father speak kindly to her mother of the love he had for her too. There was nothing more important for her little soul than knowing she was safe, and all was well in her own home.

"Okay," Elizabeth said with a smile as she broke from the dance, "I have to get started making dinner. Alexis, why don't we end the concert for now and you help me in the kitchen, or you can put your coat and boots on and go help your brother bring some wood inside before it gets dark."

James, their twelve-year-old son, said loudly, "Thank you! That noise was annoying."

Tom scolded him, "Don't discourage her, James! Singing is a talent, and if she's blessed with a desire to sing, then let her sing. She's a wonderful singer," he said with a nod to his daughter. "Now, go, bring some wood in for your mother."

"Have you seen the boys?" Elizabeth asked of Gabriel and Evan.

Tom smirked. "Yeah. They both walked that new girl, Tiffany, home to the Big Z." He chuckled slightly. "I'd kinda like to know how that three-way conversation went. Both of those boys are love-stricken and jealous of one another."

Elizabeth shook her head. "I hope they don't bring that home. We don't need them fighting over a girl here. She is a very pretty girl, though."

Tom nodded as he walked into the kitchen. "She is. But I have the prettiest wife in the county." He wrapped his arms around her and kissed her gently. "How was your day today?"

"Good. And yours? Anything new happening?"

"No. And that's the way I like it. Oh, Montgomery's dog was chasing Cliff Jorgeson's milk cow, so he shot the dog. Mister Montgomery is a bit upset, but there's not much we can do about that. Like I told him, at least he doesn't have to buy Cliff a new cow."

Elizabeth smiled wryly. "Maybe you should write a biography about all of your exciting adventures as a sheriff in the wild frontier. The people back east will eat it up like candy."

He chuckled. "Yeah, they would until they read it. Then they'd get about as bored as I do."

The front door opened, and Gabriel stepped inside. He closed the door behind him and stared at his parents.

"Is everything okay, Gabriel? Where's Evan?" Tom asked with concern as he looked at his son's facial expression.

"He's coming," Gabriel said softly.

"Are you two fighting?"

"No," he said and took his coat off. He untied his boots and slipped them off by the door.

"Is something wrong, Gabriel?" Elizabeth asked with concern. Gabriel looked to be troubled.

Alexis went to Gabriel and hugged his legs. "Hi sis," he said softly. He stepped into the family room and looked at his parents with a nervous expression. He looked like he was about to cry.

"Gabriel, what is it?" Tom asked, concerned.

He took a deep breath and was about to speak when he heard the door open, and Evan stepped inside, looking even more nervous than Gabriel did. Gabriel turned back to his parents. He found it hard to speak as his throat ran dry, and his chest felt like it had the weight of a freight train running across it. "Mom, is Matt Bannister, my father?" he asked, barely audible. His breathing was heavy and looked like he about ready to start weeping.

Elizabeth's eyes widened with the shock that ran through her body. She had known this day would come, but she never expected it would come today. She was most unprepared to answer the question even though she had practiced her response when the day would come. She couldn't speak.

Tom's head lowered as he sighed emotionally. "Gabriel, maybe we better sit down."

"No, I don't want to sit down," he said with an expression of horror on his face. "Mother is he my father?" he asked louder with a shaken voice.

Tears slipped out of her eyes and down her cheeks quietly. She looked at her son and said, "Yes."

Gabriel's eyes clouded with thick tears as he looked at Tom. "Y...You're not my father, Pa?"

Tom bit his bottom lip emotionally and shook his head slowly. "Yes, I am. But I'm not your natural father. How about we sit down and talk about it?"

Gabriel gasped for air as he found it hard to breathe. "I'm not your son?" he asked weakly.

Tom spoke with authority, "Yes, you are my son, and don't you ever doubt that! It's...it's complicated, but come sit down."

Gabriel shook his head, stunned. His eyes were heavy with tears that refused to fall. "Does Matt know?"

Tom answered, "Yes, he knows."

Tears made his vision blurry as he looked at his mother. "Does everyone know except me?"

Elizabeth fought to keep from sobbing as she shook her head. "No," was all she was able to say.

"Well, someone has to know because Tiffany knew, Evan knew! What about Granddad and Grandmother?"

She nodded. "They know."

"The Ziegler's? Matt's family knows too?" he asked, raising his voice.

She nodded while closing her eyes with another tear slipping down her cheek. "Yes, they know."

He stepped over to the davenport and sat down heavily. "Everyone knew..." he said quietly more to himself. "Except me?"

Elizabeth went to him and sat down beside him and grabbed his hand. "Gabriel, your father, and I were waiting for the right time to tell you."

Gabriel pulled his hand out of hers and looked at her with a disdained expression. "Which father?" he asked softly with a slight shaking of his head. His eyes hardened. He pointed at Tom. "I don't know how to feel. He's always been my father, and now, out of the blue, you're telling me he's not? My whole life's been a lie, and I'm just finding out?" he stood up and looked at Tom and then back down to his mother. "And I had to find out from Tiffany and him," he pointed at Evan. "You two never told me. I had to hear it from my friends."

Elizabeth bit her lip emotionally with an anguished expression. Another tear slipped out down her cheek. "I'm sorry, Gabriel. I am so sorry you had to find out like this."

"Gabriel," Tom said softly, "We planned to tell you, but it's a hard thing to talk about."

He widened his eyes. "You could've just told me. You had sixteen years to do so!" he yelled. "I'm going upstairs! I want to be alone!" he shouted and walked quickly upstairs.

The room fell silent except for Alexis trying to comfort her sobbing mother. Tom looked at Evan. "You told him?" he asked softly.

Evan shook his head quickly with his nervousness showing in his blue eyes. "Tiffany did. She thought it was the right thing to do."

Tom sighed. "I could almost curse Matt for telling her."

Elizabeth exhaled a deep breath. She looked at Tom and said, "We should've told him."

Tom raised his voice just a bit, "I'm not going there, and you know why. We're not going to bring up the past, and you know why. But we haven't had sixteen years to tell him. And you know why!" Tom had just found out Gabriel wasn't his son eleven months before when Matt first came back to Willow Falls.

Elizabeth covered her face with her hands and began sobbing. She quickly wiped her eyes and sniffled. She looked at Tom. "We need to talk to our son."

He sat down on a kitchen chair. "Let's leave him be alone to let it soak in for a while. There'll be time to talk soon enough. He wants to be alone, so let's leave him be."

"I told her not to tell him," Evan said, feeling uncomfortable and out of place.

"I wish she hadn't! Damn it, Matt!" Tom exclaimed angrily and hit the table with his fist. He looked at Elizabeth. "I'm going up to talk to him."

"I thought you wanted to wait?"

Tom's lips pulled together tightly, and a mist grew quickly over his eyes. With a broken voice, he said, "I can't. I need to talk to him now."

"Do you want me to go with you?"

He shook his head and sniffled. "No. Just me." He went upstairs and knocked on Gabriel's door. He wiped his eyes and took a deep breath before opening it. "Gabe, I know you wanted to be alone, but we have to talk."

Gabriel was sitting on his bed, staring at the floor. He wiped his eyes. "Is there anything else I don't know? Is mom really my mother?" he asked with a quick sob to his voice.

Tom sat down beside his son. "Yeah, she is. Gabe," he paused. "I am so sorry you found out like this. This isn't how we planned on telling you."

"When was someone going to tell me, on my wedding day?" he asked with a harsh gaze in his reddened eyes.

Tom lowered his head in guilt. "I don't know," he answered softly. "We just planned to tell you sometime."

"Pa, please tell me this isn't real," he said weakly and began sobbing in Tom's arms. Tom held him as his own face buckled in emotion, and the tears began flowing out of his eyes.

"I wish I could, Gabe. I wish I could," he whispered as he held his son. "Listen to me; it doesn't change anything. Okay? It doesn't change anything at all. You're still my son, and I love you so much, Gabriel." He held his son close as another tear fell down his cheek.

"I love you, too, Pa," he said as he pulled from Tom's embrace and wiped his face free of the tears. "I guess that explains why everyone in that family always hugs me and looks at me differently than Evan or my other friends."

Tom nodded. "Yeah."

Gabriel shook his head and reached down to grab one of Evan's dirty shirts on the floor to blow his nose on. "Is that why no one ever wanted me to talk to Mister and Misses Ziegler or anyone else in that family?"

Tom nodded slowly. "Yeah."

"And last Christmas Eve when you hit me after Granddad caught me talking to Steven, and his brothers. Is that why you hit me?"

Tom grimaced with regret. A tear slipped out of his eyes. "Yes," he whispered.

Gabriel's face showed his heartache. "I didn't know, Pa. And it wasn't my fault anyway," he said, sounding bitter. "I was just talking to them."

Tom wiped his nose. "It was my fault. I was scared they'd tell you. I am so sorry for hitting you. I was wrong."

"I know. You've already apologized for that." He paused to look at Tom. "Pa, did Matt not want me?"

Tom's eyes opened wider, and for a moment,

he said nothing. He shook his head slowly with the agony of having to talk about a past he never wanted to talk about again. He didn't want to lie, but how was he supposed to tell Gabriel that his mother committed adultery when she conceived him? Protecting Elizabeth's reputation and honor was his highest priority.

"No, he didn't," Tom answered after a moment's pause. "He left, and I married your mother. I loved her, and I loved you."

Gabriel looked to be quite hurt by the statement about Matt. "I thought he left because you two got married? How old was I when he left?"

Tom squeezed his lips painfully together. "You weren't born yet. Look, it's not all too important how all that came about. The fact is I love your mother, and I have loved you since before you were born," he said with a cracking voice and tears flooding his eyes. "I used to lay in bed and rub your mother's belly and talk to you at night. I still remember the first time I felt your little feet kick inside of her." He smiled painfully. "It was the most exciting thing ever until the day you were born. I held you and held you and showed you off to everyone I could. I was so proud of you. Gabriel, nothing on this earth will ever take those memories away from me or take away how much I love you. There's nothing that will change that. I think God lets us have children, so we will know how much he loves us, except he loves us even more. Gabriel, you may have Bannister blood running through your veins, but you're a Smith. You're a Smith child and my son.

Don't ever forget that. I'm very proud of you, son."

"Thank you, Pa," he said, getting more control over himself. "So Mom was pregnant when you married her?"

Tom paused. In truth, no, she wasn't. Elizabeth had committed adultery a week after their wedding and conceived Gabriel. Tom took a deep breath. "Yeah, she was," he said sadly.

"Matt's kind of a creep then, isn't he?"

Tom shook his head. "No, maybe, I don't know. Look, he a… just ran away when he found out she was pregnant. He didn't want to marry her, so I did. He was just young and scared of your grandfather, maybe, I don't know. What I do know is that it was a long time ago and doesn't need to be remembered, Gabriel, because it doesn't matter. You're my son, and that is all that matters to me, I hope that's all that matters to you as well."

Gabriel grimaced. "So, he ran away because she was pregnant? That's not what I heard. I heard he left Willow Falls because you two got married and he was in love with mom."

Tom shook his head slightly. "That wouldn't make much sense, would it? Wouldn't it make more sense if he skedaddled out of town and left her pregnant and then I married her?"

"Pa, if he left before I was born, then when did he find out I'm his son? Mom said he knew. Was that a lie too?"

Tom took a deep breath. "She told him…"

"When?"

Tom sighed deeply. "Before he left."

123

"What did he say?"

"He didn't say much; he just left town and never came back until last year."

"He just left her pregnant?"

Tom nodded his head slowly. "Yes. That's why he left Willow Falls."

"I don't understand. If I'm his flesh and blood, then why didn't Matt say something last year when he came back?"

Tom could feel a bit of irritation building within him. "Because he didn't want to cause any problems with our family. He figured you had enough on your plate at the time. He didn't want to ruin your Christmas."

"But he knows I'm his son?"

The words cut Tom to his soul. He nodded sadly. "He knows."

"Pa, can I take the horse and go see him?"

Tom was alarmed. "Why?"

"Because I have to know...I don't know. I just want to go see him."

"It's already nearing supper time and getting dark. Don't you think it's getting a little late for that? It's a three-hour ride, Gabriel. Besides, don't you think you should talk to your mother a bit first? She is feeling so bad right now that it would be nice if you let her know how you feel at least. Besides, tomorrow's Wednesday, and we'll be pretty busy preparing for Thanksgiving. Matt will be at the Big Z on Thursday, I suspect, why not wait until then?" He stood up and ran his hand anxiously through his hair. "Gabriel, I can't stop you from seeing Matt, because you're bound to run into him sooner or later. I don't know if he'll want a relationship with you or not, but if so, just know..." Tom's voice began to shake. "I love you. Okay, Son?"

"I love you too, Pa. So can I go?"

Tom was stunned by his urgency to leave. "Not tonight. Like I said, how about you wait until Thursday or Friday when he's here in town."

Gabriel had his mind made up to go, but he knew he was never going to get permission to leave. "Okay, Pa. Tell Mom, I'll be down in a bit and do my chores. I want to be alone for a while."

Tom nodded once contently. "See you downstairs."

When Tom left, Gabriel began dressing for colder weather and went downstairs.

"Gabriel, can we talk?" Elizabeth asked as she stirred dinner on the cookstove. Tom stood near her.

"Mom, we can, but I'm still trying to digest everything. If you don't mind, I'm going out to do my chores, and I'll be back in. After dinner, we can talk, okay?"

She smiled tight-lipped. "Okay."

Evan stood up, "I'll go with you."

"No, I'd prefer to be alone if you don't mind. I have a lot on my mind."

"Oh," Evan said like his feelings were hurt.

Gabriel put on his boots and pulled on his coat. He grabbed his hat to keep the rain off his head and went outside. Out in the barn, instead of milking the cow, he saddled their horse and rode it out of the barn. He sped past the house as the front door opened, and Tom yelled, "Gabriel!" He never looked back as he ran the horse down the road.

Tom gritted his teeth to restrain himself from cursing. He looked back at Elizabeth. "He's going to go see Matt."

"What?" she asked, astonished. A wave of dread went through her like a whirlwind picking up the dust of the past and throwing it in her face so thick it was blinding her. Her eyes filled up with thick layers of water. "Go get him and bring him back here!" She exclaimed as a sense of panic over-whelmed her.

Tom shook his head sadly. "No. Let him go."

Elizabeth looked at Tom through her falling tears. "Life's never going to be the same, is it?" she asked through a broken voice.

"No, it's not. We might've lost our boy today."

"Don't say that, Tom. Please." She sat down on the davenport and buried her head in her hands and wept.

13

Matt and his two deputies, Truet Davis and Phillip Forrester, rode out of Branson with a saddled horse tethered to each of their own. They were riding out to Slater Silver Mine's employee housing community known as Slater's Mile, or more commonly known around Branson as "Slater's slums of shacks and rats." They left the main road leaving Branson for about two miles and then rode down an access road that went slightly downhill through a thin forest of trees and brush to a wide area that had rows of tiny shacks that were built to give the basics of living and nothing more. It was laid out like a city plan map with nine small blocks with three roads going vertically and three going horizontally. The cabins lined the vertical streets and faced each other across the road. There was very little space between cabins to the side or the back. The small cabins were compacted together to fit as many as they could in the space available. Privacy and comfort for the company employees were never a concern. Simple housing close to the mine was the objective, and it was thrown together as fast as they could build it. To accommodate the hundred and fifty cabins, there was a long outhouse with eight stalls in each spread out on every block. Four stalls faced the left side of the road; four stalls faced the right side to serve the homes on that side of the street. The outhouses were separated by a couple of hundred feet from each other placed near the center of each block. The company housing community that was supposed to be a benefit for the mine employees may have at one time been an attraction, but it had become a slum of discarded trash and filth leading to a hefty rat population. As they rode into the employee housing complex, the stench of an overcrowded and uncared for community overwhelmed their senses even in the cold rain that fell gently down in the fading light.

Matt stopped his horse and looked back at Phillip. "There's a time to be nice, Phillip, and there's a time not to be. Now's not a time to be. We're going to go in there aggressively. This is you're first time coming with us to make a dangerous arrest, so expect the unexpected because you never know what can happen. Keep your guard up." Phillip Forrester was a deputy Marshal who was a young twenty-five years old and new to the job of a lawman. His primary responsibilities were to stay in the office, and manage the front desk, manage the jail responsibilities and run errands. It was Phillip's first opportunity to get out of the office and get into the grit and physical side of law enforcement.

Phillip nodded nervously.

They rode to cabin number twelve and tied their horses to a small wooden hitching rail that served that block of cabins and walked back to cabin twelve. Matt pulled his revolver as he stood off to the side of the main door, Truet as well pulled his revolver and stood across the doorway from Matt. Matt opened the door and pushed it open casually before peeking in and stepped inside, followed by his two deputies. The cabin was dark, dusty, stale, and stank. The cabin was nothing more than a small room with a cookstove in it and a door going back to a bedroom. The door was half-open.

From inside the bedroom came the rough voice of an angry man. "Gertie, I'm going to crack your head open! Where the hell have you been, woman?" The door was jerked open, and a big overweight man with neck length greasy black hair and a long black beard stared at Matt and Truet, who had their revolvers pointed at him. He stood with a surprised expression on his rough-looking face. He was shirtless, showing a large hairy chest and belly while standing in his canvas pants.

Matt spoke shortly, "Turn around and put your hands behind your back!"

The man's dark eyes glared at Matt with hostility. "What the hell are you doing here?"

"Turn around now!" Matt ordered forcefully.

The big man turned around slowly and placed his hands behind his back. "What am I being arrested for, Marshal? Painting on your window?"

Matt put his revolver away and said, "Get yourself dressed. If you try anything, I'll shoot you. Hurry up!"

"Can I ask why I'm being arrested? I haven't eaten anything today!" He glared back at Matt bitterly as he faced the wall.

"That's too bad. I'm counting to twenty, and if you're not dressed, that's fine. I'll take you outside and put you on a horse anyway."

"Fine." Leroy Haywood said as he dropped his hand and stepped towards his bedroom. "I'll be out by tonight anyway, tomorrow at most." He sat down on his bed and pulled on his wool socks and grabbed his filthy boots to put on. He stood up and grabbed a stained undershirt that smelled terrible from four feet away and put it on — followed by a heavy torn-up sweater and a brown flannel shirt. He stopped to pull his suspenders up over his shoulders. He reached for his hat but paused. "Where's my hat?" he looked around the floor. "I can't find my hat."

"Get your coat, and let's go."

Leroy Haywood grabbed his heavy coat off the floor and put it on. "I'm dressed. Now, what's this all about? I have the right to know, don't I?"

"Turn around and put your hands behind your back."

"Fine. Someone saw me painting your windows, huh?" he chuckled.

Matt shackled his big wrists and turned Leroy around to face him. "No. You're under arrest for two counts of murder, assault and attempted murder, and yeah, we'll throw in some vandalism too.

I hope you'll be hung for the murders of Chee Yik and Kat-Kho-Not."

Leroy Haywood chuckled. "Speak English, Marshal." He laughed at his own joke without concern. "You're wasting your time. No one's going to hang me for that. Hell, I'd kill a dozen of the little yellow bastards if I could. Besides, when I go to court, my wife and everyone else will say I was here sleeping. I even worked today if you look at the time books."

Matt looked at him harshly. "Well, I'm going to do my best to convince them that you deserve to hang. And when they see what's left of Ah See's back, and your whip, it might be enough to turn the juries stomachs enough to put you away if not hung."

Leroy's face slowly changed from humor to an angry grimace. "I'll get out. Just you wait and see."

"That's up to the jury, but until then, you're in my custody. And you're not going to like me. I promise," Matt said with his eyes burning into Leroy's.

"I don't already."

Matt nodded. "Good. Now, let's go." He led Leroy outside, and his deputies Truet and Phillip put him on his horse.

Matt closed the door and locked it with a key he got from Gertie. "Okay, one down and two more to go. Let's go get Oscar Belding next in cabin thirty-five."

They rode to cabin thirty-five. Matt looked at Truet. "I'm going to take Phillip in with me this time. You watch Leroy."

Matt neared the door and heard a woman's

voice and those of children. His heart sank, and he looked at Phillip and sighed. "They have children in there. Dang, I hate this." He knocked on the door and waited. A woman opened it in her late thirties with plain straight brown hair that fell to the top of her shoulders. She was barefoot and wore a dingy blue dress that looked like it could've been dyed burlap with holes cut out of it for her head and arms. She wasn't too attractive, and her eyes widened in fear when she saw Matt standing at her door. Two blonde toddlers clung to her legs as they also stared at Matt. She didn't say a word.

Matt spoke, "Ma'am, is your husband, Oscar Belding here?"

She nodded silently. She backed up and pulled the door open.

"Who is it?" Oscar asked from the small dining table. He was in the middle of eating his dinner. Oscar was a stout man of medium height with dark brown curly hair that was at his mid-ear and a thick mustache that went down to his chin. He stood up when Matt and Phillip stepped inside. Oscar looked shocked to see them and backed against the wall staring at Matt like he'd seen a ghost.

Matt motioned to Oscar's wife and children with his hand. "I don't want to scare your family, so don't cause us any trouble. You are under arrest for the murder of two Chinese men last night. Now, calmly turn around and put your hands behind your back," he said softly, not to scare the children.

"I'm John...you got the wrong man! Um, Oscar's not here," he said desperately.

Matt looked back at Oscar's wife. "Ma'am, I'm going to ask once, and if you lie to me, you'll go to jail too. Think about your children before you answer. Is this your husband, Oscar Belding?"

Her mouth tightened as she grit her teeth emotionally. She looked at Oscar and seen him shake his head fearfully. She dropped her head in shame and nodded while she covered her mouth and began to cry.

Matt looked back at Oscar. "Face the wall. Come on, don't make me get violent in front of your children, please."

Oscar turned towards the wall and put his hands against the wall. His body convulsed as he fought from sobbing. "Please, it was Leroy and Roger that did it. I didn't do anything to those men. Leroy is the one you want!"

Matt grabbed Oscar's right wrist and pulled it behind him and shackled his wrist. Oscar began to sob and fought from giving Matt his left wrist. Suddenly, he pushed himself off the wall and threw his head backward to headbutt Matt. He connected with Matt's forehead. Matt let go of Oscar's right wrist to protect himself, which allowed Oscar to spin around quickly and throw his right arm around, swinging the open end of the shackles towards Matt's head. Matt was too close for the opened shackle to hit him, but the opened end of the shackles connected with Phillip's cheek as he stepped forward to help Matt. The thin flat steel of the shackle ripped into Phillip's cheek and tore through it with the momentum of Oscar's body swinging around and then being pushed back against the wall forcefully by Matt.

Phillip began screaming as his cheek was ripped open midway up his jaw down through the corner of his lips. His mouth filled with blood and poured out onto the floor. Knowing his cheek was torn in two, he began to panic and cried out for Matt in sudden pain, but mostly from the paralyzing panic of having his face ripped open.

Matt's eyes turned ice-cold as he drove his knee up into the crotch of Oscar as hard as he could, and when his body went stiff and bent over, Matt grabbed his hair and drove a hard knee up into his face. Oscar fell to the floor sideways, struggling to catch his breath from the blow to his crotch. Matt looked at Phillip and quickly grabbed Phillip's hand to pull it away from his cheek.

"Truet!" he yelled, noticing the lady was quickly ushering her terrified children into the bedroom through her sobbing and closed the door.

"What happened?" Truet asked, quickly entering the door with his gun in his hand. "Oh no! Let me see, Phillip. Oh damn. What happened?" he asked Matt.

"He got hit by an open-ended shackle. You're going to have to take him to Doctor Ambrose immediately! I'll take care of these three men." Matt slipped his buffalo coat off and removed his badge from his shirt and pulled his shirt off. "Let me wrap this around your face, Phillip." He and Truet tied the shirt around the lower half of Phillip's face while he groaned and filled the shirt with blood.

Matt looked at Phillip in the eyes to make sure he heard him, "You're going to be fine, Phillip. The Doctor will have you sutured up in no time. Calm down, okay? Just relax and know, you'll be okay." He nodded reassuringly.

Matt looked at Truet. "Go ahead and go."

Truet eyed Oscar with hostility. "Alright. Come on, Phillip," he said gently as he guided his young friend out the door. Immediately the sound of Leroy laughing entered the house. Matt looked out the filthy window and watched Leroy laughing as Truet lead Phillip to his horse. Truet pointed at Leroy and said something about seeing Leroy in jail. Leroy stopped laughing by the look in Truet's eyes.

Matt went to Oscar and turned him over to his stomach and jerked his left arm behind him and shackled his wrist as tight as he could. "Get up!" he ordered and forced him outside.

Leroy was smiling as Truet and Phillip rode back towards town. "Nice one, Oscar!" he laughed. "That was bloody great to see!"

Matt lead Oscar beside the horse Leroy was sitting on. He grabbed Leroy's leg and lifted it and threw him out of the saddle onto the muddy street. Leroy landed face down with a heavy hollow sound as he landed. He gasped in pain with his hands secured behind his back. Matt placed his muddy boot on the back of Leroy's head and pressed his head down into the mud. He looked at Oscar who was weeping and looked like he was thinking about running away. "If you run, I'll make you hurt worse than you do now."

He turned his attention back to Leroy, who was cursing Matt bitterly with the side of his face buried in mud. Matt removed his boot from Leroy's head and quickly stomped down of Leroy's kidney. Leroy cried out in pain and arched his back in reaction to the pain. He rolled over to his back with a grimace.

Matt put Oscar on a horse and went back to lean over Leroy. "I don't want to hear another word out of you until we get back to the jail. Do you hear me?"

"Yeah," Leroy said painfully.

He helped Leroy stand up and get back into the saddle. Leroy noticed the small crowd of wives and children coming out into the rain to see what was going on.

Matt ignored the small crowd that watched in interest and rode to the cabin of the third man involved in the killings, Roger Lavigne. In a way, Matt wanted Roger to fight his arrest too, but Roger surrendered peacefully.

Matt didn't say a single word on the way back to town. He was furious that he had allowed Phillip to get hurt. It was a bad wound and would leave a nasty scar for the remainder of the young man's life. He was lucky it had not connected with his eye socket or his throat. Matt was filled with frustration, guilt, and anger; all three emotions roamed around inside him. It was his job to protect his deputies. It was his responsibility to watch over and teach them all he knew about using caution and trying to stay safe in the duties of a lawman. Phillip was a local boy who knew numbers and organization in a business setting. Matt had hired him for the relatively safe position of maintaining the office and all the business details that Matt didn't want to do. One never knew what was going to happen when you dealt with people, and the most unexpected things could happen when arresting someone, and unfortunately, it did to a young man Matt thought so much of. Matt was responsible, and it weighed heavily on his heart. He had failed and Phillip would always have a large ugly scar on his cheek for the rest of his life to remind him of that.

Matt led the three men into the marshal's office and took them back through the solid heavy steel door to the jail cells. The walls were solid granite blocks with a concrete floor. The jail cells had no windows and had heavy iron bars making the jail virtually escape-proof. A center granite wall separated the two cells, and each cell had two bunkbeds capable of putting four people in each cell. Albert's dog barked and howled loudly in the first cell, and a foul smell assaulted all of their nasal passages. The dog had obviously had a bout with loose bowels and relieved itself all over the cell floor. The food bowl was empty, but the water in the bucket was half full. His brother Albert was supposed to get the dog that day but hadn't while the office was open anyway.

Roger Lavigne gasped. "You don't expect us to stay in here, do you?"

"What's this? Are you arresting dogs?" Leroy asked with a chuckle.

Matt bit his bottom lip agitated by the mess. He regretted ever offering to hold the dog. He opened the second cell that was clean and pushed all three men inside it after removing the wrist shackles and closed and locked the door. He spoke over the howling dog who's bark echoed against the granite, making it even more annoying. "I'll get you all some dinner a bit later. I'm afraid my man hired to watch the jail was injured tonight, so you men get to use those buckets under the cots as a privy. You can thank your friend Oscar for that. Have fun."

Oscar said with a frightened voice as he grabbed the bars staring at Matt desperately, "Marshal, I have a wife and kids, I shouldn't be here! I didn't do anything. They did it all!"

Leroy answered, "Ah, shut up, Oscar. We'll be out of here soon enough."

Matt looked at Oscar. "Your friends might leave if the jury decides not to indict them. But you injured my deputy, and with deadly intent, I might add. You're not going anywhere for a while."

"I wasn't trying to kill anyone!" Oscar pleaded.

Matt shoved a finger in his face. "If that had hit Phillips throat instead of his cheek, he'd be dead! That was your decision and your action that caused that, nothing else. So, don't tell me you weren't trying to kill anyone."

"Can you shut that dog up?" Leroy yelled.

"I didn't..." Oscar began to plead. "Marshal, please...it's almost Thanksgiving, and my family has nothing to eat. Please, I didn't do anything!"

"I'll be back later with your dinner," Matt said

and stepped away to look at the foul mess that was all over the floor in the next cell. The dog stared at him howling and trying to jump up on the iron bars. Matt shook his head with disgust. "You are one stinking dog. I don't know what I'm going to do with you, but come on." He unlocked the jail door and the dog jumped up on him leaving a trail of the dog's wet diarrhea from its feet on Matt's pants.

"Get away from me!" he shouted crossly. The dog ran out of the jail cell into the main office.

"Marshal, my wife is in danger out there alone! Please, let me go home. I need my kids, Sir."

Matt's eyes hardened as he looked at Oscar. He spoke harshly, "You know that was my thought when I arrested you. Children should never have to have to pay for their parents' crimes. They need to be kept safe, loved, warm, and fed by their parents, not sitting at home going hungry and wondering if their father is ever coming home from jail or not! You should've thought about that before you went with those two last night or when you fought me earlier. You're not going anywhere!" he yelled before leaving the cell block and closed the steel door with a loud slam. He locked it and looked at Albert's dog that was squatting over the floor of his office squirting a pool of diarrhea on the wood floor. "For crying out loud!" he shouted with a scowl. "Alright, you have to go! You're not staying here another night. Bark, howl, and crap is all you can do! My word, Albert, is going to pay for this. Never again!"

The bell tied to the office door rang as William Fasana stepped into the office. "What stinks in here?" he asked with a distasteful grimace.

Matt pointed at the dog as it began to howl at William.

"Is that Albert's dog you were talking about last night at dinner?"

Matt scowled. "Yeah. Do you want it?"

"No! Are you looking to get rid of it?"

"Any way I can! It's crapped all over my jail and now in my office, and I just let it out here! I want to see Phillip at Doctor Ambrose's, but I can't take this thing with me, and I can't leave it in the jail either because I've got men in there. I want this dog gone!"

"Hey, I have an idea," William said and stepped back outside. He yelled down the street, "Chusi! Hey, Chusi, come here." He stepped back inside and pointed at the dog. "That's a hunting dog, you know. Chusi can probably train it to hunt whatever he wants. You might even offer him a few dollars to clean up your office and jail. It might smell better."

"I will."

"How come you didn't come get me to go with you today? If you needed help, I told you I'm available anytime. I heard about Phillip, and I'm sorry. If you need help, just say so," William said.

"I wasn't expecting to need any more help than we had."

Chusi Yellowbear stepped into the office and shook off the cold. He was an old Shoshone Indian with gray taking over his long black hair. He had become a vagrant of the Branson streets who begged for part of his money, fished and hunted to provide for himself, and sold what he could. He was known as the town drunk and had few friends in town. "Hi, my friends," he said, curious to know what William wanted.

William smiled slightly, "Come on in and warm up, Chusi. Matt wants to know if you want a new hunting dog? It's free for the taking on one condition that you be willing to clean the dog crap up in here and in the jail. Then it's yours, free and clear. It's a red bloodhound. Easy to train to hunt whatever you want," William explained as he leaned on Phillip's desk.

Chusi stepped closer to the dog and kneeled to call it over. He pet the dog while he looked into its eyes. "Yes, I want her."

Matt offered, "You can have her. And if you want to clean up the mess, it's made in here, and in the jail, I'd appreciate it and pay you five dollars to do that and take the six horses outside back to the livery stable for me."

Chusi looked at Matt with raised eyebrows. "That's a lot of money for an hour's work, maybe an hour's work."

Matt took a deep breath. "It crapped everywhere in the jail, and I don't want to clean it up. It's got diarrohea and tracked it all over my office now too. It's crapped everywhere, Chusi."

Chusi nodded. "Of course. She's scared. Does she have a name?"

Matt shook his head. "No."

"I'll give her one. Yes, I'll clean it up and take the horses back for you. And thank you."

Matt went into his office and opened a desk

drawer and counted out five-dollar coins. "Here, I'll trust you to complete the job. I have to go see Phillip, so William's going to stay here with you and close the office up for me."

"No, I'm not," William argued.

Matt tossed him a U.S. Marshal's badge. "I need you to if you wouldn't mind. Here is the key to the jail; it unlocks the big steel door and the cell doors. I have three men in the second cell. Don't unlock that cell door for any reason. They have a bucket if they need it. The dog was in the first cell. There is a cleaning brush, rags, and a pail in the closet. Make sure to lock everything up when you leave."

14

Matt stepped into Doctor Ambrose's office and stepped into the back room where Doctor Ambrose had Phillip lying on his table unconscious while he was carefully suturing the outside of Phillip's cheek back together. Behind him sitting against the wall was Phillip's parents and his fiancé, Truet also sat in the room with them.

"How is he?" Matt asked quietly.

Doctor Ambrose paused and stood up from his stooped over position over Phillip. "I had to put him out to suture the inside of his cheek. That was difficult, but he'll be fine once I get him finished up here. I just wanted to get this done before he does wake up."

"Don't let me hold you up," Matt said to the doctor and moved nearer to Phillip's parents and his fiancé and knelt in front of them. All of them looked upset. "I'm sorry this happened to your son. I really am. The man who did this is being charged with assault with a deadly weapon and attempted murder, if that helps at all."

Phillip's father was in his late fifties and was a big and strong man with a rough no-nonsense expression. He had balding gray hair and a long gray beard on his square and weathered face. He was a timberman and worked his way into a timber falling supervisor position for the Seven Timber Harvester Company before being promoted to the logging division manager. He looked at Matt. "It's a risk that comes with the job. He's not dead, and we have to count our blessings with that. In my business, I've had to tell many parents that their son, husband, or father was dead. Some of those men were crushed to death by fallen trees, logs breaking loose or a few unlucky men were cut in two by a snapped cable, you just never know what can happen in a split second. It's not your fault, Matt. It's the risk that goes with the job."

Matt frowned with a troubled expression on his face. "It is a risk, but I still feel bad. That man was trying to hurt me, not Phillip. Phillip's too great of a young man to have a scar like that."

Phillip's mother was a bit younger than her husband but had a few gray hairs in her brown hair. Her oval face was still attractive for an older lady in her late forties. She looked at Matt with glossy red eyes. "He won't be able to eat very much for Thanksgiving now. And that's going to be a very big scar on my handsome boy's face. I told him not to work for you." Her eyes glared into Matt.

"Martha, it's not Matt's fault. It's a risk Phillip was willing to take when he took the job," Big Bob

Forrester said. He looked at Matt and continued, "I never wanted my boy to work in the woods with me because I know the dangers. I wanted him to get educated and be a teacher or something so he wouldn't have to feel the pain I do every morning from laboring so hard all my life. Times are different, and he doesn't need to do what I did. But the boy was excited to be a U.S. Deputy Marshal. I can't blame him, it would be exciting here and there, but I always wondered if he had the stomach for it."

Matt smiled lightly. "Time will tell. He may not be so interested after today." He looked back at the doctor, "Be sure to bill me for this and any future care of this wound."

The doctor nodded as he used the needle to suture another stitch in Phillip's cheek.

Truet Davis asked Matt, "Did you have any problem arresting Roger or with anyone on the way back?"

Matt shook his head. "Not at all."

Truet smiled. "I saw you throw Leroy off his horse. You had a little fun with him, did you?"

Matt nodded. "He's been pretty quiet since then." He looked at Phillip's fiancé Heather Winkler, "How are you, Heather?"

She smiled sadly. She was a young twenty-three-year-old lady with a small frame, thin and fragile as a girl could be. She had blonde hair that was pulled into a quick ponytail. "I'm okay. I hate to see Phillip in so much pain."

"Truet got him here as fast as he could, I'm sure." He looked at Phillip's father, "I need to go feed my prisoners, will you let Phillip know I will work Thanksgiving, so he doesn't need to worry about that. Tell him to take as much time off as he needs. The office will be there waiting for him."

Big Bob Forrester nodded and said, "Matt, I heard your father is in town. He may not remember me. but tell him hello for me anyway."

Matt paused. "You knew him?"

Bob nodded. "Believe it or not, I probably wouldn't be married to my misses, if it wasn't for your father."

"How so?"

Big Bob smiled as he thought back and grabbed his wife's hand gently. "Oh, he told me if I loved her to let her know it because if I didn't, I'd always regret it. That little bit of persuasion changed everything. I didn't know him well, but it was the best advice I've ever received. How is your old man?"

"Fine, I guess. I really don't talk to him. He's at the Monarch Hotel if you want to say hi to him."

"He's gotta be getting pretty old by now. He was about ten years older than I was. You should talk to him because he knows a lot of the history around here. Your grandfather and your pa were pretty important folks around here back in the early days. This city wouldn't be what it is today without them."

"Is that because he lost all his money and land in a poker game or because he sold it all to settle a saloon debt?" Matt's bitterness came out loud and clear.

Big Bob Forrester frowned and shook his head

slightly. "No. He helped people start businesses and kept others from starving to death in the winter quite often. He had a big heart; he was a good man."

Matt smirked slightly. "I didn't see that side of him. Anyway, let Phillip know I'll come to see him tomorrow and not to worry about anything, just heal well."

Matt went to a saloon and ordered three dinners, instead of going to the Monarch Restaurant for his prisoner's nightly meal. He wanted to avoid his father at all costs. He took the meals to the Marshal's office and fed his three prisoners. The office and empty jail cell were clean, and the smell of a foul dog was eliminated by the scrubbing of Chusi, who had done a great job at cleaning up. Matt went home and sat down on his davenport and closed his eyes. It had been a busy day starting first thing that morning, and now at nearly eight in the evening, he was ready to relax before going to bed. The silence was nice, and it let his body drift in a falling sensation of relaxation that felt most pleasurable. He kicked his feet up on the davenport and put his hands behind his head to close his eyes for a moment. He knew Truet would be coming home shortly, and they could discuss the day, which they hadn't had a chance to do yet. He had tossed a badge to William and the keys to the jail, but he knew William would return the badge and keys the following day. William was willing to help Matt whenever needed, but he had no interest in becoming a deputy Marshal for any length of time.

Truet Davis walked in through the door and

hung up his coat and took off his gunbelt. He walked over to the smaller davenport and sat down tiredly. "Long day, huh?"

Matt nodded with his eyes closed. "That darn dog had diarrhea and crapped everywhere, even in the office when I let it out of its cell. I paid Chusi five dollars to clean it all up, and he took the dog."

Truet smiled. "Does Albert know you gave his dog away?"

"Not yet, but I doubt he'll care. Did the doctor say any more about Phillip?" He opened his eyes and looked over at Truet.

"Not much. Phillip won't be eating, talking, or singing anytime soon. The scar will be quite noticeable but will heal. It's just the darndest thing how that happened, though. I think about getting shot, stabbed, and hit maybe, but I never considered how dangerous a wrist shackle could be."

Matt closed his eyes. "I've never seen that happen before. And dang it happened to a good kid."

"By the way, I'll stay here on Thanksgiving so you can go spend it with your family."

Matt shook his head. "No, you go spend it with Annie and get to know the family better. I'll stay here and spend it with Christine and listen to her sing."

Truet grimaced and shook his head slightly. "No. Annie told me this is the first Thanksgiving you'll spend with your family in sixteen years. I won't let you take that away from your Aunt Mary. She's excited to have you all there for the first time in forever."

"Annie would like you there," Matt said.

"She'd prefer you there, though. So, I'll stay, and you go."

There was an unexpected knock on the door. Truet stood up and walked over to the door and asked, "Who is it?"

A voice barely audible could be heard.

Truet repeated louder, "Who?"

"Gabriel Smith"

Truet looked at Matt oddly. "Gabriel's here."

15

Truet opened the door and was surprised to see Gabriel soaking wet, standing in front of the door soaking wet and shivering in the cold. "Gabriel! What are you doing here, young man? Come in," he said pleasantly. He opened the door for Gabriel to enter.

Gabriel stood where he was. "Is Matt here?" he asked in a shaking voice.

"Yeah, come in out of the cold," Truet invited.

Matt stepped to the door. "Come on in, Gabriel, what are you doing here? Are your parents here?" he asked, looking around the street noticing the one horse tied to a hitching post at the edge of their yard. It had no saddlebags or bedroll, just the plain saddle, and looked as wet and cold as Gabriel did.

Gabriel shook his head quietly.

Matt narrowed his eyes and grew concerned. "Is something wrong? What's happened? Come inside and tell me."

Gabriel remained on the doorstep staring at

Matt with reddened eyes that filled up with emotional tears.

"What?" Matt asked, fearing the worst. "What's wrong, Gabriel?" he asked more firmly.

Gabriel moved his lips, but no words came out. He cleared his throat as a tear mixed with the rain that ran down his face. "Are you my..." he swallowed hard. "My father?"

Matt's throat felt like it was closing with the sensation of his soul dropping down into the pit of his stomach with the weight of a cannonball. He was struck across the face with a question he didn't know how to answer. He never wanted to cause any trouble in the Smith home but was faced with a question that was far too complicated and painful to answer.

"Are you?" Gabriel asked, staring at him with trembling lips. They trembled not only from the cold but from the unsettled emotions that ripped through him like a storming sea.

Matt's eyes filled slightly with moisture, and his tongue suddenly felt too dry to speak. Matt squeezed his lips together and exhaled. "I am," he said softly.

Gabriel's lips began to tremble more as the words struck his ears. He squeezed his lips together and fought the storm of tears that filled his eyes. "You knew?"

Matt nodded. "Gabriel, come inside, please."

Gabriel stepped inside, slowly looking like he was poleaxed. "You're my father?" he asked again in disbelief. "And you knew that?"

"Gabriel, let's get you into some dry clothes, and we can talk about it, okay?" Matt asked.

Gabriel looked at Truet. "Mister Davis, you knew that too?"

Truet smiled compassionately. "I did."

Gabriel turned back to Matt. "Does everyone know that except for me?"

Matt shook his head. "No, just the people in my family."

"All of them? Steven? Annie? All of them?"

Matt nodded slowly. "Yes. Let me get you some clothes to put on and then we'll talk, okay? Follow me." He led Gabriel into his room and found some clothes for him to change into. While Gabriel changed, Matt stepped back into the main family room.

"Wow," Truet said softly. "I think you two have a lot of talking to do."

Matt exhaled and widened his eyes with a heavy sigh. "I guess. I don't know what to tell him. I don't know what to say."

Truet padded Matt's shoulder. "You'll be fine, my friend. If there's anything I know about you, it's you'll be fine. But I'm going to leave for a while so you two can talk without me here listening in." He shouted towards Matt's room, "Hey Gabriel, do you mind if I take your horse to the livery stable to get it fed and someplace to dry out?"

"Where are you going to go?" Matt asked quietly.

Truet shrugged. "I'll go patrol the town or something. Don't worry, my friend. You'll do fine."

"I don't have any money for that," came Gabriel's

response.

Truet frowned. "Don't worry about that; I'll take care of it. I was just letting you know."

Truet left, and soon, Gabriel came out of the room wearing some of Matt's clothes. He carried his wet clothes to be hung up to dry. They sat down facing each other on the two separate davenports with an odd silence between them. Matt asked, "Do your parents know you're here?"

Gabriel nodded. "They should. My Pa said I couldn't come here, but I left anyway."

There was a silence that felt as thick as a city block between them. Matt's lips moved, but his question didn't come out. "When did you find out?"

"Today." He paused as he stared down at the floor. "Tiffany told me."

Matt sighed heavily with a shake of his head. "She wasn't supposed to do that. She promised me she wouldn't."

Gabriel's eyes shifted up to Matt. "Why would you tell Evan and Tiffany, but not me? You knew I was your son, and you never said a word!" He glared at Matt.

"No, I didn't."

"Why? I don't understand how everyone else can know, but I'm not allowed to know. It's my life, isn't it?" he snapped. "My Pa said you got my mother pregnant and left town when you found out. Did you not want to be a father? Do I have other siblings out there from other women you got pregnant and left behind? It's no wonder my grandfather and parents hated you for so long!"

Matt frowned as he thought about what Tom told the boy. "What exactly did your father say about me?"

Gabriel's eyes widened. "Well, apparently, you're my father!" he spat out with disgust.

"Apparently so. So, what did he say?" Matt asked, irritated by Gabriel's tone.

"He said you got my mother pregnant and left town when you found out. He married my mother because you wouldn't! He raised me knowing I was your son."

Matt raised his eyebrows as a slight flame of anger passed through him. It wasn't quite true at all, but he understood what Tom was doing to protect Elizabeth. He nodded slowly. "Well, that sounds... about right."

"I found out today that my father isn't my real father! I found out that everyone knows that, including you, and no one had the decency to tell me this? I'm sixteen years old now, and I'm just finding this out? Were you ever going to tell me?" he asked bitterly.

Matt shook his head slowly. "No."

Gabriel's brow narrowed. "You weren't? Ever? What kind of a father are you anyway? I would think you would want to get to know me, maybe? It's not my fault that you got my mother pregnant! I wouldn't be here bothering you if you hadn't of done that. If someone had told me the truth, it wouldn't be such a shock after sixteen years of thinking my father was my father, but he's not, you are! Why would you leave when you found out she was pregnant? Didn't you want me?"

Matt shifted uneasily on the davenport. "Gabriel, there's a lot you don't know..."

Gabriel stood up and walked around the davenport as he talked, "I know you were courting my mother and got her pregnant. Everyone knows you left Willow Falls in a hurry, and it was because my mother was pregnant, and not because my mom married my Pa, wasn't it? You couldn't handle the responsibility of being a father, so you left! You left her to raise me alone. If it weren't for my Pa, my mother would have been a mother with a child out of wedlock! I see how it all fits together now. I used to think you were a great man, but now I think you're nothing but a coward! How could you hear my mother say she was pregnant with your child and run away like a coward and never come back again? You knew she was having your child, and you left her! I didn't matter to you, did I? I still don't. You are a heartless man, just like my grandfather always said. I would never get someone pregnant outside of marriage to begin with, but if I did, I sure wouldn't run out on them like a coward! Sure, you're brave enough to kill, but not man enough to marry a woman and raise your child!" He paused and took a deep breath before gasping to fight his emotions. He sat back down. "I don't want to be your son," he said and buried his head in his hands weeping.

Matt had been cut to the bone by his scathing words, but he couldn't respond. Tom Smith had not told Gabriel the exact truth of how Elizabeth had become pregnant or the fact that Matt and Tom both learned the truth of Gabriel's paternity just eleven months before when Matt had returned home. It had been a devastating blow to Tom, who had always believed Gabriel was his son. And it had been quite a shock to Matt as well. In truth, years before, when Matt and Elizabeth were teenagers, they had been courting for a long time when her father ended it. His forbidding her to see Matt wasn't as effective as he wanted it to be, so he forced her to marry Tom after he talked Tom into proposing to her. It was a hurried wedding, and Matt was devastated. One week after their wedding, Elizabeth came to Matt in tears and shame for betraying her love for him by marrying Tom. They were in love, and the legal bond of marriage didn't matter to them when their love for one another took over in the hayloft of the barn. Matt pleaded with her to run away with him so they could be together and raise a family like they always planned and get away from her father and Willow Falls. Elizabeth was too afraid to defy her father's will, and she was not ready to leave the bond she had with her mother. She refused to leave with Matt, and reluctantly went home to Tom. Matt packed his things that night and disappeared before daybreak, refusing to come back to Willow Falls for another fifteen years. The pain of seeing his beloved Elizabeth living as another man's wife was just too much to bear. When Matt came home for the first time, this past Christmas was the first he heard that he had a son named Gabriel.

The version that Tom told Gabriel was a lie

meant to save Elizabeth's honor and reputation for Gabriel's respect. Matt understood that and gave Tom the credit he deserved for trying to do so. Matt was in a position to tell the truth and save his reputation, but it was better to take Gabriel's fury and lose his respect than for Gabriel to lose respect for his mother.

Matt looked at his son, sitting across the room, crying. He longed to hold him and tell the boy he loved him, but he couldn't. Instead, he remained seated and watched Gabriel with a heart yearning to tell the boy the truth. And the truth was Matt loved Elizabeth very much and had no idea she was ever pregnant. If he had known, he never would have left Willow Falls and would be married to Elizabeth to this day. "Gabriel," he said. "It may not make any sense, but I want you to know that I am proud of you. And I... loved your mother." His own eyes filled with moisture, and his voice cracked as he said it. He wanted to tell Gabriel he loved him, but the words didn't come out.

Gabriel looked up at him with an angry expression. "You don't even know me! You wouldn't even have acknowledged me on the street, let alone acknowledge me as your own blood! You just said so yourself! You don't have anything to be proud of. You sure as heck didn't have anything to do with raising me! And if you loved my mom, you never would've left her! I don't even know why I'm here; I just wanted to know if you knew about me, and you did! My Pa said you did, and he was right. I don't know what I was expecting." He stood up. "I gotta go. I'll grab my clothes."

"Wait," Matt said softly. "Sit down, Gabriel. It's getting late, and it's pouring rain, so you might as well stay here tonight. I'll take you back home tomorrow if that's alright with you? I'm going to the Big Z for Thanksgiving anyway."

Gabriel shook his head. "No, I want to go home." Gabriel looked at Matt with narrowed eyes of disgust. "All those books I have about you, even the one you never signed, I'm going to throw in the woodstove when I get home. You're not the man I thought you were, and..." he looked up into the air, unable to speak, "You're my father. You know, I don't even know who I am anymore! I grew up knowing I was my Pa's son, and now I'm not. My brother and sisters are only half brother and sisters. Why did you ever tell Tiffany anyway? I never would've known if it wasn't for her, and I would've been happier never knowing that!" he said with an anguished expression. "Why did you tell Evan and her? Were you hoping they'd tell me?"

Matt shook his head sadly. "No. Evan heard your mother tell Donovan Moskin that. And Tiffany," he paused to shift uncomfortably. "I had no idea I was bringing her back here when I told her that. Gabriel, I know you're my son. And believe it or not, I am proud of you. That's why I told her about you."

"So, you said! I'm not proud of you, and I hate being your son. As I said, I wish I had never known. How am I ever going to look at your family now knowing they know I'm related? I'm just a bastard child by one of their own."

"No one's ever spoken like that." Matt closed his eyes as it felt like someone was carving out a large hole inside of him. "One of the first things my Aunt Mary said to me when I came back was, I needed to tell you who you were. She said you needed to know who your family was."

"But you didn't!"

Matt shook his head. "No, I didn't. What good would it have done, Gabriel? Your mother was in danger, and we had other things on our minds. I knew telling you would shake your world to its core. Who am I to want to do that to you? No. I wasn't going to tell you. I can be just as proud of you without you knowing about me as I could with you knowing. I'm sorry you found out the way you did, but here you are. Are you happy about it? No, you're not! So, I was right. You should never have known."

"And you'd be fine with that?" he asked bitterly.

"Yes, I would," Matt said and swallowed hard enough, he almost choked. "I wouldn't have much of a choice, now, would I, Gabriel?"

"Yeah, you would!"

"How so?"

"You could've told me!" he yelled.

"For what purpose?" Matt raised his voice. "I just said I knew it would tear your world apart, and I didn't want to do that to you. I don't understand why that's so hard for you to understand!"

"Because I'm your son! Doesn't that matter to you?"

Matt paused before he spoke. He wanted to tell

159

Gabriel he just found out he had a son, but the story Tom had told Gabriel kept him from doing so. His eyes watered just a touch as he said, "It's better that I carry the pain than for my son to. Of course, you matter to me. I am human, after all. Gabriel, I figured I would live with the heartache and spare you from it. I never wanted you to find out that Tom wasn't your father. He's a good man and a good father. You know this must be painful for him and your mother as well. I hope you're not mad at them."

"I am! They lied about that for all of my life. And I don't know what's true anymore. What other secrets are there? Come on, you haven't said one word about how I came about, and I remember up on the mountain there was far more to you leaving Willow Falls than you told me. You hid the truth from me, and my parents betrayed me, or at least I feel like they did. I don't know if I can trust them anymore, and you didn't even want me, so where do I belong?" he said with a slight shaking to his voice. "It just feels like I'm falling down a very dark hole, and there isn't a bottom or anything that I can grab hold of," he said shaking his head with a sniffle.

Matt frowned. "What happened with your mother was a very long time ago. We've all changed a lot since then."

"So, you just got her pregnant and left town?" he asked with disgust in his voice.

Matt frowned. "Yeah. I did." He neglected to add the rest of the story or pleading with Elizabeth to leave with him. As he had told Gabriel, it was better for him to feel the heartache than for his son. He would let Gabriel leave the house, thinking his biological father was nothing more than a cowardly womanizer with low morals. It was better than ruining Gabriel's respect for his mother.

Gabriel sat back down on the davenport heavily. He sighed. "Who am I?"

Matt looked at him sadly. "You are Gabriel Smith. The son of Tom and Elizabeth Smith. But you have Bannister and Fasana blood running through your veins. You're the same young man you've always been except for one difference, and that's a whole new family and heritage."

"It's not that easy, Matt. That means my Grandma and Grandpa Smith aren't my grandparents. That whole family history they talk about doesn't belong to me. My ancestors didn't come over on the Mayflower or whatever boat it was on, or partake in the revolution. Those were Smith's, and I'm not one. Do you know how proud of that I was? It doesn't apply to me anymore. That's what I'm saying, Matt, I don't know who I am anymore because all that I knew was a lie. And they all knew it. Steven, he's always been my friend, now he's an uncle. Annie's my aunt and Charlie Ziegler, a man I was always taught to fear, is my uncle. Do I have any other siblings out there somewhere?" he asked solemnly.

Matt shook his head slowly. "No."

"You're sure you didn't get any other women pregnant and leave them behind too?"

The statement irritated Matt, and he bit his lips

tightly. "I'm pretty sure."

The front door opened a few inches quietly, and Christine Knapp peeked into the room. "I'm sorry, I should have knocked," she said as she entered the house. "But, I wanted to introduce myself to Gabriel." She closed the door behind her. She was dressed in a long wool black coat with a hood that protected her hair from the rain. She carried a wicker basket in her hand and smiled as she entered.

"Christine?" Matt questioned, he was startled by her unexpected arrival. "What are you doing here?" She was supposed to be working at the dance hall.

"I brought you, boys, some dinner." She turned her attention to Gabriel and reached her hand out to shake his. "My name's Christine. Your father is one of my best friends. I am so glad to meet you."

"I'm Gabriel Smith, Ma'am," he said, standing up politely and staring at the beautiful woman in front of him.

She shook his hand with a friendly smile. "Are you hungry, Gabriel? I brought some chicken and other things from the dance hall. Please, make a plate and eat. I even brought a peach pie that I made earlier today."

Gabriel followed her into the kitchen. "I am hungry. I haven't eaten since this morning."

Christine raised her eyebrows towards him, fondly. "Then it's a good thing I brought a lot of food. Please, eat as much as you want, and don't be shy."

"Thank you, Miss," Gabriel said softly.

"Christine. I like to think we're friends, so call

me Christine." She turned to Matt. "Come eat, Matt."

Matt frowned as he approached. "Thank you." He wanted to ask how she knew Gabriel was there, but she started talking to Gabriel before he could ask.

Christine spoke as Gabriel began fixing his plate. "I have to admit, I overheard you talking about your grandparents when I came in. So, I have to ask, did Matt tell you his father is in town? I think your timing is perfect to meet him. Would you like to meet your grandfather, Floyd Bannister? I think you'd find the Bannister's have a pretty unique and interesting history too. Did you know your great grandfather was almost Oregon's Governor?"

"Um, no, I didn't know," Gabriel said uneasily.

"I think it's important that you meet him, because this may be your only chance to. How about you finish eating and then we'll go, okay?" she asked. She looked over at Matt and said, "Don't you think he should have that opportunity, Matt?"

Matt looked at her irritably. "I don't think that's necessary, no."

Christine tilted her head with a discouraged expression on her face. "It's his grandfather, Matt. Your personal feelings don't change that. And this may be the only chance he ever has to meet him. Can you tuck away your animosities for a bit and introduce him to your father? And maybe you can let him have his own judgment about his grandfather without your input. People can change, and I'm sure your father would love to meet his grandson.

You probably didn't even notice the look in his eyes when he looked at his other grandchildren, did you?"

"No, I didn't. But it's getting a little late, don't you think?"

"It's not so late, yet. Come on, Matt. Let's introduce them. It's the only chance he may have to meet him."

Matt had no interest. "He can meet him tomorrow."

Christine widened her eyes and looked at him sharply. "Yes, he could. But I'd like to be there, and I'll be busy in the kitchen at the dance hall all day tomorrow. It would mean a lot to me to be a part of their meeting. Please."

Matt sighed heavily. "Why's that so important to you? Yesterday you agreed to go to dinner with him; then, you got mad at me for not being nice to him. I have nothing nice to say to him! Why do you want Gabriel to meet him? Why would that mean anything to you?" he raised his voice slightly.

She looked hurt. "Because they're both a part of you," she said softly. "I loved my grandfather, Matt. You know how important my grandparents were to me. I think Gabriel should have the opportunity to meet his. Whether he continues that into a relationship or not is totally up to him, but I think he should have the opportunity at least. Don't take that from him."

Matt thought about it for a moment and then looked at Gabriel. "Gabriel. Let's go meet your grandfather."

Gabriel questioned, "You don't like your father?"

Christine was quick to answer, "I think you should meet him without hearing what he was like thirty years ago. People change, but the wounds left behind can fester, and trust me, you don't want to hear the pus that comes out of Matt's mouth."

"What?" Matt asked sharply.

She shrugged lightly. "You have to squeeze the pus out before a wound can heal. Right? Let's go."

16

Joe Thorn's eyes burned with indignation as he glared over a large group of men on the muddy street of Slater's Mile. He stood on a wooden chair and raised his hands to quiet the men and women that dared to stand in the rain.

"Hush! Joe's talking," his friend Allan Rosso yelled to quiet the group.

"You all know me. And you all know Leroy, Oscar, and Roger too. We're all a family out here away from town. When Billy Jo needs sugar, she can go to Sally, or when Sally needs some flour, she can go to Lucille's. We're family out here. We're family in the mine shaft because we're all we've got. We look after one another in the mine, stamp mill, in town and out here. Who wouldn't step up and protect someone else's family, wife, or children if they needed help, huh? Well, we're all facing a threat, whether you believe it or not. Look at how fast that Chinatown in Branson is growing. It's doubled in size, and the closer the railroad gets to here and the longer gold is found here, the more the Chinese show up to take over our livelihood. It's not just here, everywhere they are taking over jobs, and the money that belongs to us Americans is being sent overseas! The federal government understands the threat to us Americans and made the Chinese Exclusion Act just last year! Has anyone walked through Chinatown recently? The filthy rats are bold enough to walk out onto the streets after dark in their neighborhood like they have nothing to fear at all. The law is, no Chinese are to be outside after dark! So, why are they permitted to ignore the laws of our county, state, and country? And do you not think there are shiploads of Chinese being loaded in China right now to be sent to this country despite the Exclusion Act? They're being smuggled in, and don't you doubt it! It's an invasion of our country to make it like their own. Trust me; if we the people don't stand up and fight back, we'll be speaking Chinese by the time your kids are grown! You won't have a job, and I won't have a job. Look, we have forty-eight Chinese men working for Slater Silver Mine now. How many worked here last year? Don't know? I can tell you, five! Forty-three Chinese have been hired in the last year by the Slaters. How many white men? Don't know? I can tell you, twenty-five. That's a two to one difference. Worse, the Chinese work for less money! It's true! Those yellow rats are working for a dollar a day, and we make two dollars and fifty cents a day. Do you see where we are being run out of our own jobs? And then we'll be out of our homes! Do you see the seriousness of the threat? It's a yellow plague! The Black Plague killed millions in Europe way back when, and if we don't act, and start acting like men on the brink of extinction, the yellow plague is going to run all of us right out of the mine, timber industry, farming and everything else until we'll all be taking a ship back over to China because they'll all be over here!" he yelled and then paused to take a deep breath.

"What do you want to do, Joe? How can we stop them?" a man asked with a scowl on his rain covered face.

Joe raised a hand to quiet the crowd that was being worked up. "A few weeks ago, a white man named Pick Lawson was hung by the neck over the quarry pit of the Fasana Granite Quarry. Listen to this, nailed into his chest, not pinned, but nailed into his chest was a note written in Chinese! The note said it was just the beginning of what the Chinese would be doing to us white folks here in Branson! Three Chinese men hung a white man! It's already starting! If your white, they're a threat to your life, your wife's, and your children's lives too. Now listen, the quarry is in the Marshal Matt Bannister's jurisdiction, and what did he do? Absolutely nothing, he let the murderers go and tried to blame some other group of guys. Now our Sheriff, Tim Wright, did an investigation knowing Matt lied and arrested those three Chinese men that lynched Pick! He had them in jail, and that half breed marshal, Matt Bannister, turned them loose by threatening the Sheriff's life!"

"What? Why that…" A man yelled out angrily.

"Are you kidding me?" someone else yelled.

"I'm not done!" Joe yelled above the crowd. "Last night, two of those yellow rats Matt released were thrown over the edge of that quarry pit by their own kind to teach the other yellow rats a lesson. The third China man was whipped as punishment for getting caught in the first place! This is a war they're starting, and they don't want any foul-ups like getting caught! Remember I said Matt accused other people for hanging Pick? Well, now he's accusing our friends Leroy, Oscar, and Roger of throwing those Chinese over the pit and whipping the third! The Marshal came out here into our community, and forcefully took our friends to his jail. He should have arrested those yellow beings from hell in the beginning, but he didn't because they work for his uncle! That's right; those three murdering Chinese men worked for the Fasana Granite Quarry. Who owns that? Matt Bannister's uncles! Billy Jo's father. Matt's corrupt, and it's sickening! It's all about money! And protecting cheap labor puts money in his pocket while the Chinese to take over our jobs, our homes, and our livelihood! He lets the killers of a white man go free and then protects the yellow rats that did it! Why?" he shouted. "Because it's money in their pockets! Us, white people will be losing our jobs and then forced to leave our homes, and Matt and his brothers will be buying up every empty house in town that they don't already own! Where are we going to go when we lose our jobs at the mine and the Chinese move in here? Think about it! If we lose our jobs, we lose our homes! But it's money in the Slater's pockets too! They don't care what happens to you or if your children are freezing to death before they can starve to death! It's all about the money in their pockets! The company owners want cheap labor and will replace us with Chinese labor. It's a dollar fifty less a day per man! Add it up! The big business owners around here have always controlled the power and now have an agenda to squeeze us hard-working Americans out and put in cheap Chinese labor. Where's that extra money going? Follow the money; it's going to the one man who is protecting the yellow rats! I can promise you the Bannister family is going to have a big Thanksgiving feast, and a lot of it will go to waste. What about you Fred, is your Thanksgiving looking meager? Mine is. It's already beginning my friends. The Chinese are being protected, and we white folks are being framed, fired, and run out of town!"

"Now, here's what we can do to stop this yellow rat-infestation before it goes too far to stop. We can grab a twenty-pound sledgehammer and a chisel and bust our friends out of that jail and stand our ground and say we have had enough of the yellow plague! We can shut down the marshal's office and burn Chinatown down and run every China man out of Jessup County! I'm keeping my job! What about you all? If you're with me, then let's go into town and bring our friends home! Who's with me?" he yelled.

A crowd of men cheered and cursed Matt's name

along with the Chinese.

Lawrence Barton stood in the crowd and frowned nervously. He knew Leroy and his friends were guilty because Lucille had told him about walking into town with Gertie. Gertie was no longer living at the housing camp of Slater's Mile. She had taken the ride out to her place and gathered her few things and got a ride back into town. She was paid the hundred dollars by Matt and took all the money that Leroy had saved up in his Arbuckle's coffee can. She had already bought a ticket for the next stagecoach heading west.

"Lawrence, you are coming, right?" a man asked.

"No. My child is sick, and I don't feel like being in the cold rain either. You guys go ahead." He stood back with around forty others while a dozen or so men left Slater's Mile with a fight in their eyes.

"Fools," a man named Howard Reed said to Lawrence. "I'm all for standing tall, but breaking into the marshal's office to free guilty men is foolish. Especially when that marshal is deadlier than any man out here."

Lawrence chuckled. "Exactly."

17

Floyd Bannister had spent the day with a certain melancholy hanging over him even though he was able to visit with Lee's family and spend the day with his granddaughters and visit with Albert's family for a good part of the afternoon. He still could not pull his spirits out of the muck and mire that his fourth son's words had thrown his hopes of reconciling into. It weighed heavy on his heart and wouldn't leave his mind. A man could live with a broken heart, and he could live with regret too, but hearing the venom of his son's animosity was a stinging memory that sucked the life out of him. It was hard to love someone so much and hear they never wanted to see you again. For Floyd, there was no turning back; he had come this far to make amends and failed. Some risks are worth the chance, even if they end up being failures. When it came to Matt, the trip east to Branson had been a waste of money and time. It was clear that the relationship with Matt was broken and would remain so. Some bridges can't be repaired, and a new crossing had to be developed. However, with Matt, that crossing would never see a foundation laid nor a stone or plank collected. Floyd had resigned to let Matt have his way and no longer try to reach out to him in any way. His hopes to build a relationship with his son were over.

He had been invited to travel out to the Big Z Ranch for Thanksgiving by Lee and Albert, but Floyd had declined because he knew Matt would be there, and his presence would cause friction and ruin it for everyone else just as it had at dinner the night before. Floyd wasn't too keen on invading the home of Charlie and Mary Ziegler without their inviting him anyway. His last visit there hadn't been well received. He was warned then, never to come back, and it was a warning he had heeded. Floyd wasn't exactly a weak man or a cowardly man, but he feared his former brother-in-law just the same. He planned on staying around Branson for the next two days while all his children were out of town, and when Matt came back, he would rent a coach and drive over to Willow Falls and visit with his three other children and his grandchildren for a few days before they went back home on Monday.

Rhoda sat down on the hotel's davenport and picked up her yarn to knit a blanket for Floyd's only daughter, Annie. Rhoda was anxious to meet her and the other boys, Steven and Adam. She was unimpressed with Matt, which was a big disappointment for her. She liked Lee and Albert and their families just fine, but more than anyone, she looked forward to meeting Annie. She knew she would never see Matt again, and she was fine with that because quite frankly, all he did was tear her husband down. Rhoda knew she wasn't the most cordial person, but she had tried so hard to be friendly and make a good first impression to all of Floyd's children. It was just too bad she couldn't make the connections she had wanted to.

Floyd glanced over at her. "I think I'm about to call it a night. What about you?"

"No. I'll wait up for Maggie to get home. I can not believe she is enjoying time with that annoying nephew of yours."

"He's a... bit different. He takes after his mother, I think. That blonde hair and a wild streak that comes with it. She was an interesting lady when I knew her."

"I think he's too wishy-washy for Maggie. She needs someone more focused on life than cards. I'm beginning to worry about her starting to like that wishy-washy maggot."

He smiled comfortingly. "She'll be fine."

There was a knock at the door. "Expecting someone?" she asked.

He shook his head. "No," he said as he got up and went to the door. He opened the door and saw Matt standing beside Christine and another young man behind them. "Oh, hi," he said, surprised and yet stunned to see Matt at his door. "Well, come in," he said opening the door wider.

"Thank you," Christine said with a smile as she entered. Matt stepped inside without a smile. He didn't want to be there.

"Son," Floyd said, reaching his hand out to shake.

Matt shook his hand reluctantly without saying a word. Hearing Floyd call him "son" struck a nerve that caused him to want to leave with repulsion immediately. It was Christine's idea to bring Gabriel to meet his grandfather thinking it would help Gabriel find some answers to at least some of his questions about his newly found family. Matt agreed to come for that purpose.

"Who's this?" Floyd asked as his eyes focused on Gabriel. His eyes narrowed a bit with a touch of unspoken recognition.

Matt took a breath and said, "Gabriel, this is your grandfather, Floyd Bannister. This is your grandson, Gabriel."

"What?" Rhoda asked loudly and stood up quickly.

Floyd's eyes widened, and his mouth opened in silence for a moment. A large smile slowly came across his face. "Yours?" he asked Matt as he grabbed Gabriel's shoulders to look at him proudly.

Matt nodded.

Floyd laughed and hugged his grandson. "It's great to meet you! I had no idea Matt had a son! You have your grandmother's eyes. Has anyone ever told you that?"

Gabriel shook his head slightly. "No," he said uneasily.

"You do," Floyd said as moisture filled his eyes.

"Give me a turn," Rhoda said as she stepped between them and said, "I'm your grandmother." She hugged him tightly.

Christine explained, "Gabriel just found out Matt was his father today. So, he's getting used to that whole idea. We," she motioned towards Matt and herself, "thought it would be a good idea if he got to meet you. Maybe you could tell him some Bannister history? And I'd be interested in hearing that too."

Floyd looked pleased. "Absolutely! Well, first, I'm your grandfather, and this is my wife, Rhoda, your grandmother. Your eyes don't look like her's though; they look like your grandmother's, meaning Matt's mother."

"Oh," Gabriel said a bit overwhelmed.

Rhoda waved a hand towards Floyd. "Don't listen to him. Your grandmother died a long time ago. I'm your grandmother now. Come sit down and visit for a while," she said as she led him towards the davenport and chairs.

Matt felt a surge of animosity flow through him, and it showed in his eyes to hear Rhoda speak so indifferently about his mother. Christine picked up on it and gave him a small understanding smile as she led the way to the furniture.

Floyd pulled a padded chair in front of the davenport to create a seating arrangement where they could all face each other. Floyd sat down so he could look at Gabriel. "Let's talk. Tell me about you first. I'm excited to meet you!"

Matt sat in silence and listened to Gabriel speak about his home and his likes, hopes, and his family. Matt watched his father lean forward with interest, laugh, smile, and be intrigued to learn more about Gabriel. Matt wasn't excited to talk about Elizabeth, and to his relief, the subject of how Gabriel came about didn't come up, except for Floyd saying he knew Elizabeth and Tom when they were little and remembered them well. He even told a couple of stories about them that Matt hadn't heard and forgotten about over the years. As he sat there listening, he could feel his own eyes begin to water slightly as the man's voice, laughter, and presence took him back to better memories of his early years. Floyd's laugh was a forgotten sound that was resurrected from better moments of his childhood. Family retreats up at the lake cabin during the Summer, Christmas morning, and random memories on the ranch where Floyd would laugh and be in high spirits without the alcohol or the wrath it brought out of him. Days when he was a father and played, taught, and loved his family. Memories of riding on his father's lap holding the reigns to the mules leading the wagon, being pushed in the swing behind the house, and being sprayed in the face by the fresh milk while being taught how to milk the cow, followed by that same laughter he heard now. He remembered his father's smile then and looked at his father now. He had aged well enough but carried the weight of his burdens in the lines of his face and the sadness in his eyes. He still had a nice smile, though. A touch of a smile twitched the corners of Matt's mouth and a sniffle that brought attention to him.

"Are you alright, Son?" Floyd asked with concern.

Matt nodded. "Yeah," he said as he noticed a tear sneaking down his cheek. He wiped it off with a bit of an embarrassed smile. "I'm just listening."

Floyd chuckled. "I don't think he can believe it either. I remember when your father was born, Gabriel. I'll never forget the first time I held him in my hands. I just stared down into his eyes, and he stared into mine. The boy didn't cry like the others. Adam didn't cry either, but the rest sure did. Anyway, Matt was a very quiet and well-behaved child. He was a very inquisitive young man. I always thought he'd grow up to be a doctor, myself."

"Because I gutted Salamanders?" Matt asked dryly.

Floyd frowned and said sincerely, "No, because you were smart, you caught onto things very quick and still thought of better ways of doing things. You were just a smart kid."

Matt nodded sadly.

Floyd chuckled, "Granted, the autopsy's you'd perform on frogs, and Salamanders hinted to that as well, Son."

Christine scoffed with a light slap to his shoulder. "Salamanders are so cute!"

He smiled faintly as his eyes went to the floor. The word, Son, was a word that only his father had called him. No one else had ever called him that word growing up, and it was so foreign to him that it felt oppressive. Yet, to hear it again was haunting. It stirred something inside him that was much too unsettling. To hear his father talk about his childhood and things he had no memory of only added to the frustration that grew within him. He wasn't mad; he wasn't sad; he was…torn and confused by a mixture of emotions that couldn't be identified until the soot of his past, as Christine had put it, had found a place to rest.

A gunshot echoed down the street, and Matt's head lifted as he listened intently over the others who questioned it. He could hear the faint sound of a crowd yelling in the street. He stood up quickly. "I have to go! You two stay in here until I get back," he said to Christine and Gabriel pointedly.

"What's going on?" Rhoda asked, followed by Gabriel.

"I'm going to find out," he said and neared the door.

"Be careful, Son," Floyd said.

Matt looked back at him and saw a legitimate concern on the older man's face. He nodded and went out the door.

"Does this kind of thing happen a lot around here?" Rhoda asked.

Christine nodded. "Unfortunately." She began telling them about a few weeks before when Matt confronted Bloody Jim Hexum outside of the hotel and ended up killing him. She explained that was when Felisha Conway ended her courtship with Matt, which led to the story of how Christine had been kidnapped mistakenly when two men mistook her for being Catherine Eckman, a missing railroad tycoon's daughter.

The story she told intrigued Gabriel, and he

couldn't stand to stay in the hotel any longer as the yelling outside grew louder. He had seen Matt kill someone before and never wanted to witness something like that again, but he was too curious to know what was happening to stay where he was. "I'm going to see what's going on," he said and stood up.

"No, you're not, young man!" Rhoda said firmly.

"Matt told you to stay here," Christine reminded him firmly.

"Gabriel, sit down," Floyd said calmly.

Gabriel ignored them all and went to the door and went out of the hotel room.

Christine stood up to go after him, but Floyd's firm voice stopped her.

"Stay here, Christine! I'll go get him," Floyd said and went to grab his boots quickly. He slipped them on and tied them, grabbed his coat, and left with the worried words of Rhoda to be careful.

18

Shamus O'Shea was the fifteen-year-old son of Michael O'Shea, a miner at Slater's Silver Mine, and lived at Slaters Mile. Shamus was sent by his father to run as fast as he could through the woods to get to Branson before the men leaving the housing community did and warn Matt Bannister that the men were coming to bust Leroy and the others out his jail. Shamus had run fast and hard through the rain and the mud to get to town but found the Marshal's Office closed and no one around on the street. He didn't know where Matt lived, so he went to the Sheriff's Office and told the only deputy on duty, Mark Thiesen.

Mark went to Sheriff Tim Wright's house and told him. The Sheriff told Mark to gather the other deputies and have them meet at the Marshal's Office. When Mark commented on stopping by Matt's house to tell him, Sheriff Wright discouraged him from doing so. Tim explained quickly that he wanted-ed to stop the men from destroying the Marshal's office himself.

When Mark left, Tim smiled and put on his boots, gun belt, coat and hat and left his house. He walked up Main Street and stood under the porch of the Marshal's Office until he was joined by two of his deputies, Thirty-seven-year-old Bob Ewing, who was Tim's main deputy and twenty-seven-year-old, Alan Garrison. They waited until they heard the voices of the men nearing the office. They walked out into the street to meet the angry miners as they approached.

"Evening boys," Tim said as he puffed on his cigar with a smile.

Joe Thorn drank the last of a bottle of whiskey and threw it against the granite block wall of the Marshal's Office; it shattered upon impact spreading broken glass across the boardwalk. "Hope you're not planning on trying to stop us, Tim. Or did you send your boys to get Matt?"

Tim shook his head. "Nope, I was told to keep my nose out of the Marshal's affairs. So, have at it. I watched him take my prisoners out of my jail; I suppose it's only fair. I should watch you all take his out of his jail," he said with a smile.

Joe nodded and looked at his brother. "Bust that door down."

Deputy Alan Garrison was uneasy. He had always been sent out of the office every time Matt came in to talk to the Sheriff. He had no real knowledge of what was going on between the two, but he knew they didn't like each other at all. "Are you sure that's a good idea, Tim? Matt's going to be mad."

"Alan. I don't need you here after all, so will you go tend to the office until we get back?" Tim said, barely looking at him. "Go, please."

"Sure. But you're asking for trouble if you let them do that," Alan said as he stepped away displeased with his boss.

Tim turned towards him. "Alan, I don't need to hear that from you! I'm the Sheriff, not you. Are we clear?"

"Yes, sir."

"Then go, tend to the office until Mark gets back."

Deputy Bob Ewing added to Alan, "You need to learn to keep quiet. If you did that, you could enjoy the show."

Ritchie Thorn swung the twenty-pound sledgehammer and hit the lock of the front door. The lock gave away, and the door flew open, shattering the window on the impact of the door hitting the wall.

"Nice hit!" one of his friends yelled as they all stepped inside except for a few who broke out the two bay windows with the painted words on them. The sound of glass shattering echoed through the quiet night.

Tim chuckled with pleasure.

Inside, Ritchie again swung the sledgehammer against the lock on Matt's private office door. The door burst open as easily as the other one did; the window shattered upon impact as well.

"Find the keys to this door!" Joe said, looking at the steel door that blocked their access to the jail.

Ritchie and two others tore Matt's office apart looking for a key but came up empty. The other men searched the desks in the main office, and no one found a single key to anything. Richie stepped out of Matt's office. "There are no keys in there. I found some money and Leroy's whip, though."

Joe looked at the whip. "Have Jerry or someone hide that in their coat. That's evidence he took to frame Leroy! We need to take that with us just in case the Marshal returns before we can get this door opened." The steel door had a heavy-duty lock and wouldn't be easy to break loose. The door had an outside lip that covered the door jam making it difficult to wedge open and impossible to force open with the sledgehammer. They had brought chisels to bore through the jail locks with the sledgehammer, but he feared if he bent the steel door's lock or the bolt that went into the door jam that they wouldn't be able to open the door at all. He had no way of knowing if the jam was made of wood or iron. He looked at the Mahogany wall beside it and said, "Bust through the wall. Come on, boys, tunnel through the wall!" He stood back as Ritchie and Alan Rosso took turns beating the beautiful mahogany siding. The wood cracked and fractured with every blow and began breaking down, exposing a layer of plaster and then a solid granite block wall.

"It's granite! Just like outside." Alan Rosso said, exasperated.

"Tunnel through it! This is what we do every day! Get to work," Joe ordered harshly with a few curse words added in for good measure.

"Why don't we punch the lock out of the door? We have a punch and chisels," Alan suggested.

Joe scoffed. "Because steel's pliable and granite isn't. If that lock or bolt bends, our friends could be stuck in there for a week before the door is fixed, that's why. Bust that wall down!"

"Give me a chisel, and we'll break the cement and take them out one block at a time," Alan Rosso said. "Hold the chisel," he said to a man named Brian Barns, who brought the two-foot-long steel chisel with a flattened tip about an inch wide. Brian held the tip in the thin layer of concrete in between the blocks. Alan swung the sledgehammer expertly and hit the chisel square on the top, driving the wedge into the concrete. He swung again and again. Brian pried the chisel back and forth to loosen it. He put it on the side of the block to loosen the concrete on the other side of it. When he had done all four sides of the block, Alan began hitting the block one side at a time to budge it through to the other side. Slowly, it gave way and fell to the floor in the jail.

Joe stuck his head in the hole and could see an empty cell with four beds and another granite block wall. He could hear the men talking behind the block wall. He yelled, "Leroy, can you hear me?"

"Loud and clear, Joe!" he laughed. "Hurry up and get us out of here before the Marshal comes back!"

"Oh, don't worry about him, we'll have Alan knock him in the head with his handy sledgehammer. We'll have you out of there in no time. Keep going, men," he said to Brian and Alan.

"We should burn the place down when we get Leroy and them out of there!" Richie Thorn exclaimed bitterly.

Joe looked at him and nodded. "When we're done empty the lanterns and do it."

The second block fell out easier than the first, and they started in on the third. "Give us five minutes, and we'll have a hole big enough for you to fit through Leroy. Maybe that is, I don't know if the whole wall would be big enough," Joe joked.

"Just hurry up! Joe, is Gertie at my house?" Leroy yelled from the jail.

"No, she's not. She disappeared before we got home from work. If she were, we'd bring her here so you can make her see things straight and clear."

"I'd put to her to my whip is what I'll do," he cursed.

"We found your whip in the marshal's office. We'll be taking that too."

Outside, Deputy Jed Clark and Mark Thiesen walked up to Tim Wright and Bob Ewing. "What's going here?" Jed demanded. He held a shotgun in his hands.

Tim couldn't hide his satisfied smile. "Relax. It's none of our affair."

Jed scowled. "None of our affair? They're destroying federal property, and you're standing here doing nothing?"

"Well, the Marshal has told me before to mind my own affairs, so I am."

"This is our affair. I'm going to stop this now!"

"No, you're not!" Tim spoke harshly. "Your job is to do what you're told, and I'm telling you to go home if you don't like it." His eyes burned into Jed's.

Jed shook his head uncaringly. "Not this time. Fire me if you will, but I'm stopping this right now!"

"Do not disobey me, Jed!" Tim warned harshly.

Jed waved him off and stepped in front of the office and fired his shotgun into the air, getting everyone's attention. He yelled, "Get out of there, now! All of you!" Jed was the oldest deputy at thirty-eight-years old and was an old cowboy from Oklahoma originally before moving west with his family. He wasn't the biggest man at five foot ten or so, and he wasn't the broadest at about a hundred and sixty pounds, but of the Sheriff's four deputy's, he was the fiercest. He had short brown hair and wore a mustache that continued down to his chin. He was a tough man and it showed in his hazel eyes that he wasn't one to back down.

Joe Thorn looked at him surprised and then pointed his finger at him. "Mind your business, Jed. The Sheriff already said he'd not interfere."

"The Sheriff's not interfering, I am! Get out of there, now!" he shouted and pointed the shotgun at Joe.

Some of the men nearest to the door slowly stepped outside with their hands up, but Joe, Ritchie, Brian, and Alan Rosso all remained where they were standing, silently debating what they were going to do. A fifth man, merely a boy of sixteen named Mitchell Gaylord, stood near the Marshal Office's gun cabinet that he had broken into. It contained six rifles of various calibers, including two shotguns. Mitchell wasn't known for being too bright, but he wasn't a troublemaker either. He had been drinking on a bottle of whiskey shared with him by other men on the walk into town, and he was visibly intoxicated. He kept looking at the nearest shotgun in the gun cabinet. He knew if he could grab it and get a good round off at Jed, they could all get away without being arrested. Mitchell normally wasn't so daring to try it, but he wasn't normally drunk on whiskey either.

Jed shouted out, "I'm not telling you, men, again! Drop the hammer and get out here! Boy, if you go for that gun, I'll shoot you. Don't make me do that!"

Joe Thorn knew he was caught. He knew they'd never be able to break his friends out of jail now that Jed had fired a shot and alerted the townspeople, possibly even Matt. He raised his hands slowly with a bitter expression on his face. "Jed, you don't know what you're doing. You're starting a war."

"And I suppose you're the general, right? Well, General Thorn, I think you're a piss-ant. Now get out here, all of you. You're all under arrest."

Tim Wright stepped forward awkwardly with Bob. "Now, no, they're not. Put the gun down, Jed."

"I will not! Get out of there, Boy! You're under arrest too."

Mitchell Gaylord shook his head. "I can't go to jail. My momma needs me at home."

"Then maybe you shouldn't be in there, huh? Rosso, get moving!" he shouted at Alan Rosso.

Jed saw Mitchell's hand moving slowly towards one of the rifles. Chances were it was unloaded, but Jed couldn't risk taking a chance. He aimed quickly and fired the last shot of the shotgun. The pellets filled Mitchell's hand with lead and shot off two of his fingers immediately. Mitchell started screaming with the combination of pain and the terror of seeing his hand becoming a mangled mess.

Tim Wright tried to grab Jed from behind but was met with the stock of the shotgun being rammed back into his gut. Tim bent over, trying to catch his breath. Bob Ewing tried to draw his pistol but was blindsided by the end of the shotgun's barrel spinning around and slamming across the side of his head. Bob fell into the mud, dropping his revolver in the process. Jed tossed the shotgun towards Mark Thiessen and pulled his revolver and pointed it at the miners who were standing there watching in amazement while others ran away while they could. The men inside had gone to help young Mitchell. "Get out of there," Jed shouted, verifying that none of them were trying to reach for any of the rifles in the gun cabinet. He turned his head to look at Tim and Bob. He shouted angrily, "I'm sick of standing by and watching you pick and choose what's legal and what's not! Those men are under arrest, and I don't care what you say!"

Tim still bent over, looked up at him with a nasty grimace. "You're fired," he said painfully.

"No, I quit!"

Matt Bannister had run down the street with his revolver in hand. He glanced at Tim and Bob, who was lying on the street, unconscious while bleeding from a small head wound. He looked at his office and the broken windows, doors, and the hole in the wall going into the jail. He looked at the men standing outside who appeared to be afraid now that Matt was there with his legendary gun in his hand. His eyes were hard and mean.

Jed spoke, "Tim could have stopped them before I got here, but he didn't."

Alan Rosso, Joe, and Ritchie Thorn were bringing Mitchell out of the office with his mangled hand outward and bleeding all over the ground. "You didn't have to shoot him!" Alan yelled at Jed.

"I warned him," he said simply. "Where do you think you guys are going? You're under arrest!"

Joe Thorn grimaced, "We have to get him to the doctor!"

Jed shook his head. "No, you're not."

Matt pointed at two men in the crowd. "You two, take him to Doctor Ambrose's house, now!" He turned to Jed. "What have you got going on here? Who's responsible for this?"

Jed nodded at the Thorn brothers, Alan Rosso and Brian Barns. "They caused most of it."

Tim forced himself to stand up. "My deputy is arresting them, so they'll go to my jail."

"I'm not your deputy, not anymore."

"What about the rest of these men?" Matt asked Jed.

"No. The primary ones were these four."

"Let's get them inside." Matt turned to the others standing there, anxious to leave. "Go home. And I may be knocking on your doors later. But for now, get out of my sight!"

Tim put a hand on Jeb's shoulder. "Let's go back to the office and talk this over, Jed."

Jed pushed his hand off his shoulder quickly. "Get away from me, Tim! I told you, I'm done with you and your favoritism. I quit!"

Tim shook his head. "You can't quit on me. You'll never work around here again. I'll see to that!"

Matt shook his head with a disgusted chuckle and looked at the four men Jed was arresting. "You men wanted in my jail so bad; now you can have a closer look. You're not going to like it, I promise you."

Truet Davis ran to a stop and stared at the broken windows and door as he caught his breath. "Oh my gosh! What happened?"

Matt nodded at the four men. "They wanted into the jail pretty bad, so take them in and put them in a cell next to their buddies. I want a few words with the Sheriff."

Truet shook his head irritably. "I was down on Rose Street, walking around when I heard the shots. Yeah, I'll put them in there, alright. Let's go!" He walked them into the office and then cursed loudly when he saw that they had broken four large granite blocks out of the wall. "I should throw every one of you through that hole headfirst!" he yelled angrily.

Matt looked at Tim squarely. "You sat back and watched?"

Tim smiled uncomfortably. "No, I stood." He

chuckled nervously. "Well, you said I should mind my own affairs."

Matt shook his head. "No, you told me that. That's fine, Tim. All this can be repaired before too long. But your reputation as a coward is going to multiply fast when word gets out that you were too scared to stop a bunch of unarmed men. It tells me what a piece of trash you really are. From this point on, I won't be there to back you up when you need it."

"That's fine, Matt. Just stay out of my business, too, then."

Matt looked at him pointedly. "Keep things legal, and you'll have nothing to worry about. If not, then I'll be the biggest pain in your side that you can imagine."

Bob Ewing began to sit up from being knocked unconscious for a few moments. Tim looked at Jeb. "Help me pick him up."

"Pick him up yourself."

Tim looked around and saw Mark Thiesen. "Mark, come help me."

Mark reluctantly did so.

Tim looked at Jeb bitterly. "You're done. You might as well move out of town. You won't work in this town again!"

Matt looked at Jeb. "Wow. He must be a pretty powerful man. You have a family to feed, don't you?"

"I do."

"So, you'll be looking for a job?"

Jeb sighed. "That I am."

"Do you get along with Truet and the two other boys I have working for me?"

Jed looked at Matt with interest. "I do."

"Are you a bigot, or do you think you can treat everyone the same? The color of a man or woman does not matter in my office. We do what's right and treat everyone the same. We can't be bought, and we protect, help, and serve anyone, even the worst of society. We don't hit women or abuse a child, and we stop someone if they do. And we're all Christians and believe in the bible. Do you have any issues with any of that?"

Jed shook his head. "No, I do not."

Matt put out a hand to shake. "Then, there's a job open with me if you want it."

Jed smiled. "Really? I'd be honored to join the U.S. Marshal's Office."

"Then, you're hired." He looked at Tim, who was furious. "Well, he's working again right here in your town, and he'll probably become a thorn in your side too. Maybe even more so than I am."

Tim's eyes burned with anger. "Come on, boys, let's go," he said to Mark and Bob, who was holding his bleeding head. They started walking down the boardwalk to stay out of the mud of the street.

Truet came out of the office, looking angry. "I'd like to hurt every one those men. Do you have any idea how much damage they did? I have to replace every window, two doors and door jams, those blocks, which I'll have Luther help with because he might have to chisel one down to fit back in there correctly. They broke one of them in half!" he yelled, irritated.

Matt looked around and saw the gate ripped off the hinges of the three-foot partition fence, and another part of the partition fence was broken down as well. He sighed. "It's bad, but it can be fixed, right?"

Truet nodded. "Yeah, but it's going to take some work." He looked at Jed for the first time and put out his hand. "Evening, Jed."

"Jed is joining us here at the U.S. Marshal's Office," Matt said.

Truet smiled slowly. "It's about time. I've been telling him for a while that he should come to our side of the street. I look forward to working with you."

"Thank you. I'm excited to join up with you all," Jed said.

Matt looked at the broken bay windows. "Do we have anything to fix those windows with tonight?"

Truet shook his head. "No."

Matt groaned with frustration. "Well, we can hang some tarps up for tonight." He walked over to the hole in the wall and bent down to look through it. He spoke to his prisoners through the hole, "It's going to get cold tonight. You all can thank each other for that."

Matt was greeted with a volley of curses from a number of the eight men in his jail. Matt laughed quietly and looked at his new deputy, Jed Clark. "I know it's a lot to ask, but how would you like to stay here tonight and keep your eye on these men? I'll make it fair. I'll pay you five dollars for one night's work, and I'll even make it fun for you. How would you like to keep those men up all night playing a trumpet? Just sit here by the fire and play the trumpet as loud as you can all night."

"I don't know how to play a trumpet," Jed answered honestly.

Matt smiled. "Perfect. I didn't want you to know how. I want you to play as poorly, and as high pitched as you possibly can all night long. In the morning, you can go home and get some sleep and Truet, and I will come in here and get the windows covered and doors repaired. And have Uncle Luther look at the wall. It sounds like a plan to me, if it's okay with you?"

Jed shrugged. "Can I go tell my family?"

Matt nodded. "Of course."

19

Gabriel Smith had never been in Branson after dark, nor ever experienced the light from the ten-foot-tall ornamental light posts illuminating from their height. He had seen a man with a ladder lighting the oil lamps under the white glass globes earlier in the evening, but as the darkness grew, the light was far more evident. Willow Falls didn't have any light posts, the only light at night came from windows of homes, or maybe one or two lanterns hung outside. The city lights were probably taken for granted by the people of Branson, but for Gabriel, they were a new experience, one of many he'd found attractive that made him want to move to the city. He wasn't thinking about the lights, though as he ran down the plank sidewalk along Main Street towards the Marshal's Office. There had been two loud shotgun blasts and he'd already passed two men leading a young man, who looked to be barely conscious with a bloody hand that looked to be disfigured beyond repair. The young man moaned as the two men hurried him by without saying a word.

The thought of Matt lying on the street with lead pellets in him from the second shotgun blast frightened him. He knew Matt had his revolver on him, but the deep percussion of a twelve-gauge shotgun sounded a lot different than a Colt .45. Gabriel feared the worst, and that anxiety kept him running. Ahead, he saw three men walking towards him. All three had badges on their coats that flickered in the available light. One of the men held a handkerchief against the side of his head to stop a bleeding head wound. They took up the width of the walkway.

Gabriel came to a stop in front of them and bent over to catch his breath momentarily. He asked, "What's happening down there? Is Matt okay?"

Sheriff Tim Wright's lips curled in anger. He was already furious about losing one of his best deputies to Matt, and just hearing his name brought a deeper rage that he couldn't control. Unexpectedly, his right hand swung around and connected with Gabriel's cheek with a hard-stinging slap across his face. Gabriel stumbled back and caught himself against the wooden wall of a building. He was stunned by the unexpected blow. Tim grabbed him by the coat lapel with both hands and jerked him forward and then slammed him back against the wall as hard as he could. "Why'd you run into me, huh? You were trying to fan my pockets, weren't you?" he accused and slapped Gabriel again with a vicious right across the same cheek. "If there's one thing I can't stand, it's a damn thieving pickpocket! Well, I caught you now, didn't I?"

Gabriel was dumbstruck and shook his head as his eyes filled with terrified tears. He could hear his heart pounding in his ears and felt the adrenaline running through his body. "I didn't," he said weakly. He recognized the Sheriff and the deputy holding the blood-stained handkerchief to his head from when they came to Willow Falls the year before when Matt brought his mother home after being kidnapped. Gabriel had great respect for the well-dressed Branson Sheriff then. He had thought he was a well-poised man with a confidant and an easy-going composure. At the moment, none of that was true.

Tim glared at Gabriel with a cold and angry glare. "Yeah, you did! Didn't he Bob?"

Bob Ewing nodded, "Yeah." He was annoyed that Tim would even waste his time with the frightened boy.

"No, sir, I didn't. I just asked a question." Gabriel's voice shook weakly.

Tim cupped his right hand and swung it low and upward into Gabriel's crotch. The blow was received with the boy exhaling quickly and bending over. The blow to his testicles sent a shock wave of pain up into his stomach and took his breath away at the same time. As Gabriel bent over, Tim grabbed Gabriel's jaw with his left hand and squeezed his cheeks against his teeth and rammed his head back against the wall and held him there. Tim drew close with a sneer on his face. "I think we finally caught the kid that's been pickpocketing everyone out here, Bob. What's your name?" he asked and squeezed his cheeks harder against his teeth.

A tear fell down Gabriel's cheek as he tried to speak through his gripped mouth, "Ga..brel."

"What was that? I couldn't hear you." Tim said with a wicked snarl. "Well, it doesn't matter. Tonight, you're going to find out what happens to thieves around here. Let's go. You're under arrest!" He let go of Gabriel's cheeks and grabbed hold of the young man's ear firmly and started to walk him down the boardwalk towards his jail. He saw an older man with silver hair and goatee, pointing at him from twenty feet away and walking quickly towards them.

"Let go of him now!" Floyd Bannister demanded loudly with his deep and authoritative voice. "Get your damn hands off my grandson right now!" he shouted with his finger pointed at Sheriff Wright.

Bob Ewing stepped in front of Tim and held up his left hand to stop the old man. "He's under arrest, old-timer. You can get him out of jail tomorrow."

Floyd's eyes burned with anger. He slapped Bob's hand out of his way. "What do you think you're arresting him for?" he asked bitterly.

"Pickpocketing," Tim replied. "I caught his thieving little hand in my pocket."

"Bull!" Floyd exclaimed sharply. He pointed his finger at Tim. "There is no way that boy pickpocketed three lawmen! Do you think I'm stupid? You three are if you think I'm going to let you beat on my grandson and then take him to jail for a crime he didn't commit! There's not one person stupid enough to try to pickpocket three lawmen! Now let him go! And let him go now!" he shouted with a fire in his eyes that showed he was a man that wasn't going to walk away.

"Grandpa, I didn't..." Gabriel stated and then buckled under pain of his ear being twisted in Tim's grasp. "Ouch," he cried out with a high pitch.

"Let him go, I said! You son of a..." Floyd yelled and tried to reach Tim but was pushed back against the wall of the building by Bob Ewing. Bob was a much larger man than Floyd.

"You better calm down before you have a stroke," Bob said with a slight smile. He stood between Floyd and Tim protectively with a stream of blood running down his hairline and neck.

Floyd pushed Bob with more force than he was expecting and stumbled backward a few steps. Floyd stepped towards Tim with his wild eyes burning into him.

Tim held up his right hand to create some distance and pulled his left hand that held Gabriel's ear back behind him slightly. He spoke quickly, "I'm the Sheriff, and I'm warning you right now. Walk away, or you're going to jail too. And I won't promise that you'll look as good when you get out!"

Floyd's lips tightened into a snarl. He shouted as his temper had reached its limit, "And I'm telling you to let my grandson go! I may be old and not what I used to be, but I'll do my damnedest to make you hurt! All of you! And I don't give a damn if you're the sheriff! I'm from Portland and have seen lots of corrupt lawmen willing to do the unthinkable for a dollar!" He pointed at Tim with a hard glare. "You're not taking my grandson anywhere without me!" he shouted.

Tim raised his eyebrows slightly humored. "Fine. Bob, arrest him, and let's go."

Bob reached for Floyd's arm, but Floyd hit it away with a quick wave of his left arm. "Don't touch me, or I'll knock your teeth out!"

Bob chuckled. "I'd like to see that old-timer. Trust me, I've heard that a dozen times from old men who still think they have something left and haven't met one yet who does. Now, we can do this nicely, or if you want, I can be rough. I'll try not to break any of your crusty old bones in the process."

Floyd's head tilted slightly as he listened to Bob's words. "Fine. Do your best," he said with a slight smirk on his lips. He had looked past the Sheriff and saw Matt and another man walking quickly towards them. It amazed him how even nearly thirty years later, he could still read his son's body language and knew Matt was furious.

Bob stepped closer to hit Floyd, and as he did, Floyd moved his left foot to act like he was going to kick him. Bob immediately lowered his hands to protect his crotch from a kick exposing his jaw for a right cross. It came with fury as Floyd unloaded a clean right fist into Bob's cheek that caused him to stumble three steps and caught himself on a porch support post as he fell. He held onto the post for a moment and spat out some blood from a split cheek. "Still have my teeth old-timer," he said in a low and dangerous voice. He looked at Mark Thiessen, who looked unsure about the whole situation. "Hand me that shotgun."

Mark shook his head. "It's Jed's. I need to give it back to him," Mark replied hesitantly, not wanting to hand it over.

"Give it here!" Bob demanded as he snatched it from Mark forcefully. He stepped towards Floyd. "I'm going to bust your crusty bones!"

Floyd glanced towards the Sheriff to see where Matt was, and then smirked as he looked at Bob and backed up just enough to keep some distance and said, "You're not brave enough to use your fists against an old man?"

Bob stopped to respond. "Oh, I am!"

Matt knocked the Sheriff's derby hat off his head and grabbed a handful of hair and jerked his head back while at the same time pulling his revolver and pointing it at Bob. "Put it down, now!" he ordered firmly. Bob's eyes widened in alarm to have Matt's gun aimed at him. He lowered the shotgun to the walkway slowly. "Truet, grab that gun."

Truet grabbed the shotgun and without saying a word, rammed the stock into Bob's gut. Bob bent over and stepped backward, missing the boardwalk and collapsed to the edge of the street on his knees, holding his stomach. "You piece of crap! You were going to beat an old man with this?" He kicked Bob in the face with a hard kick that drove him down into the mud. Truet looked at Floyd. "Are you alright?" he asked heatedly.

Floyd nodded with an excited smile. "I am."

"Let go of his ear," Matt hissed in Tim's ear. His voice was noticeably restrained.

Tim grimaced. "He's a pickpocket. I caught him reaching into my pocket," Tim said as he let Gabriel go.

"That's not true!" Gabriel answered, stepping away from Tim. "He hit me for no reason and accused me of trying to steal from him, I never touched him," Gabriel spoke heatedly with tears falling from his eyes. Floyd stepped near and wrapped an arm over his shoulders.

Matt looked at his son while keeping a hold of Tim's hair. "Are you okay, Gabriel?"

He nodded.

Tim chuckled nervously. "Matt, you're interfering in my business again."

"Am I?"

"Yeah, ask Bob when he can talk. Your deputy had no right to do that to him, by the way. We're making an arrest. You're pissing me off, Matt." Tim said strenuously due to his head being tilted backward and held in place by Matt's strong grip on his hair. "Didn't he try to rob me, Bob?" Tim asked.

"Yeah," Bob croaked out painfully as he got his breath back.

"I don't believe either one of you," Matt looked at Mark Thiessen. "Mark, what did you see?"

Mark was uncomfortable. "I didn't see anything, except the Sheriff hitting him."

Tim tried to speak, "The kid's a thief! And you're interfering with my job!"

Matt put his mouth close to Tim's ear and spoke

with a slow, restrained voice, "That boy is my son!"

"Huh?" Tim asked, nervously. "You don't have a son."

Truet Davis chuckled lightly while he turned Gabriel's chin to look at his reddened cheek. "You'll be okay, Gabe." He turned back to Matt. "He was smacked pretty hard."

"I do have a son, and not only did you hit him, you just tried to frame him. And that old man you all were threatening to hurt is my father! You were going to let Bob beat him with a shotgun?" He let go of Tim's hair and pushed him against the wall of the building harshly. He rammed his left hand up to Tim's throat to hold him tight against the wall. He glared into Tim's eyes with a wild expression. He put the barrel of his gun to Tim's head. He spoke slowly, "I want to hurt you! I really do. I want to beat you and beat you until you can't show your face around here again. I want to take that badge and shove it so far down your throat that it'll never be found again. I am trying very hard not to give in to what I would love to do to you. But I am losing that battle the more I stand here looking at you!" He looked at Gabriel. "How many times did he hit you?" he could see the reddened cheek on Gabriel's face.

"Two, three. I don't know." The fierceness of Matt's eyes took Gabriel by surprise.

Floyd offered, "He hit him in the Bannister jewels too."

Matt clenched his jaw tightly as he fought to control his temper and beat Tim senseless. "I already broke your nose. What else do I have to do, Tim?" His breathing was becoming heavy.

Tim was frightened and it came out in his voice. "Matt, I apologize for hitting your son. I had no idea he was your son. He never mentioned it, did he, boys?" he asked Bob and Mark desperately.

"No," Bob answered, taking a seat on the boardwalk to rest against a support post.

Matt sneered, "He shouldn't have to. That's the whole point, Tim! No one should have to fear being falsely accused by you!" Matt placed his revolver in his holster and then quickly slapped the face of Tim with a loud crack that echoed down the street and then did it again as fast as he could. "Do you like that?" he shouted. He slapped him again, ferociously. "I'm sure my son didn't either! But you were happy to do it, weren't you? Put your hands down!" Matt yelled when Tim covered his face with his hands. Tim's hands came down. Matt slapped him again, ferociously. A bead of snot came out of Tim's nose stretching across his cheek. Matt took a deep breath. He spoke softer, "I want you to get out of my sight, Tim. Don't ever do this kind of thing again. The people here have enough trouble without the Sheriff trying to set them up for crimes they didn't do. Rest assured, in the next election, everything will come out because I'll make sure the townspeople know what kind of a man you are. Your time is limited. And if you and I have any more trouble…I will hurt you. And I'm not talking about just slapping the snot out of you. Apologize to my son and my father and get the hell out of my sight!" Matt let go of his throat.

Tim wiped his face and glared at Matt for a moment before picking up his derby hat and looked at Floyd, who had his arm around Gabriel's shoulders. Floyd was smiling with a bit of adventure in his eyes, while Gabriel looked humiliated by the Sheriff's actions. "My apologies to you both. Have a good evening," he said and looked back at Matt bitterly. "I didn't know he was your son."

"You shouldn't have to."

Matt watched the three men walk away and sighed heavily. He looked at his father. "Thank you for watching out for him."

Floyd nodded. "He's my grandson. I would've fought to the death for him. Luckily, I saw you coming and didn't have to," he said with a chuckle.

Matt looked at his father, awkwardly, and looked away. Strangely, tears filled his eyes for no reason that he couldn't understand. The sound of his father's yelling had rung out like a ghost from his past. The haunting tone and the anger expressed through it was its own sound that he could never forget from years past. It was initially terrifying like a forgotten nightmare, and yet it drew him outside faster than any other noise he could think of, including shots being fired. The sound of his father's yelling could still scare him. But this time, it wasn't manifested in alcohol or directed towards another helpless loved one. It was to protect a grandson that he had just met and claimed to love. "I appreciate it," Matt said, glancing back at his father.

"Oh, hell, I'd do the same thing for you too. I haven't been that fired up in years." He chuckled as he looked at Gabriel proudly. "Someday, you'll be able to tell your children that you watched your father and grandfather take on the local law and win just to protect you! That's a pretty good story to tell, I think." He messed up Gabriel's hair affectionately. "Well, shall we go back to the hotel?"

"Yeah," Gabriel said, still downcast.

Matt waved his hand towards Truet. "This is Truet, by the way. Truet this is my father, Floyd Bannister," Matt introduced them awkwardly. He didn't know how to address his father. Should he call him Father, Pa, Dad, or maybe old man as some folks referred to their fathers? The whole concept seemed as foreign as being called Son. When he was a child, he called his father Pa, but now that he was grown, it seemed too intimate, like a father and son who had a relationship like it was supposed to be. Matt was distant, detached, and could only refer to the man as "my father." That reference was a fact and showed no personal relationship.

Truet smiled and shook his hand. "Nice to meet you, Sir."

"Likewise."

"You'd be interested to know Truet's courting Annie."

Floyd looked closer at Truet and nodded with a smile. "Oh. Well, congratulations." An expression of sadness came over his face. "I'm afraid I didn't have much to do with raising her at all. But um, I sure love her, and I'm glad to know she's courting a good man. I can tell you are one. So yeah, congratulations and take care of my baby girl for me." He sniffled as his eyes watered a bit.

Truet nodded. "I will, Sir."

"Well, shall we go back," he asked Matt and Gabriel with a slight smile as he forced the sadness away.

Matt answered, "I'll be a bit still. I have just a little more to do. They broke up my office, trying to break the prisoners out of jail. I'll be along in an hour or so and tell you about it. If you would ask Christine to wait for me and if she doesn't want to, will you walk her home for me? I don't like her walking alone at night."

"Of course. It would be my pleasure."

"Gabriel, stay with your grandpa, okay?"

Gabriel nodded.

"Do you know where William is? I am surprised he isn't here."

Floyd shrugged his shoulders. "I have no idea. He is out with Maggie somewhere."

"Okay. I'll see both in about an hour."

"Be careful out there, Son."

Matt nodded. The word Son just didn't seem to fit him well after nearly thirty years.

20

Matt and Truet had borrowed some tarps from the livery stable and tacked them up over the two front bay windows for the night. They cut a portion off one to tack up over the door window as well to keep the rain off the office floor. When Jed had returned with warmer clothes and a pot of soup to keep heated on the stove, and everything was about as well as it could be, Matt was about an hour later than he expected when he walked back to the Monarch Hotel and went up to his father's room. It was late, and he didn't want to knock on the door if Christine had already gone home, and everyone else was sleeping. He put his ear close to the door to listen when he heard Christine ask, "Floyd if you don't mind me asking, where did you meet Matt's mother and what was she like?"

Floyd's facial expression took a downward turn as his mind went back to the day he had first seen Ruth Fasana. His mouth opened to speak, but no words came out. He took a breath and spoke with deep sincerity, "The first time I saw Ruth, I was down on what's called Premro Island now. Back then, it was just called the Falls. Branson wasn't anything more than a few blocks of homesteads and not much more than a store or two back then. Mister Fasana, Ruth's father, was a big man and ornery as a cantankerous bull. We were all scared of him. He was an old trapper and just a tough kind of man with a full-blooded Indian wife. Luke was a stonemason, that's how the Fasana Granite quarry was started by the way. Matt's uncles own it today," he said sadly. "The first time I ever saw Ruth quite a few us were swimming down in the pool at the bottom of the falls right at the south side of the island, and I was standing on the edge of the water getting ready to jump in when I saw her shadow cross in front of me. I looked up to see who was up there and there she stood with her little sister, Mary. I was dumbstruck. She was so beautiful. Her father brought them out to the falls to swim while he was replacing the millstones in the first mill here. It was a hot August afternoon, and we were all there swimming. It's odd to think that we were all so young and now we're all so old. That was the first time I ever laid my eyes on Ruth. She was the most beautiful girl I'd ever seen, and I was lovestruck. I knew right then that I wanted to marry her. I couldn't get her off my mind, and all I wanted was to get to know her. Eventually, three years later, I began courting her and ended up marrying her." He stopped and smiled as Matt stepped into the room quietly.

Matt waved at everyone and sat down near Christine. He looked at Floyd, "Please continue."

"Well, I was telling Christine and Gabriel how I met your mother. And to answer your other question, Christine, Ruth was the kindest, most generous, and the nicest person you could ever meet. There wasn't a mean bone in her body. I look back now, and if there was any flaw about her, it was marrying me," he said with a sad but pain-filled expression.

Christine frowned. "Did you not love her?"

"No, I loved her very much." He looked towards the bedroom where Rhoda was sleeping and then looked back at Christine and spoke softer not to be overheard, "Ruth is still the love of my life. But I ruined it. We all have things that we regret, I suppose, but if I could go back and live my life over again knowing what I know now," he paused as his chest filled with air and his eyes filled with moisture. "I'd do it all over again, but I damn sure wouldn't do it the same. I'd change a lot of things." He sniffled and wiped his nose with a handkerchief.

"What would you change most? If there was just one thing you could change, what would it be?" she asked softly.

His eyes filled with large thick tears that hovered over his eyes. He wiped them before they could fall. "I think it all boils down to one thing, and that's drinking. I'd never pick up that bottle." He opened his hands and shrugged faintly. "The only time I ever yelled at my wife was when I drank. The only time I ever laid my hands on her, hit her...was when I was drunk. I was a mean drunk, a stupid drunk, and I lost everything I knew, loved, and needed the most because I had become a drunk. I lost everything that mattered, and then nothing mattered anymore. When Ruth died, I left my children behind. I had lost just about everything my father and I had built together. I guess if you wondered why I went to Portland, it's because I couldn't stay here anymore. There's just too many memories and too much sorrow." He looked away from the others and wiped his eyes silently.

Matt stared at the floor with an angry expression.

Christine asked softly, "When you got drunk and laid your hands on Ruth as you stated, did you ever wake up the next day and see what you had done to her? And if so, why would you keep drinking if you loved her? Forgive me if I'm asking very personal questions, but I think it's a good question. I guess it's more of a question of how you could keep doing that to her and not so much of why. I'm not casting judgment on you, Floyd, I'm just asking because I think it's important to know or think about at least." She took hold of Matt's hand, knowing he was deeply uncomfortable with the conversation by his breathing.

Floyd sniffled and shook his head in shame. "I've spent the past twenty-eight years thinking about that," he said slowly with an anguished expression on his face. "It's too easy to blame it on the alcohol and leave it at that. Yeah, I would wake up in the mid-afternoon or whenever and see her with a black eye, a bloody mouth. A tooth knocked out or crying over the pain of her broken ribs..." He squeezed his lips together tightly and fought from sobbing as his body convulsed a few times. "I saw her broken nose and blood all over the room, and it killed me."

Christine looked over at Matt and seen his lips tightly squeezed together and his moist eyes staring down at the floor. She squeezed his hand softly with a soft, comforting smile.

Floyd continued, "So many times, I swore I would never drink again! So many times, I swore I would never hit her again. I promised her that I would give it up and be the husband that I promised to be on our wedding day. I would be good for a while, and we'd go to church and do family things, but when her wounds were healed and the bruises were gone, it would happen again. Every time it seemed like it got worse, and it was never her fault. She was going to take the kids and move in with Mary and Charlie, and I pleaded with her to stay. I loved her, you know. I begged her to stay promising I would never drink again, and I meant it. She stayed and that's when Annie was conceived. But nothing changed. I'd get frustrated or angry and go to town and buy a bottle. I'd go to town for business and give in to temptation and buy a bottle. I even took the three older boys to town with me just so I wouldn't be so tempted, and sometimes that worked, but the last time..." he paused to swallow and fought from sobbing. "I went in with a friend for one drink and ended up staying in there and came home drunk. The boys were already mad at me, but when we got home, we found out Ruth had died in childbirth. We finely had a daughter."

"And that's when you took your children to their aunt and uncles?" Christine asked with tears of empathy in her own eyes.

He nodded and wiped his moist eyes. "Yeah. Now managing a saloon, I see men I know doing the same thing to their wives, and they always say it's the woman's fault for making them mad. Even some of the women will tell you they deserved it too. That was never the case with Ruth. She never deserved being hit on. She deserved far more than that. That's what I mean by saying if she had a flaw, I was it. I was her only flaw. I ruined my family, and I missed out on the blessing of watching my children grow up and being a part of their lives. What's the one thing I would change? I would never let alcohol touch my lips. And that alone would change everything."

Matt looked at his father severely. "But you make a living selling it?"

Floyd nodded. "I do. But I don't encourage it, and I would rip that bottle right out of Gabriel's hand and hit him across the head with it if I caught him taking a liking to the crap. It ruined my life, Son. I don't want it ruining any of you kids' or my grandchildren. I know I messed up, but if your mother was ever proud of anything I've ever done, it would be telling you all not to do what I spent my life doing."

Matt's lips tightened. "Do you ever regret hitting Mom?"

Floyd answered sharply, "Every damn day! Are you kidding me? I know what I did, and I can't change it now, but it leaves a nasty aftertaste in my soul even today. All I can do is say I am sorry I did that to her and what that did to you. I never considered the damage it would cause my children to see and hear that. My anger and taste for alcohol blinded me. I was a damn fool. I really am sorry, and if you can, I ask you to forgive me. The only reason I came here is to ask you to forgive me for all the times I made our home hell. For not being there when your mother passed away and for leaving you with your aunt and uncle and then disappearing from your life. I could keep going because I've done nothing right, except for leaving you all with Charlie and Mary. That's probably the best thing I could have done for you all. I ask for your forgiveness for all the crap I put you through, but I left you there because I loved you all enough to do so."

Matt frowned and looked down at the floor again. "Why did you bring me a dying blind calf knowing it was going to die?"

"Hmm?" Floyd asked, not immediately remembering the calf he brought Matt. "Oh! The calf, yeah. Did it die?"

Matt looked at him, coldly. "Uncle Charlie shot it that afternoon. It had scours so bad maggots were eating its hindquarters."

Floyd frowned. "I remember now. I didn't know it had scours. I stopped by my friend's dairy over in Natoma before coming over, and he had a blind bull calf; he had no use for it. I knew it was blind, but I thought it would make a nice pet for you. He put it in the wagon, and I drove it over to the ranch to see you kids. I didn't realize it was that sick until Charlie pointed it out. I figured you were such a lover of critters, and Charlie is such a good man that I thought you'd raise it as a pet instead of live-stock." He paused. "I had the best intentions, Matt."

"Oh, that's sweet," Christine said.

"I hoped," Floyd said with a disappointed shrug.

Matt stood up. "It's late, and I have to get up early and try to get my office secure at best anyway. Nice talking to you. I'll see you tomorrow, possibly." He put out his hand to shake Floyd's hand.

Floyd shook his hand. "I love you, Son."

Matt nodded. "Have a good night."

Christine hugged Floyd. "I appreciate the time we've had talking. I've learned so much, so thank you and tell Rhoda thank you as well."

Floyd smiled appreciatively. "Well, come back anytime." He looked at Gabriel and hugged him. "You come to see me tomorrow before you leave, young man. I want to give you my address so you can write to me, or if you ever get to Portland, come see me." He looked at Matt. "I've missed out on all of your lives; I'd like to be a part of those I can."

Matt nodded, with no emotion on his face. "Goodnight."

21

Matt and Christine left the Monarch Hotel and walked Gabriel to Matt's house and left him there to get some sleep. Matt walked with Christine along 9th Street towards Rose Street, which was eight blocks away. It was cold out, but the rain had stopped, and a slight fog was expanding across town from the river outward. Like most weekday nights, it was quiet and peaceful as they walked across town, but Rose Street would be busier with the men going to the saloons, gambling halls, prostitutes, and other various means of entertainment including the dance hall, of course.

Christine was bundled in her wool coat with a scarf around her neck and a hat to keep the rain off her hair. Her hands were in her pocket as she walked beside Matt at a casual pace so they could talk. "Matt, are you ever going to forgive your father? I found it disappointing that you ignored that whole part of his conversation. That's what he's here for after all."

"I know."

"But you're going to ignore him?"

"Just because someone asks for forgiveness doesn't mean you have to forgive them."

"I suppose not, but aren't we as Christians supposed to forgive those who hurt us? You remember the Parable of the Unmerciful Servant, right? In today's money the servant owed the King over a million dollars, and he couldn't pay the debt of course. The King ordered that the servant's wife and children were to be sold to pay that large debt he owed, but the servant begged and pleaded with the King to be patient with him until he could pay it. The King had compassion on the servant and cancelled the entire debt completely. Can you imagine the joy that servant would have felt to be debt free after having owed over a milliom dollars to the King? Then moments later, that very same servant went out and found a man who owed him a few dollars, like three dollars at most. It was hardly anything. The servant beat the man and demanded to be paid those few dollars right then and there. The poor man didn't have any money and fell to his knees and begged the servant for some more time to pay him, just like that very same servant did the King moments before. But the servant wasn't so forgiving and had the man thrown in prison until he could pay his small debt of a few dollars. Other people saw it happen, and went and told the King what this servant did to the poor man. The King called the servant right back to him and was very angry. He said, 'I cancelled the million dollars you owed me which is a lot, because I felt compassion for you when you begged me to give you time to pay it. I could have sold your wife and children, but I forgave your debt. Shouldn't you have had mercy on the man who owed you three dollars? I had mercy on you for a whole lot more!' Then he threw the servant in prison until his impossible debt could be paid, which it never would be. And then Jesus said when he finished the parable, 'This is how my heavenly father will treat each of you unless you forgive your brother from your heart.' I think, forgiving people is important or Jesus wouldn't have told the parable or said that."

Matt smiled slightly. "Yes, I know that parable. I knew what my father was getting at, and I think, who is he to show up here and expect me to forgive him and everything's supposed to be good after all these years? The truth is it was never good with him around. Moments come to mind of him being nice and doing fatherly things with us, but the memories that stand out are of him screaming and hitting, and how am I supposed to forgive that? I know other people have worse fathers than mine, and I never once said I had it worse than anyone else. What I am saying is, how am I supposed to forgive my father for what he did to my family and me? Families are not supposed to be broken. Fathers are supposed to be there when you need them, and he wasn't. His choices affected everything and every aspect of my life. He brought me into this world and then made it a painful place to be. I've been asked why I don't trust anyone? Well, who's supposed to teach a child to trust? The parents! I was failed by my father and left to be raised elsewhere while he was out playing, drinking, and doing whatever he was doing. Now, he wants me to forgive him?" He stopped and turned to look at his friend. "How can I?"

"I can take that question two ways. How can I to mean you want to, but you don't know how? Or how can I to mean, you refuse to? That's the question you have to answer."

Matt sighed and started walking slowly again. "It's a little of both, I think."

She spoke softly, "He asked you to forgive him because he loves you and knows he did you wrong. All those things you just said, he knows what he did to hurt you. He can't forgive himself if you don't forgive him because the guilt is always going to be there like an invisible wall. He loves you and wants to get to know you, but that barrier of guilt will always be there like an impenetrable wall to him, and like years of soot building up in a chimney within you. Which one do you think is more destructive, a trunkload of guilt chained to your waist or years of soot building up in a chimney that's never been cleaned? I talked to your father for a while, and he's very sincere, I think it would be a good thing if you were able to forgive him."

Matt walked in thought without saying anything. "Why is that so important to you?"

Christine continued, "You mentioned not trusting anyone. So how can you forgive someone who broke all your trust? It's not as easy as it sometimes sounds, I know. The wounds can be much deeper than saying the words that can possibly heal. Why is it important to me, you asked? Because the soot from the fires of long ago can be an unexpected danger that can burn your whole house down if you don't sweep it away. Forgiving someone isn't about forgetting about what happened or trusting them again. It is about sweeping the soot of the past out of your heart and no longer holding onto that old charcoaled log that's darkening your hands. It's old, it's cold, and the fire's not coming back. So why hold onto the ashes of the past with a tight grip when there are twenty other pieces of oak waiting to warm up a frozen heart? Maybe the hardest thing in life is simply letting go of all we knew and hang on to, but in time we realize it's just the soot we're holding on to. It's not a real tangible piece of firewood that we're trying to start a fire to warm our hearts and put some light in our lives with. Forgiveness is letting the past go; all the bitter feelings and the anger and all that is blackening your joy, your light, and your life. You let go of that charcoaled stick and wash your hands of it. Those men who clean chimneys are covered in soot from head to toe and I think that's a good example of what a father's or mother's bad choices can do to a child. All those children grow up not knowing they're covered in the soot of their past and they become bitter, angry and mistreat their children because of all the soot in their own lives." She stopped to look at him. "Matt, you're an amazing man with so much to offer, but as I've said before, you have to get rid of the soot of your childhood before you'll really be free. So, decide to drop the old charcoaled log of your past and go before the Lord and bathe in His forgiveness, and then reach out for a new piece of oak for a brighter future. When you can forgive your father, you'll be able to pick up a beautiful piece of white birch without leaving a trace of that ugly old soot on it. And in case you're wondering what my goofy analogy means, the oak is your future, a future hope, a future wife maybe. And the beautiful white birch is your future children. Don't spread your soot onto them. Forgiveness is important because without it, your children will pay the price of it through your actions. Afterall, soot spreads and gets all over everything. Choose to forgive the people now who hurt you, so the soot doesn't continue to spread any further along. And that, my friend, is something for you to think over tonight." She stopped in front of the dancehall and looked at him fondly. "I'm not going to see you for a few days, am I, Matt? Well, think about what I said, and we'll talk more about it when you come back to town. I hope you have a wonderful Thanksgiving, my friend."

"Thank you. You have a nice Thanksgiving as well. Remember to sing with all your heart, and enjoy the moment."

She smiled. "I will. Goodnight, Matt."

"Goodnight. I'll see you this weekend."

She stood on the porch and watched him walk back towards Mainstreet. He looked back at her and waved as he turned the corner. She smiled and waved before going back inside.

22

Matt didn't feel like going home just yet. He had far too much on his mind between the damage to his office, Gabriel learning that he was his father, and Matt's father and the conversation they had that evening. He needed the time alone to sort out his thoughts and get control of his mixed emotions that were all over the place. He was angry about his office, and a bit overwhelmed with the presence of his father. There was a sense of excitement about getting to know Gabriel and yet a bit anxiousness about how Tom and Elizabeth would react to him now that the truth was out in the open. He was fed up and sick of Sheriff Tim Wright stepping over the edge of the law and getting away with it. He had a slurry of emotions tumbling around inside of him, but the one thing that weighed heaviest on his mind at the moment was how he should feel about his father.

On the one hand, he wanted to stay away from his father and live as he had always done, leaving

Floyd Bannister nothing more than a distant memory. However, that distant memory had resurfaced and called him "Son." Forgiveness was a good thing, and Matt was no stranger to it, but when it came to his father, it was a harder thing to do than just saying it to appease his father. However, on the other hand, he had learned something he never knew. He had never heard the story of how his father met his mother or much about their courting and marriage. He had only known what he could remember and what was told to him by his brothers and by his mother's siblings, which was probably more impartial than not. There was a bit of curiosity that floated around in the inside of him. What else did he not know? Floyd had explained a lot, and as much as Matt had resented his father for bringing him a dying calf, the explanation made it all too clear that it was an innocent mistake on his part. Giving him a dying calf had become the metaphor Matt used to describe the kind of father Floyd was. It had become clear that there was more to the story than his understanding at nine years old knew.

Matt wandered up the street to the Modoc River and crossed the bridge onto Premro Island thinking he'd sit by the river where his parents met and pray. Premro Island was a large basalt landmass that separated the Modoc River as it dropped in elevation just outside of Branson's city limits. The island was surrounded on both sides by channels of fast-moving water that hurled down the natural shoots over a series of turbulent waterfalls and rapids. The force of the current created a perfect power source for water wheels to power the equipment of multiple businesses that took advantage of it. The island was part of the main thoroughfare that went south to the silver mine or across the Blue Mountains to Prairieville on the other side of the mountains. The bridges were heavily supported and used frequently by multiple businesses with heavy loads. The first bridge leaving Branson was over the narrow twenty-foot wide channel of rapids that fired past the island in a wild flow of white water on the northside of the island. On the south side of the island, the other bridge covered the main channel of the river by the Seven Timber Harvester Company sawmill. The main channel of the river was much larger with far more greater volume of water cascading down a steep incline of roaring power as the whitewater dropped significantly as the river came out of the Blue Mountains and entered Jessup Valley. The two forces of water came together in a deep pool at the western end of the island.

The fog was thicker on the island, and all Matt could hear was the rushing water as it fell over the falls. Most all the businesses had lanterns burning which lit up part of the darkness, but the western point where the forces of water converged was dark. Matt took a path through the brush and trees on the lower part of the island, where it was undeveloped and overgrown. This end of the island was a popular swimming hole in the summer with a fire pit that was used almost every summer night, but now in November, it was cold, unlit and dark as he neared the end of the island. It was uncanny to walk to where his brother-in-law Kyle had made a fatal leap into the rocks below the bank a few months before. He walked through the brush, and as he neared the point, he noticed a faintly lit light reflecting through the fog. He stepped out of the brush line and saw a lantern sitting on the ground beside a man dressed in black sitting on a block of wood at the edge of the ten-foot bank overlooking the dark water below. The man was wearing a black coat and a derby hat over his short silver hair. As Matt stepped closer, he recognized his father sitting there alone.

"Reminiscing?" Matt asked his father. He was surprised to see him there.

Floyd was startled by the unexpected voice. "Oh! Geez. You scared me." His father said, jumping up from his wooden block. "What are you doing down here? I thought you were going home?"

"I have too much on my mind. I thought I'd wander down here. I thought you were going to bed?"

"Well, it looks like we have something in common. Pull up a block of wood and join me. You can't see much in the fog, but it's good to listen to the river."

"I'm not interrupting?" Matt asked.

Floyd chuckled lightly. "No! I borrowed a lantern from the mill and was just sitting here. Grab a seat." He waved to the fire pit, which was nothing more than a pile of burnt ashes and sticks surrounded by river rocks. Around the outside of it were several round wood blocks that people used for seating.

Matt grabbed a block of wood and set it a few feet from Floyd and sat down.

"So, this where you met Mom, huh?"

Floyd nodded with a distant look in his eyes. "Yeah. She was standing right here where I'm sitting. I was down there on the rocks." He pointed down at the edge of the water. "I don't know if people really fall in love at first sight or not, but I believe I did. I remember trying to show off as kids will do to get her attention. It never occurred to me that I already had it. I still remember the very first words I ever said to her too. It was a quote from Romeo and Juliet, which I had been reading at the time. 'Have I ever seen true beauty until this day?' The quote may not have been exact, but I had to say something." He smiled slightly in reflection. "And she answered, 'Maybe you should get up early enough to watch a sunrise.' I think I knew I loved her right then. She was beautiful, Matt. Kind of like Christine. I can see why you are so taken with her. She's a very nice person. You should marry her."

Matt smiled slightly. "Well, I'll keep that in mind, but I'm not going to rush it. Did Mom know it was Shakespeare you were quoting?"

"No," he chuckled. "And she didn't like the story when she read it years later either. She thought it was ridiculous and not about love at all, but infatuation and childish nonsense. She had a huge heart for people but was very practical about living. Finding beauty in a love story about two impetuous teenagers committing suicide disgusted her." He took a deep breath. "I like Christine, though.

She reminds me of your mother a little bit. So, how do you like being a father?" Floyd asked.

"I've never really been one. I found out about Gabriel last Christmas when he was fifteen. I didn't know he existed before that. We, Elizabeth and I, decided it was best he didn't know. I always figured he'd find out someday, but I wasn't expecting it to be so soon. Tom didn't know until last Christmas either, so it was very awkward for me and really tough on him."

Floyd grimaced. "Ouch! That would be excruciating. Wow. Well, I appreciate you bringing him by to meet us. That was very special to meet a grandson I never knew existed either," he chuckled. "Thank you for that. He's a great young man."

"Yeah, he is," Matt said.

There was an uncomfortable silence for a moment when Floyd offered, "I went to lay down and couldn't sleep. Talking about your mother got me thinking about this place, and I decided to come on down here to sit for a while. Everything on the northside has changed; everything down here is the same. It's strange how life goes by, you know. It doesn't seem so long ago when I was young and swimming here with my friends. Time moves faster the older you get, so don't waste time on foolish things. Start investing your money now, so you have it when you're my age and retire as your uncles did. You don't want to be on the backside of sixty and still forced to work for a living like me. Save up while you can. Marry someone that you love and loves you and treat her like gold. Christine's falling in love with you, you know. I can see it in her eyes when she looks at you. I know I've never been much of a father to you, but if I could give you some fatherly advice, you should ask her to marry you."

"One of these days, I might take that advice, but I'm not ready to get married yet."

Floyd spoke sincerely, "It's smart to take your time. There are a million men out there who wouldn't waste a day to ask someone like her though. Myself included, I suppose. Now that you have a son, can I give you a little advice?"

"It couldn't hurt," Matt answered with a shrug of his shoulders.

"When it comes to Gabriel, don't do what I did. Be a part of his life, and don't let him slip away from you, okay? I'll tell you what, Son, if I could do it all over again, I would never have left here. I would never have left you, kids. I think that hurts more than anything else the older I get. You're all grown now and have children of your own, and I missed it all. I was never invited to a single wedding, never got to walk my daughter down the aisle or, for that matter, got to know her." He looked at Matt with a glimmer of light reflecting off his watery eyes. "I know you don't need me and probably don't even want me coming around. I guess I don't blame you for that. I haven't done much right. But if I can, I would sure like to make things right between us. I'm not going to live forever, and I'd sure like to see my family more often before I do depart for the mansion in the sky. I'd like for my family to know who I am."

Matt spoke slowly, "You could've come back. You could've told us where you were or if you were alive. You came back that one time with the calf and then sent that knife the next year for Christmas, and came back that last time pretty drunk. That was the last I ever heard of you until I heard you were at my house in Cheyenne." He looked at Floyd critically. "Where were you when I could've used you? If I had known where you were when Tom and Elizabeth got married, and I was running away, I might've come to live with you, because I had nowhere else to go. I remember a lot of bad things, but you weren't always bad either. I remember a few good times too."

Floyd lowered his head. "Son..." He exhaled deeply. "I've never been a strong man. I could lift and plow and do all of that okay, but I hated being alone. I was never good at it. Ruth was my strength. I know that makes no sense because I treated her so bad, but without her, I was nothing. I wasn't like my father, and I wasn't like your uncle's Joel or Luther. When they lost their wives, they worked their butts off and raised their children. I couldn't stay away from the bottle or gambling tables. I had no self-control around those or my anger when I did drink. I was a weak-willed man. When I left here, I was running away too. Probably for the same reason you did. I didn't want to be reminded of the pain I felt, so I left. I buried my sorrows in alcohol and bad relationships. I said I didn't like to be alone, so I lived with several women. None would be acceptable to introduce to my mother."

He smiled slightly. "I think you got your strength from your mother, and your running away from me. Work on that, because it's not a good quality."

"You did the same thing I did?"

He nodded. "Yeah. And probably for the same reason, just different circumstances."

"I was gone for fifteen years."

"How many times did you write home?" Floyd asked curiously.

Matt shook his head. "Not often."

Floyd looked at his son. "Me neither. Maybe we have more in common than we know."

Matt frowned. "I don't mind being alone."

"Neither did your mother. She and I made six children together, and it's amazing to me how alike you all are, yet how different. Adam takes after your grandfather Fasana, Lee takes after my father, Albert, reminds me of your Uncle Joel, Steven takes after me, I was a good, fun-loving man too, once. He's just smarter than I was and left the liquor alone. Annie reminds me of your mother almost exactly. You," he paused. "are the perfect combination of your mother and me. Your bad traits probably come from me. If nothing else I'm not a complete failure, I helped create six wonderful children who your mother and I have every reason in the world to be proud of. We did well, her and I, even with all the rubbish I put you all through."

"Uncle Charlie and Aunt Mary have a lot to do with that too, I think. But I wish Mom was still here," Matt said quietly.

"Me too. I wish I were still married to her today."

"What about Rhoda?"

Floyd chuckled. "Rhoda's great, but you never quite get over the love of your life. That doesn't mean the first love; it means the love of your life. And there's a big distinction between the two. Your mother has always been and is still the love of my life. I'm not trying to take anything away from Rhoda. I love her a lot, and I'm glad we're married, but your mother was...my life."

Matt grimaced and shook his head. "You know, I keep going back to the same thought if she was the love of your life, how in the hell could you hit her? I don't mean to kick a dead horse, but that's all I can think of."

Floyd tightened his lips sadly. "Matt, I never hit her when I was sober. You know how alcohol changes people. Look, I can't change what I did all those years ago. I am guilty, but I'm not the same man I used to be either. I am who I am today, and I don't touch the stuff anymore. I wish I could change the past, but I can't. I have no excuses and no reason why I did it. I can only ask for your forgiveness, Son. That's all I can do. But I'll be honest with you; I have a hard time living with it."

Matt stood up and stepped away.

"Are you leaving?" Floyd asked, concerned.

"No," he said and went to the fire and picked up a partly burned stick. He carried it back to his seat and sat back down to look at it.

Floyd frowned. "You're going to get ashes all over you if you keep rubbing on that stick."

Matt smirked. "I already do." He looked at how

quickly the charcoal of the stick spread to his hands and stayed on his skin like a permanent stain. He tried to wipe it off, and it stained his other hand. Christine's words were far too true, the soot of ones past contaminates everything it touches. His eyes filled with water too quickly to stop them from pouring out and falling down his cheek. He looked at the soot on his hands and fingers. He took a deep breath. "Dad, I forgive you. And just so you know, I love you too."

Floyd smiled with a warmth filling his eyes. "Well, Son, I'd hug you, but I just had my coat washed and don't want ashes all over it."

Matt chuckled. "I don't want them on me either. Not anymore anyway," he said and threw the stick out into the darkness into the river. It was an unspoken symbol to free himself from the soot of his past.

23

Matt had stayed up late talking with his father and finally went home to get some sleep. He woke up early and left before Gabriel woke up. He went to the Marshal's Office and went inside to find Jed Clark sitting at a desk sipping coffee. He looked tired and doing his best to fight from falling asleep.

"Any problems?" Matt asked as he closed the door. Truet had hammered the door jamb back together the night before so they could close the door.

Jed shook his head. "None."

"Are you holding up, alright?"

Jed nodded.

"Did you play that trumpet all night?"

"No. My cheeks began hurting around two in the morning or so. I've never played one before."

Matt grinned. "Did our guests like it?"

Jed shook his head with a chuckle. "No, they did not. I almost couldn't hear myself play with all their screaming and yelling."

Matt laughed. "Good. Where is it?" He picked up the trumpet and opened the door to enter the jail. All six of his prisoners were sleeping soundly. Matt put the trumpet to his lips and blew as hard as he could.

Joe Thorn woke up abruptly and sat up in his bottom bunk and immediately began cursing with a loud yell. He was as angry as were the other men who jumped out of bed and glared at Matt with outraged expressions while yelling at him to stop blowing into the trumpet.

Matt stepped nearer to the cell with his eyes on Joe and his brother Ritchie and moved his head back and forth as he continued to blow into the trumpet and press the keys in a horrible and inexperienced rhythm that could make anyone cover their ears.

"Stop! Okay? We're awake!" Ritchie screamed, followed by some personal expletives towards Matt.

Matt removed the trumpet from his mouth and endured a moment of being yelled at by the men. They were all furious. "I call that one 'Charm in the morning.' This one is called simply enough, 'Peace.' I hope you enjoy it."

"No!

"Enough!"

Matt blew into the trumpet with one long breath and changed notes with every breath. When Joe Thorn stood at the door of the cell, glaring at Matt angrily, Matt stopped. "Did you love it?" he asked with a touch of excitement.

"No! I didn't love it!" Joe shouted bitterly.

"Oh, that's too bad because I play in here every morning when I come in. The granite walls make it sound phenomenal to me. I'm practicing for the city band," he said with a sincere expression. "Do you want me to play another song?"

"Matt, if you blow in that thing one more time, I'm going to throw this bucket of piss on you!" Joe warned.

"Hmm, that wouldn't be a good idea, Joe. I'll tell you that right now. But if you want to test me, go for it." He began blowing in the trumpet again.

A moment later, Jed came into the jail with a smirk on his face. He tapped Matt on the shoulder to get his attention from his awful playing. "There are some people here to see you," he said with a chuckle.

"Oh, okay." He looked at the men in jail. "That one was called, 'I told you, you're were not going to like it here.'"

He left the jail cell being cursed bitterly and entered the main office, surprised to see six Chinese men standing inside the office. Wu-Pen Tseng was again standing in the middle, surrounded by the same two men at his side dressed in black. Behind them were three other Chinese men who wore a plain dirty white or light gray clothes. All of them their long hair in queues and seemed to be looking around the office with interest.

"Marshal Bannister, good morning," Wu-Pen said with a friendly greeting.

"Good Morning. How is Ah See doing?"

Wu-Pen nodded once. "Very well."

"Great. How can I help you?" Matt asked.

Wu-Pen shook his head. "We're here to help you. I heard this was done because you arrested those responsible for Ah See, Chee-Yik, and Kot-Kho-Not. This is true?"

Matt nodded. "It is. I arrested three men for those crimes. Their friends decided to try to break them out. I have four of them in jail too."

"Did they like your songs?"

Matt laughed. "No."

Wu-Pen pointed back at the three men with him. "That is Jin King, Hui-Chao Hung, and Shing Xiang. They are master craftsmen with wood and stone. They will start fixing your office right away. They speak no English but know what they are doing. Others are bringing the supplies and tools for the windows shortly. We don't have glass to fit but can seal up your office securely until the windows come in. We will order them and pay for the damages in gratitude for what you have done for us."

Matt frowned. "Wu-Pen, I appreciate the help. But I only arrested them. The court of law is who will decide if they're guilty or not. I hate to say it, but I have doubts they'll be convicted. I'll do my best to make sure they are, but the jury is going to decide, and I can't promise you that they'll find them guilty because...well because Chinese people aren't equal in some people's eyes. So, before you pay for all this damage, which is not your responsibility, do know it may be for nothing."

Wu-Pen smiled slightly. "I understand. But you are our friend. Let us take care of you. Now, may I see who killed my friends?"

"Sure. Come on back." Matt led the way into the jail and bypassed the first cell and stopped at the second cell where Leroy Haywood, Oscar Belding, and Roger Lavigne all were. "You boys have a visitor, and it isn't your wives. Especially not yours, Leroy."

Leroy looked up at Matt bitterly and then focused his sight on Wu-Pen and his two men standing beside him. He scoffed and shook his head. "What? Did you bring the yellow rat's family here? Well, give me my whip, and I'll whip them back to China too."

"My name is Wu-Pen Tseng. Do you have a name?"

"Wow, the golden monkey speaks English, boys." He stood up and stepped to the jail door and grabbed the bars softly. "My name's Leroy. That's Oscar, and over there is Roger. We whipped your boy good, didn't we?" he chuckled.

Wu-Pen smiled kindly. "He will be fine. I just wanted to see the faces of the men we must forgive. Good day," he said kindly.

Leroy sucked air in through his nose and sucked the snot into his mouth and spat a mouthful of mucus in Wu-Pen's face. "No need to forgive me! I'll do the same thing to all of you yellow rats sooner or later!"

Wu-Pen wiped the thick mucus off his face and stepped one step closer to him. He smiled pleasantly. "Have a good day."

Leroy let go of the bar with his right hand and

reached out quickly to grab Wu-Pen's clothing. His hand was caught in mid-air by one of the two men that stood close to Wu-Pen, and with just his fingers latching onto Leroy's palm, he twisted Leroy's wrist and had Leroy crying out in pain and quickly retreating to his knees. The Chinese man's eyes were hard as steel as he increased the pain and snarled something in Chinese while he held Leroy's twisted hand. Leroy was in great pain and begged him to let go. Wu-Pen spoke a single word in Chinese, and the man let go of Leroy's hand. Leroy pulled his hand close to his body and held his wrist in pain.

Wu-Pen smiled ever so gently as Leroy yelled out threats and curses as they exited the jail.

Matt was surprised by the speed and accuracy the man displayed. He looked at Leroy as he got back up to his feet, slightly embarrassed to be forced to his knees by a Chinese man. "Are you alright?" he asked.

Leroy cursed him. "Why didn't you shoot him? He attacked me?"

"You deserved it." Matt followed them back out to the office. "Wu-Pen, who is your friend? Does he speak English?" Matt asked, stopping them before they walked out of his office.

Wu-Pen shook his head. "He does not. His name is Bing Jue. He is, how should I say, a temple guard. And this is Uang Yang." He motioned to the other man in black on Wu-Pen's other side.

"I've never seen anyone's hands move so fast. That was amazing."

Wu-Pen translated to Bing Jue. He smirked slightly and nodded and bowed slightly. Matt bowed his head in return.

The other three men had already torn down the canvas tarps from the window and measuring the width and height of the bay windows with a cloth measuring tape of some kind. One of the men was looking at the door jamb of the front door and making measurements as well.

"Have a good day, Marshal," Wu-Pen said and left the office.

Matt looked at Jed. "That man stopped Leroy's hand in mid-air and forced Leroy onto his knees with just his fingers. I never saw that man's hand move. It was just like, bam! And Leroy was on his knees, begging him to let go. It was incredible! I don't think I'd ever want to fight that man. I wouldn't see anything coming."

Jed raised his eyebrow. "Wish I would've seen it."

"Here's your night's pay like I said. Go home and get some rest. And Jed, have a great Thanksgiving."

"Am I working? I know someone's got to be here."

"Do you want to?"

"I'm bottom of the totem pole, Boss."

"I'll let you know. I'll leave that up to Truet. Go on home and get some sleep."

24

Elizabeth Smith found it difficult to get any sleep with all that was going through her mind. She had no idea what it felt like to learn that the man you knew as your father wasn't, and a man you met a few times was. She always knew the truth would have to come out someday, but she planned on being the one to tell Gabriel that Matt was his father, not some seventh-grade girl at school. On the one hand, Elizabeth was angry at Matt for telling the young lady to begin with. On the other hand, she was angry at herself for not telling Gabriel sooner. Gabriel had ridden away unexpectedly, and Tom was sure he had ridden to Branson to confront Matt. Elizabeth knew Gabriel was upset; it wasn't uncommon for him to go off by himself or for a ride to think things over. She hoped he'd return, but he hadn't, and she worried. They both knew Matt wouldn't leave him out in the cold, but still, she worried. What if's constantly ran through her mind. What if Matt rejected him? What if he had to sleep out in the cold rain? What if he wanted to live with Matt? What if he was so disgusted and angry at her that he never wanted to speak to her again? The what-if questions never ended of possibilities.

Her home was once a sanctuary of peace and loving warmness, but suddenly it felt cracked like a fragile egg waiting to be exposed for the whole community to see the core of their yolk and the secrets buried inside. By now, everyone in Willow Falls knew her darkest secret, and a childhood decision would forever tarnish her reputation. Her father, the honorable Reverend Abraham Ash, would be tarnished as well by her indiscretion coming back to haunt them from so long ago. Her whole family would be under scrutiny, and the judgments of the community and the weight of rumors could ruin far more than just their reputation. People were like sponges sometimes; they would soak up all the gossip they could hold before they spat it out further along with a bit of added filth along the way. Too often, there was no defense because one never knew what was being said about them nor by who. A so-called friend's gossip could ruin a marriage like a weathered fracture on a cliffside during a torrential rainstorm or tear a church apart like a lion savagely digging for the heart of it. Regardless of the consequences, it was her fault; she should have told Tom the truth a long time ago and raised Gabriel knowing who his birth father was. The truth would have been a bitter task to tell, but one that would have been better off now.

The evening had been a tough one as they had

to sit all the children down and explain that Tom was not Gabriel's father. For their twelve-year-old son, James, and nine-year-old Racheal, it was hard for them to understand that Gabriel didn't share the same father as them. six-year-old Alexis had no real comprehension of what they were saying. To her, Tom was their father, and that was the end of the story. It had been a humbling and humiliating experience for Elizabeth to tell her older children that she had gotten pregnant by another man aside from their father. They neglected to tell them the whole story of how it came about; the outcome was most relevant. Their adopted son, Evan, felt out of place and guilty for being part of the cause of the whole ordeal. He had apologized multiple times and needed to be reassured that neither Tom nor Elizabeth were angry at him. In truth, though, she was angry. She was angry at the situation and the fact that it should never have been brought up in the first place. She was angry at Tiffany Foster and Evan as well, even though she tried not to be. The fear of the unknown future and how it would affect their home hideously transformed into anger, and she couldn't help it no matter how many times she tried to deny it.

Wanting to speak with her parents and get their advice, she left Alexis in the care of her siblings and dressed warmly for the walk into town. She left her long blonde curly hair down freely and put on a knitted stocking cap. She grabbed her knitted scarf to wrap around her neck and coat. Stepping outside into the cold, cloudy day felt rather nice after being inside all day. The sky was gray and threatened to rain more than it had already done. The road to town was muddy and had its share of mud puddles along the way. Some she had to walk off the road to get around. Her heart was heavy, and her sadness was clear to see in her face.

"Lord," she prayed. "It was almost a year ago when I prayed on this same road that you would keep my family together over this very same issue. I never wanted to hurt Gabriel, but I'm afraid I did. Jesus, I don't know what to say, I made a mistake a long time ago and I'm still paying for it today, just in another way. You helped keep my family together last year, and I pray that you'll do it again now. Tom's hurting, I'm hurting, and so is Gabriel, I'm sure. I hope he won't treat Tom differently or become bitter towards me. I'm the one who should have told him. I just want my home to be the same. I pray that I'll still have a relationship with my son and that he won't hate me for lying to him all these years. And Lord, I know Tom feels the same. He loves Gabriel just as much as I do. Lord, I pray that nothing will come between the relationship we've always had with him. I love that young man so much." She wiped her eyes. "I know the town's going to think differently of us, maybe I'll even be shunned by some, and I don't really care. What I do care about is having my son back and that he'll talk to me because he wouldn't yesterday. And that breaks my heart." She wept.

She walked into her parents' home and began crying as soon as she wrapped her arms around her mother. After sitting down in the family room with her parents, she told them what had happened the day before. With tears of shame in her eyes, she said, "I'm afraid Tom and my relationship with Gabriel will be ruined. I'm afraid he'll never want to talk to us again; he climbed out his bedroom window yesterday and ran away towards Branson and hasn't come home yet."

Abraham Ash was an old man thin man with short gray hair and long gray sideburns. He shook his head slightly with his strict emotionless face. "He might be upset right now, but he'll come home. He might be Matt's seed, but he's yours too. You and Tom both have too strong of a relationship with Gabriel for him to have nothing to do with you. Matt didn't have that in his life, Gabriel does. Things might change a little, but it's out in the open now, and that might be a blessing too. It's my experience that, more often than not, the Lord uses moments we fear the most to teach us to trust him. Most of the time, what we fear turns out to be nothing at all." He smiled at his daughter slightly. "Elizabeth, I think you all will be just fine. I really do."

"You don't think Gabriel will run away like Matt did?"

The Reverend chuckled lightly. "No. Keep in mind Sweetheart that by Gabriel's age, Matt had lost his mother, been abandoned by his father, not to mention all the fighting and violence he witnessed between the two before she passed away. Matt's upbringing and Gabriel's upbringing are not comparable at all. Gabriel may be Matt's son, but Tom raised him, and there's a lot more of Tom's mannerisms in that boy than Matt's. Gabriel will come home and absorb this blow. He's a resilient kid. Where that comes from can be from either one of them or you; a combination of you three maybe. Sweetheart, he's going to be fine, and so are you."

Elizabeth sat on the davenport with her mother's arm around her. She wiped her eyes. "Thank you, Pa. What about the church, though?"

"What about it?" he asked.

"The gossip is going to get around, and I think some people might shun me for living a lie. It's going to ruin my reputation and maybe yours, too."

Reverend Ash grimaced light-heartedly and shook his head slightly. "Oh, Elizabeth, I used to get so uptight about that as you might remember. I think you learn as you get older that people's opinions aren't as important as it seems when you're young. I think of the story when Jesus came to the rescue of the adulteress. Here are all these men wanting to stone her to death for her sins, and Jesus makes an amazing statement. 'He that is without sin among you let him first cast a stone at her.' Grace trumps judgment, Elizabeth. Gabriel is an exceptional young man and not a mistake. God does not create mistakes, even if the way the baby was conceived was wrong. Everyone sees who he is now, and not how he was conceived. Not even the Lord remembers that sin, he tossed it as far as the east is from the west. So should you. Remember, Sweetheart, there is no condemnation for those in Christ. Don't beat yourself up for what happened years ago; just do what's right today, and you'll be fine. And if anyone wants to cast stones at your past, we'll have to remind them of that too."

Elizabeth sniffled. "I have to go to the Mercantile, and it's the day before Thanksgiving. People are going to be there, and if they've all heard about it already, I don't know what I should say if anything. I don't know if I should be humiliated, ashamed, or just what? All I know is I'm afraid of going there."

Reverend Ash frowned empathically. "You have nothing to be ashamed of. You made a bad decision once and have a wonderful son because of it. Listen to me, Elizabeth; if someone values you, this will pass without losing your value to them. And everyone here loves you and your family. Go do your shopping and just be you. Besides, it doesn't sound like Tiffany told anyone except Gabriel. So chances are you're worrying about something that won't happen."

Her mother, Darla Ash, spoke softly towards Elizabeth's ear, "And if they did hear, I bet that half of the women here in town will be jealous when they find out Matt's Gabriel's father."

"Ma!" Elizabeth shouted out with a surprised laugh.

Abraham looked at his bride. "What?" he asked with a slight grin.

Darla shrugged with an embarrassed smile. "Well, I bet!"

Abraham shook his head with a humored smile.

Elizabeth entered the Mercantile, and the owner, William McDermont, was pleased to see her as always. She did her shopping and carried an armload of goods up to the counter. She paid her bill and stopped on the Mercantile's porch when she saw Annie Lenning stop her team of horses pulling a covered wagon in front of the store. Annie and her children, Rory Jackson and Tiffany Foster, all climbed out of the wagon to enter the store.

"Elizabeth," Annie called out to make sure she wasn't walking away. Annie wanted to talk to her. "If you want to, you can put your box of goods in the back of the wagon, and we'll drive you back home."

"No, thank you," she said with a touch of irritation in her voice as she looked at Tiffany.

"Yeah, it'll be fine. Ira, take that box from her and put in the wagon," Annie ordered her Eight-year-old son.

"Okay, Ma," Ira said and reached out to take the wood box away from Elizabeth.

"Really, Annie, it's okay. I can carry it."

"Nonsense. By the way, Tiffany has something to say to you, don't you?" Annie questioned Tiffany with a harsh expression.

Tiffany's eyes filled with shameful tears. "I am sorry for telling Gabriel that Matt was his father, Misses Smith. Matt told me not to, and I did, anyway."

Elizabeth allowed Ira to take the box of goods as she focused on the pretty fourteen-year-old girl with long blonde curly hair. Elizabeth was upset.

"Gabriel ran away last night and hasn't come home yet. I am the one that should have told him that! I don't know if my son will ever talk to me again or if he's gone for good. Matt is his father, after all," she said to Annie. She looked back at Tiffany. "I am very upset, young lady!" She paused to take a breath and regain her composure. She spoke more gently, "But at the same time, I should have told him a long time ago. I'm sorry to be so rude, I'm just..." she began crying.

"Upset, I understand." Annie finished for her. She put her arms around her in a comforting hug. "Gabriel's smarter than Matt ever was. He'll be home in no time. I suppose you don't know where he went?"

"Matt's, we're pretty sure," she sniffled, regaining some control of herself.

"Well, I'll tell you what, if he went to Matt's he'll be coming home soon. Matt never has food and can't cook even if he did. Plus, his house stinks. Honestly, Gabriel will come home. Matt wouldn't let him get too far even if he did try to run away; he'd track him down and kick Gabriel's butt right back home to you. I know my brother, that's what he'd do. Besides, he's coming out here today, so if Gabriel's with him, he'll be home today sometime."

"Thank you, Annie. I'm glad to hear that. Forgive my tears; I'm just tired. I didn't sleep at all; I don't think."

Tiffany wiped the tears from her eyes. "Misses Smith, I am so sorry. I only thought it was right to do."

Rory Jackson spoke in a motherly tone, "As I told you, it just wasn't your place to do it, Tiffany."

"I know."

Annie added with a sharp look towards Tiffany, "And you know who's going to be the most disappointed in you, right?"

Tiffany lowered her head and nodded. "Matt."

Elizabeth could see the sincerity written all over Tiffany's face. "Young lady," she said, getting Tiffany's attention. "Thank you for apologizing. You are forgiven."

"Thank you."

"You're welcome. And I can see why Gabriel and Evan are fighting over you. You are a beautiful young lady."

"They are?" she asked quickly as her face lit up with interest. She blushed while Annie and Rory both laughed. "Thank you, I mean."

"Yeah, that's what you mean, alright!" Annie teased. She looked at Elizabeth. "It's beginning to rain, so if you hold on a moment, we'll take you home."

Elizabeth smiled. "I really would like that."

"I figured. Get on in and stay dry."

25

It was just before noon, and William Fasana shook his head as Matt told him about what had happened the night before. "The only night I take a lady to my sisters to visit and play a few games is the night I miss all the action. I can't tell you how disappointed I am. I would have loved to have gotten ahold of Joe Thorn this time." He had beaten Richie Thorn and broken his nose a few weeks before. "I suppose that's why I never court women; I miss all of the excitement when I do!"

"Are you courting Maggie?" Matt asked over the hammering and noise that was going in his office.

William grimaced. "No! She's my cousin. Heck, Matt, you ought to know that she's your sister!"

"She's not my sister, and she isn't your cousin. Come on, seriously, William, are you interested in her? I've not seen you so taken by a woman since... Well, I never have."

William shook his head defensively. "Rhoda told me she was my aunt. That makes Maggie, my cousin, and your sister."

"Fine. Are you interested in your cousin, Maggie?" Matt asked with a growing grin.

William sighed. "Yes and no. She makes me laugh. She's about as witty as I like a woman to be, and she's not a whore. She has every bit of moral fiber that Christine or any of your sister in laws, or my sisters have. We went over to Georgina and Ron's place and had a lot of fun. Georgina and Ron liked her a lot. Yeah, I'll tell you what, Matt, I'll be sad to see her go back home. She's a horrible dresser, probably a good butcher the way she talks about it, but she is a lot of fun to be with. I was more than less joking when I asked her to go for a buggy ride in the rain." He chuckled. "Who takes a buggy ride when it's raining in the dark, huh? But I'm glad we did. I enjoy her company."

"Are you going to follow her to Portland?"

"No. I'll wave goodbye and watch her, Aunt Rhoda and Uncle Floyd leave town. I'm not falling in love; I just enjoy her company. By the way, I invited her to join me at the Big Z for Thanksgiving. I thought you were going there today?"

"I am later. I have to take Gabriel back home. He's hanging out with his new Grandpa today. I'll be at the ranch tonight. But with the office being damaged, I thought I'd stay here for a while and oversee the repairs."

"How'd you find the Chinese men? They're doing a good job it looks like."

"A man named Wu-Pen brought them over. He was grateful for me arresting Leroy and his friends and wanted to help repair the damages. He's not charging me for the labor or supplies even though I told him those men will probably go free with the way folks look at the Chinese around here."

William leaned back in his chair. "Be careful with him. If he thinks you owe him anything, he'll expect repayment. And from what I understand, that can be dangerous."

"Who? Wu-Pen?"

"Yeah. It's my understanding he's like the...I don't know, leader of China town or something."

"Really? I was wondering who he was. He always has the same two men with him. I watched one of those guys grab Leroy's hand with his fingers and drop Leroy to his knees, begging that man to let him go. It happened so fast; it was pretty amazing. Wu-Pen said he that man was a temple guard."

"I don't know Wu-Pen. I just heard about him. The sheriff knows more about him than I do. Ask Tim, but those two men with him are his guards. Maybe Wu-Pen thinks he's important enough to be a temple."

Matt chuckled lightly. "I don't know. But that man who grabbed Leroy seemed like an able-bodied man. Like I told Jed, I wouldn't want to fight him. He's fast and obviously knows something more than I do."

"If you ever do have to fight him, shoot him. He's not faster than a bullet; I'll bet you."

"I don't think we'll have any issues."

"Probably not. They keep to themselves pretty well."

"Hello?" a man hollered over the noise of the Chinese men working. "Marshal Bannister, are you here?"

"Excuse me," Matt said to William and stepped out of his private office. "Hello," he said, walking forward to meet a finely dressed man in his late forties with a clean-shaven face and clean looking haircut, wearing a finely tailored black suit over a perfectly pressed white shirt.

The man held a leather bag by the strap in his left hand and held out his right hand to shake Matt's. "I've not met you yet, Marshal. My name is Delbert Van-Arden, Attorney at law. I know your brothers fairly well, though."

Matt shook his hand. "Oh. Nice to meet you. Well, I'm Matt Bannister. You'll have to excuse the mess and noise. I had some men break in here last night. So, how can I help you?"

"Well, that's why I'm here. I am representing the seven men that are currently in your jail. You see by the papers here that all seven men have made bail and are to be released immediately." He reached into the leather bag and pulled out a file, and set it on Phillip's desk at the front of the office and took out the papers to hand Matt.

"Wait, what are you talking about? Truet just took the arrest reports to the courthouse to file them and hasn't even returned from the courthouse yet, and you're telling me they made bail? How is that possible?"

"Marshal, with all due respect, you make the arrests, file the reports, and the District Attorney and the Judge take over from there. With Thanksgiving being tomorrow, all the new cases were expedited through the proper channels, and with my representation, all seven men have made bail. I don't need to name them all, do I? Here is the paperwork for your records. As you can see, there are court dates scheduled for preliminary hearings. There's nothing extraordinary about making bail and being released to enjoy Thanksgiving with their families."

Matt glared at him and took the paperwork. "This is a crock of crap! I barely finished writing those arrest reports an hour ago. Who's paying their bail?"

Delbert Van-Arden sighed tiredly. "That's confidential information. But I do represent all seven of these men and will be representing them through any trials if there should be one."

Matt was angered. "There will be one! You look for yourself at the damage the Thorn brothers, Alan Rosso and Brian Barns, did to my office. We can go look at what Leroy and his pals did to Ah See's back and take a look at the dead bodies of his friends too. There will be a trial!"

Delbert smiled. "As I said, you make the arrests and write reports. The District Attorney, myself and the judge and jury will decide everything else. Your job is done, aside from being a witness for the prosecution, of course." He nodded once approvingly. "Good job arresting them. Now, if you would, you have a court order signed and dated by Judge Jacoby to release each man listed here to his own recognizance as soon as they sign these release agreements. It is Thanksgiving, Marshal; a little grace is a good thing on the holidays, don't you think?"

Matt read the documents he was handed and shook his head in disgust. "No, I don't think it's a good thing."

"Are you refusing to release them?"

"No. But I think it's a load of crap!" he said bitterly and went back to his office to grab his keys. He unlocked the jail's steel door and went in to unlock the cell doors. "You're free. Get out of my jail and get out of my sight!"

Leroy laughed. "Told you fella's, we'd be out of here today!" he looked Matt in the eyes. "See you again, Marshal. Now I'm going to find my wife and force her to make Thanksgiving dinner. Joe, Richie, you guys want to help me find her?"

Joe glared at Matt. "Love to."

Oscar smiled as he left the cell. "Thank you, Marshal."

Matt followed them out of the jail as they all walked through the office and stopped to sign pieces of paper that Delbert had spread out across two desks for each man to sign his release agreement. They all introduced themselves and thanked their attorney.

Matt spoke, "Mister Van-Arden, if those men harm another person, it will be on your head."

Delbert Van-Arden chuckled. "Marshal, have you ever heard the story about the China man who wanted to fly?"

"No."

"He was found at the bottom of the quarry. It happened twice. Chinese smoke opium and think they can fly. It happens occasionally." He laughed lightly. "It's not a crime. Happy Thanksgiving," he said as he collected the signed papers and put them back in his file as the ink dried.

William leaned against Matt's private office with his arms crossed, watching. He hollered to Joe Thorn as the men laughed at Delbert's attempt at a defense or a joke; no one knew for sure which one it was. "Hey Joe, don't you love the look of your brother's new nose? I could give you one just like it." He said with a challenge in his tone.

Joe Thorn looked back at William. "You'll get yours eventually." He walked out of the office in a hurry and pushed one of the Chinese laborers down on his way.

William spoke after the attorney left the office, "Delbert is the Slater family's personal lawyer. He's the best in town."

Matt nodded with discouragement. "That figures."

One of the Chinese men came to Matt and made a motion with his hand of a key turning. He motioned towards the front door and made the motion for the key again.

"Oh, here," Matt said, handing his key ring over to the man to make sure the lock worked. The three men replaced both door jams and doors and put the old locks in the new doors. They sealed the bay windows by pulling the Mahogany trim off and securing the windows with boards. Verifying that the front door locked securely, the man moved on to Matt's private office door to check that lock and then returned the keyring to Matt.

"What time are you heading to the Big Z?" William asked.

Matt looked at a clock on the wall. "I don't know. Truet will be back pretty soon, and he can stay with these fella's while they finish up. We have no more prisoners, so Jed and Truet can take the next couple of days off. I don't know, pretty soon."

"I know your brothers have already left. I was just wondering if I rented a coach and hired a driver, we could all ride together. You wouldn't mind if I invited your pa and my aunt Rhoda, would you?"

Matt was hesitant. "Why don't you let me invite them. They might feel more comfortable if I invited them. My father was planning on renting a carriage from the stable for a few days anyway, so you can ride with them. Or you could rent Maggie a horse and go for a long ride with her, but not with me. I want the time to ride over there with Gabriel. We have a lot to talk about."

"Well, I knew they were renting one. I don't know if they have or not yet or if one's available right now. But I'll find out and rent one if they haven't. You don't think Aunt Mary or anyone's going to be upset to see Uncle Floyd again, do you?"

"Hope not. But they can always stay at Annie's, Steven's, or Adam's. That's what they were planning to do anyway."

26

Matt did a few errands and then walked into the Monarch Hotel and said hello to Pamela at the front desk as he walked by and went upstairs. He knocked on the door of his father's room.

"Come in," Rhoda's raspy voice hollered.

Matt opened the door and stepped inside. He was surprised to see Christine Knapp sitting in one of the side chairs talking with Rhoda and Maggie. There was no sign of Floyd or Gabriel. "Christine, what are in the world are you doing here?" he asked. "I thought you were going to be busy preparing for tomorrow?"

She stood up with a smile. "I am. But I wanted to wish you a happy Thanksgiving before you left town. I went by your office, and you had just left, so I came by here looking for you and Gabriel. These ladies were good enough to invite me in, and we've been talking about you."

"Are you hearing anything good?"

She smiled kindly. "Let me just say; I am so glad that you and Floyd got the opportunity to talk last night. According to these ladies, Floyd's a brand-new man this morning. I think that's awesome. How are you?" Her brown eyes looked at him affectionately.

Matt preferred not to talk about his emotions or other personal things in front of people he didn't know so well, but he smiled appreciatively. "I am good. It was a good talk we had."

"Did you clean the chimney of your past?"

"I'd say a lot of it was knocked down, yeah."

Rhoda grimaced. "Chimney? What's chimney cleaning have to do with the price of tea in China? We're in America."

Maggie gasped. "Ma, let them talk. It's their own private conversation."

Christine looked at Rhoda. "It's a metaphor we used in a conversation." She turned back to Matt. "I am thrilled. Now get that chimney swept clean so you can start a new flame without the trash of the past coming up again. I am so happy for you, my friend." She hugged him.

"Thank you. I'm working on it," he said in her ear. Her hair and perfume smelled wonderfully inviting. He didn't want to let her go.

"Good." She released her hug and sat back down. "It looks like you're getting your office all fixed up."

Matt nodded. "Yeah, it will be as good as new before too long."

Rhoda moved a blanket she had been covered in earlier off the cushion beside her. "Come sit down and talk to us, Matt. I have to be honest, when I first met you, I thought you were an ass. An unappreciative and arrogant ass! And you cut your father so deep that night at dinner that I swore I was going to come down to your office and give you my two cents worth of hell! I may not be that much of a threat to you, but I was going to give you a lashing anyway!" She paused to change her tone to one of soft sincerity, "Last night, when you brought Gabriel over here, it meant a lot to your father. You may not know this, but you boys and Annie are his pride and joy even though he hasn't seen you since you were small. If you think that doesn't break his heart day in and day out, you're wrong. He may have messed up royally years ago, but he's a good man. He has a very hard time trying to forgive himself for what he has done and what he has missed out on. Right now, he's out there showing Gabriel everything he knows about the history of this town. He left here last night a broken man, and I feared he went to the saloon, and he'd come stumbling in. But he came back alive and with more joy in his heart than I've seen in years. You were the missing piece to the puzzle. Thank you for meeting him at the river and taking the time to talk with him. Floyd has lost the burden he's been carrying since I met him. After all these years, it's wonderful to see him smile and hear his laugh with life in it again. So, thank you. You made your father a happy man."

Matt could feel a slight smile cross his lips. "It was good for both of us. I only wish I could have spoken to him sooner like that. I didn't meet him by the way; it was wholly coincidental. Christine has talked to me a lot about soot, chimneys, and forgiveness. I was thinking about that when I ran into him."

Maggie said, "It wasn't a coincidence, then."

"No, it wasn't," Christine agreed.

Matt continued, "There's a fire pit there, and I picked up a partly burned stick and looked at the ash on my hands and felt the cold remains of what once was a burning fire. I looked at the ash on my hands and realized I was hanging onto the hurt, confusion, pain, and anger of the past as well. I knew I had to make a choice; I could either choose to hold on to that cold, burnt stick of my past like a walking stick and limp through life, or I could throw it away and wash my hands so that the ash didn't spread to anyone around me. I tossed that stick into the river where I'll never see it again and, at the same time, decided to forgive my father. And it feels good."

Christine watched him with her elbows on her knees and her hand on her chin with a tight emotional smile and water in her eyes.

Rhoda smiled emotionally. "You'll never know how much that means to him, or me." She added more light-heartedly, "Because I was afraid, I'd be thrown in jail if I tried to slap some sense into you. And I know I'm not your real mother, but I'd sure like to be your stepmother if you'll let me. You can call me 'Mom' if you want."

Matt chuckled uneasily. "I'd be proud to have you as my stepmom. However, in all honesty, I'm not ready to call anyone Mom yet. That's just a name reserved for my mom. I hope you understand, but that doesn't take away from you being my stepmom."

Rhoda tilted her head with a caring frown. "I suppose it will do for now. But I do think of you as my son if that makes any difference."

"I appreciate that I do."

Maggie cleared her throat. "Matt, can I ask you something? Is William always such a sweet man to all the women around here?"

Matt lowered his brow weary of answering. "How do you mean?"

Rhoda clarified for her daughter, "Is he always like a desperate hound in heat knocking on every female dog owners' door?"

Maggie scoffed. "No, Ma. He's sweet."

Matt laughed slightly. "Usually, it's the female hounds in heat," he clarified slowly.

"I know that!" Rhoda snapped loudly. "You know what I mean. My daughter has had enough heartbreak without being chased around by a hound dog with no desire to settle down. A womanizer is all he is. I know them from a million miles around! He sees a new girl come into town, and he's all over her like a fly on…manure." She had paused to choose her words carefully.

Matt laughed. "Well, I'll put it to you this way, I've never seen William with a woman."

"He's a homosexual then!" Rhoda exclaimed. "I told you to stay away from him," she said to Maggie.

"No, he's not," Matt laughed. "He's just particu-

263

lar. And by that alone means he's not a womanizer. He's a big talker, but he's a pretty good man."

"I told you, Ma," Maggie said. She was sitting in a side chair with her feet tucked up under her. She was wearing what looked to be black Chinese cotton pants and a worn green sweater. She had pinned her long bangs back out of her face but her dark hair fell brushed, but plainly to her shoulders.

"I don't believe it," Rhoda said with a scowl.

Matt addressed Rhoda, "It's true. I've never seen him pay so much attention to a lady. I never have. He told me he enjoys Maggie's company. She makes him laugh."

Maggie smiled shyly. "I call him, Wooley William. I don't think he's ever been called that before. But with all that blonde hair, he looks like a sheep."

Matt chuckled. "No, I…I don't think he has been called that before."

"Well, don't tell him I told you that he'd be embarrassed."

Matt nodded with his eyebrows raised. "Yeah, probably."

Christine stood up. "I must be going back. It was wonderful talking to you, ladies. I hope someday we can meet again."

"I'll walk you back," Matt said quickly. He turned to Rhoda. "I came by to invite you all to come over to Willow Falls to the Big Z Ranch to have Thanksgiving with us."

Rhoda looked at him questionably. "Are you sure?"

"We'd love to have you. Your family, aren't you?"

She smiled. "I am. Floyd will be thrilled."

27

Matt walked Christine down the street slowly to enjoy a few moments longer together. He had told her what had happened the night before and about Wu-Pen and finally about the Slater's Attorney getting all of the employees of the Slater's Mining Company out of jail. He explained, "I think the paperwork was already in the works before I even finished writing my reports. Truet had no sooner handed them to the court clerk when Delbert Van-Arden was at my office. I'll tell you Christine; sometimes it feels like I'm wasting my time."

"That would be frustrating. We do know how corrupt this city is, right? So maybe it shouldn't be so surprising after all. Just keep doing what you're doing, and eventually, everyone will see what's happening around here. We have an election in a few months, and hopefully we can get some more honest people in office instead of the good ole boys."

"Maybe."

"Do you think that man found his wife and took

her back home?" she asked with concern about Leroy looking for Gertie.

Matt smirked. "No. Leroy won't find her. She wanted out of town as fast as she could go so, she paid Old Pete at the stables to drive her to Natoma to wait for the stage heading west there. She'll be safe enough. My concern is for the Barton's out there at Slater's Mile now. Miss Lucille Barton escorted Gertie to my office to report her husband. If there's any retaliation against them, then it's going to get ugly because they have little ones, and Lucille didn't do anything to Leroy or the others."

"Do you think there will be?"

Matt bit his lip, unsure of himself. "I don't know. I hope not. Anyway, are you getting nervous about your concert tomorrow night?"

She raised her eyebrows and widened her eyes nervously. "A little. It's the first time I'll be on the stage for the duration of the night with the band and my piano. We'll be practicing all night tonight while the girls decorate for tomorrow. It's going to be a long night and a very long day tomorrow. There's so much preparation in the kitchen to feed so many men as what we're expecting and then the dancing and singing, and then the cleaning up. Bella bought an extra fifty plates, bowls, glasses, and silverware for this event. They have invested so much money into tomorrow that I don't want to let them down by not singing well. If those men aren't dancing because they don't like the music... Uh! It'll be the last time I'll ever sing."

Matt smiled warmly. "I'm confident that you'll

do great. I've heard you sing, and it should be quite a treat, unless..." he paused.

"Unless what?" she asked with concern.

"Well, unless your voice is so mesmerizing that all the men are listening to you and not interested in dancing."

She laughed and slapped his arm playfully.

"That would be bad for business, but good for you," he added.

"Bella would never let me sing again if that happened. They invested a lot of money into tomorrow; the turkeys, hams, and all the dishes and desserts, plus the liquor and decorations. It's going to be quite a celebration. I wish you could be there."

"No, I wish you could be with me at the ranch. It's a smaller crowd."

She smiled. "I do want to meet your family sometime. Speaking of, are you taking Gabriel out to the ranch?"

"Hmm. I don't know. I'll leave that up to him and his parents. They might be downright furious that he came here. I'll find out later today when I take him home. It's going to be an awkward conversation that's for sure."

"You get along with them, though, right?"

He nodded. "I did. We'll see how they react."

"Aren't you glad I talked you into introducing Gabriel to your father? It seems like they are getting along well."

Matt smiled and cast an affectionate glance towards her. "Yes, I am. You were right."

"I know," she said with a wide grin. "I can not

believe how well they are getting along. They seem to be enjoying each other. And I'm very happy for you because now you have your son in your life and your father too. It's amazing because I can see the burden lifted from your eyes. When your father stepped into your office that day, it was like a darkness came over you, and now that's gone. Hence, the soot of your past."

"Is that how you came up with that analogy?"

"Yeah. I could see a visual change in your expression and especially in your eyes. They went from light and joyous to dark and cloudy in a second. It was like taking a clean hand and wiping the inside of a dirty chimney. Nasty, and you became nasty. But now they're brighter than ever before. And you know, I'm very proud of you, my friend."

"Well, thank you. And I mean, thank you for everything."

"You're welcome." She turned to look at him. "I'm glad you're my friend. I truly am. I pray for you all the time and will continue to."

"That's interesting to know because I pray for you all the time too."

"Do you want to come inside and have a piece of pie or cake?" She motioned towards the door of the dance hall.

"I wish I could, but I need to go find Gabriel and get him home. It's a long ride. You have yourself a wonderful Thanksgiving and sing with all your heart."

She looked at him fondly. "I will. Tell your aunt I look forward to meeting her some time, and may you all have a blessed Thanksgiving."

28

Matt walked back to Main Street and paused when he saw Floyd and Gabriel walking on the board-walk back towards the hotel. "Where have you two been all day?" he asked.

Floyd pointed towards the north end of town. "Oh, geez, all over. We walked down to the river where I met your mother and went inside the old mill to show him how the grinding wheels work. We had to look in the side yard to find the grinding wheels your grandfather made. We found two sets with Luke's initials marked on them. He always initialed everything he made."

"Really? I didn't know that."

"Oh, yeah. Look on the side of the wheel. He was very proud of the things he made even headstones, if you look hard enough, you'll find a small L.F. on the edge of it somewhere. I don't know if Joel and Luther continued that, but I'd guess so. Then we walked over to the quarry and showed him where that all began and what it is today. He's related to them, of course, and needed to know about his grandmother's family and not just the Bannister side. We've been all over town looking at things. It's been a good day, hasn't it?" he asked Gabriel.

Gabriel nodded. "It has. I didn't realize there's so much of our family history here. I would never have known."

"It sounds like there's a lot of things I don't know," Matt said. He looked at Floyd. "I asked Rhoda, but I wanted to invite you to join us out at the Big Z to share Thanksgiving with us."

"Oh…" Floyd hesitated. "Matt, you know, Charlie and I didn't get along so well the last time I was out there. I'm not sure he'd appreciate me being there at his table."

"That was a long time ago. He'll be fine with it, trust me. Come on out and enjoy yourself."

"What about your mother's brothers?"

"Luther will be there. Maybe, Uncle Solomon, I don't know. His wife keeps him over here, usually with her family. And Uncle Joel's over on the coast for the winter. But Uncle Luther will be fine too."

Floyd frowned curiously. "Did Joel move to the coast?"

"No. He's staying with Aunt Eleonore in Astoria. Uncle Joel retired from the quarry and had never seen the ocean before, so he went there for the summer. He must like it because he's staying through the winter to watch the storms. I guess they have a big house in Astoria and a smaller house overlooking the ocean or so I hear."

"Is she rich? The last I heard of her she was going

to college."

Matt shrugged. "She married Uncle Robert. I haven't seen them since I was fourteen, maybe. He's a mechanical engineer and builds ships over there. He does well, I think. They have two sons who were just toddlers when I saw them last, but I heard they're both in college now. They're the more educated half of the family," he emphasized.

"Well, I'll be. She was always a sweetheart. I'll discuss it over with Rhoda and see how she feels about it."

"She was excited when I asked her. I think you'll be coming out there. It would be nice to have all your kids around you at once for Thanksgiving, wouldn't it?"

Floyd bit his lip tightly. "It would be a dream come true."

"Then make it come true. We'd all love to have you there. I must get going before it gets dark, though. So, Gabriel, say goodbye to your Grandpa, and let's get going."

Three hours later, they had passed the old Bannister Ranch, and Matt told him about his time living there as a child. Gabriel was more than interested in hearing all that he could about his heritage and any stories he could hear. He asked Matt about a few gunfights and got more out of Matt than most people ever would. The one subject that neither of them had brought up was his parents and how he was feeling about learning he had a different father. Matt had caught on to many small, but obvious hints through their various conversations that Gabriel wanted to move to Branson. He asked, "Gabriel, what are your plans now?"

Gabriel hesitated before answering nervously, "I'm thinking I would like to move to Branson. Is it alright if I move in with you and Truet?"

Matt frowned. He had a strong feeling that the question would be coming up. "Don't you have school to finish?"

"Yes, but after I graduate. I could probably work for the granite company since they're family, right?"

Matt pulled the reigns and stopped his horse. "Listen to me," he said gently. "I already know your parents expect far more from you than that. You weren't raised to labor in a quarry; you were raised to go to college and become more professional than that. You would be far more valuable to the quarry and Uncle Luther if you went to college and became an engineer or a geologist, land surveyor, or something like that instead of a laborer. He can always find them. Listen, I don't want you going home today and having plans that changed overnight because of what you learned or the stories you heard. You had a path you were going to take; you need to keep following it. Go to college and come out more valuable for someone than two hands and muscles."

"Do you think Uncle Luther would hire me if I became a mechanical engineer or something?"

"My cousin Robert actually runs the quarry now. But you can talk to him or Uncle Luther and see what would benefit them the most. They might be needing an accountant or something like that. The point is, don't change your plans. Go to college and come out with something you'll enjoy doing."

"Okay. But I don't know what I want to do yet?"

Matt smiled, comfortingly. "You'll figure it out eventually. Gabriel, we've talked about a lot of things, but I need to know how your feeling about me being your father. How do you feel about that?"

Gabriel took a deep breath. "I feel okay. At first, I was mad, but since talking to you and meeting Grandpa, I am fine with it. I wouldn't ask to move in with you if I wasn't."

"What were you mad at?"

Gabriel frowned. "Honestly?"

"Very honestly. Now would be a good time to get it all out in the open, wouldn't it?"

"My parents. They lied to me for all these years. I thought Tom was my father, and he's not. But that's only part of it because then I found out that you got my mother pregnant and left town when you found out. I was mad at you too. I don't know how you can want to marry someone, and when they get pregnant, you run away? From what I was told last Christmas and now, it just doesn't make sense. But then Grandpa Bannister said you were not much older than I am and probably were too scared to face my Grandpa Ash. Is that true? That's why Grandpa Ash didn't like you, huh?"

Matt's frown was noticeable. "Yeah. It is true."

"I don't understand that. I wouldn't fornicate until I was married anyway, but if I did get someone I loved pregnant, I'd marry her. It would be my responsibility to do that and take care of them. I still don't know why you didn't tell me last Christmas. You do want me as your son, or do you not? Because now would be a good time to tell me. Right?"

Matt shook his head with a humored grin. Gabriel reminded him of Elizabeth when she would get upset with him. "Gabriel..." he paused. "We already talked about this. I knew you were my son as soon as I saw you. Aunt Mary, Lee, Annie, they all told me when I came home that... well, about you. I loved you right then and there when I saw you and knew you were my son. Your mother and I decided it was best that you not know until later on. I'm sorry if you think that was the wrong choice, but we thought it was best. You have a relationship with Tom, he's your father, and he loves you. I didn't want to interfere with that."

"But I'm not his," he said plainly.

Matt held up a finger to stop him from talking. He spoke sharply, "Yeah, you are! He raised you from the day you were born, and that's a love and commitment that you don't ever take for granted. I may be your father by blood, but he's your father by love. I do not ever want to hear of you telling him that he's not your father! That's a low blow and far under you. You need to respect him, his rules, and his authority. I am to you very much like my father is to me. I missed your life too. I look forward to getting to know you better, and you'll always be my son, but your devotion should belong to Tom. I would love for you to meet my side of the family and get to know them, but do not ever disrespect your mother or your father. They have done a wonderful job raising you and providing for you and love you so much. You refer to Tom as your father and never call him by his first name. I don't ever want to hear of that either! He's earned the title of Father, Dad, Pa, or whatever else people call their father's. I didn't have one, Gabriel. You know my father better than I do. Do you understand what I'm saying? You can call me Matt, and it won't hurt my feelings, but if you call your father, Tom, it will hurt my feelings. He deserves all of your respect, honor, and devotion, not me. I'll always be your father, and I won't deny it or you, but I do not want this whole issue of learning about me to interfere with your home or your relationship with your parents. You understand that, right?"

Gabriel nodded. "I've never called him anything except for my Pa."

"You just did a few moments ago. And that's what I'm ending right now. You refer to him as your Pa, Father or Dad, and don't ever refer to him as Tom to me or anyone else again. I don't want you feeling pressured to call him one thing and me another. I'm Matt; he's your father. He deserves that honor, and you nor I will take that from him. Agreed?"

Gabriel nodded. "Agreed."

"And don't let them hear you refer to me as your father, dad, or pa in front of him. He's too good of a man to be put through that. I mean, he stood up when I stepped out, right?"

"Yes, Sir."

"Then let's give him the respect and honor he

deserves. When you get home, hug him and your mother and tell them you love them. Because they are probably scared to death right now."

Gabriel stepped into the door of his house and closed it behind him as Matt waited outside. He could hear the excitement in the voices of Gabriel's siblings as they greeted him and heard Elizabeth and Tom as they came to him, wondering where he had been. They didn't sound angry but relieved to have him home. Matt waited by his horse, and soon, Tom and Elizabeth both came outside after being told he wanted to talk to them alone. They both had thrown on their warm coats and walked outside in untied boots. They had concern on their faces as they neared Matt's horse.

"Hello," he said awkwardly.

"Matt…" Tom greeted him, unsure of why they were called outside to talk. They feared the worst.

Matt spoke softly not to be overheard from inside the house. "Gabriel came to my house quite upset and asked if I was his father. He said you had already told him so…"

Elizabeth reacted sharply, "Actually, it was Tiffany. And she never should've known!" She lowered her voice, "Why would you tell her anyway?" Her eyes burned angrily into him.

"I had no idea she was coming here at the time. But that's neither here nor there now. What's done is done."

"Done?" she snapped with her angry brown eyes

burning into him. "This is just beginning! I have so much explaining to do to him, and I have no idea how it's going to affect our home. It's done for you! You can leave, but we're his family, and we'll be the ones who have to deal with him! I'm so pissed off at you, Matt!"

Matt raised his hand slowly to get a word in. "I understand, I do," he said. He explained softly, "Listen, I already talked to him about this. I told him yeah, I'm his father by blood, but Tom's the one who raised him, took care of him and loved him. You can talk to Gabriel about all that we talked about. I think you'll be pleasantly surprised; I do. I wanted to talk to both of you out here because he's under the impression that I knew you were pregnant when I left. He thinks I was afraid of your father and left you pregnant and alone to run off and womanize elsewhere."

"What?" Elizabeth asked with a foul grimace on her face. "Where would he hear something like that?"

"Hmm," Tom groaned. "From me."

Her angry brown eyes now focused on Tom. "Why? He's going to think we're always going to lie to him if we don't tell him the truth!" It looked like she was about to cry in her anger.

Matt spoke quickly. "Tom said it to protect you, Lizzy. I agreed to it as well and admitted that's exactly what happened. Keep it that way."

"No," she said with a grimace. "He deserves to know the truth! If there's anything I've learned through this, its to tell the truth and not hide it."

Matt shook his head. "Elizabeth, he has no idea what love is nor ever felt it. How could you expect him to understand what really happened? It's painful to all three of us right here, and I hate talking about what happened so long ago. But the fact is, Tom is right. Protect your honor Lizzy until he is old enough to understand. Right now, he won't, and he can't possibly until he gets his heart broke at least once in his lifetime. Let him get some life experience behind him, and maybe then he'll understand it. Until then, if ever, let it go just as it is." He pointed at Elizabeth with his finger. "Your honor is what Tom and I are both protecting! His view of me went down, and I'm okay with that. I am not okay with his respect for you or Tom going down. I'm not okay with that at all!" His eyes went to Tom. "I made it very clear that you are his father. And you've done a hell of a job. You both have. That's all I wanted to say."

"Thank you," Tom said softly.

Matt looked softly at Elizabeth and exhaled deeply. "Lizzy, he doesn't need to know the details, just the outcome. Okay? I love you all," he said and climbed up into the saddle.

"Matt," she said, "Thank you."

He smirked tightly and looked hesitant to speak. "Can I ask a favor of you two? My father is here and is coming to the Big Z for Thanksgiving. It's probably going to be the only time that we'll ever have to be all together with him for Thanksgiving. It would be nice if Gabriel could be there too. They spent a lot of time together. I know it's a lot to ask if you would, could you bring your whole family out there and enjoy the day with us? We're all family now."

"We'll see," Tom said, slightly stunned by the request.

"Your father is back?" Elizabeth asked, surprised.

Matt smiled. "Yeah, for a few days anyway. Ask Gabriel about him. I hope to see you tomorrow."

29

Matt rode out to the Big Z Ranch and led his horse into the large barn to unsaddle and put his horse away for the night. As he entered, he saw his uncle Luther Fasana sitting on a sawhorse set out for someone to use for a saddle. Standing in front of him was his daughter, Billy Jo Fasana. Luther was a big barrel-chested man with a long gray beard, square face, and short uncombed gray hair. He smiled when he saw Matt come into the barn. He stood and came forward.

"Good to see you, Matt."

"Good to see you too, uncle Luther." He was going to mention the damage to the granite wall in his office but decided to wait and see how the Chinese men had done with it. "Hello, Billy Jo."

"Hi, Matt," she sounded unpleased to see him. Billy Jo was Luther's youngest child at twenty-six years old. She was a thick boned young woman with broad shoulders and a short neck, like her father. She had a round face with a slim nose and large brown eyes. Her straight blonde hair was brushed straight down, barely touched her shoulders, and had a pink comb holding her bangs out of her face. Her countenance was melancholy.

Luther continued, "You know Joe Thorn, right?"

Matt chuckled bitterly while he unsaddled his horse. "Yeah, I sure do. He just got out of my jail this morning." He looked at Billy Jo, seriously. "You should drop him like a scorpion and stomp on his neck while you're at it! He's nothing but poison, Billy Jo."

Billy Jo and Joe Thorn had a long going off and on-again relationship that had produced two children and no wedding ring. It had caused bad blood between the Thorn family and the Fasana and Bannister families. Billy Jo scoffed and rolled her eyes irritated. "Can't I just come to the family function without being harassed about him? You and William both need to mind your own business and leave him and Ritchie alone! William had no right to beat Ritchie up the way he did! You do know Richie's nose will never be straight again, right?"

"He had no right?" Matt asked, skeptically. "Richie was robbing a woman of her money. It was Felisha; I was courting her at the time. I think he had every right! Secondly, your piece of crap man and his brother look for trouble, and here real soon, they're going to find it with me." Matt stepped closer to her and put a finger in her face. "And if he ever puts his hands on you again, he'll look a lot worse than Ritchie when I get a hold of him. I will not mind my own business; you're my cousin, and

I love you if you have a problem with that...tough! Drop him and find a real man, would you?"

Billy Jo was taken back by his heated words. Tears filled her eyes, and she refused to look at him. "I love him."

Matt grimaced with repulsion. "Why? He does nothing for you. Nothing! Think about that for a while, would you?" He looked at his Uncle Luther. "Sorry to interrupt. I'll see you two inside."

"No, I agree with you. She's living with him out at Slater's Mile," Luther explained with irritation in his voice.

"Are you kidding me, Billy Jo? Seriously?" he raised his voice. "You took your children out to that rat-infested cesspool? Well, I imagine that won't last long." He sighed to speak more even-tempered. "If it gets to the point where you're scared to leave again, let me know." He left the barn irritated over the same story it always seemed to be when it came to her. They would have a fight, and he'd beat her up, and she'd leave devastated and promising she was through with him, and a week to a month later, she was in love with him again. It was always the same story, and one Matt had a hard time digesting. It irritated him more every time he heard she went back to him.

Steven Bannister stood on Charlie and Mary Ziegler's porch with a wide grin on his face. He was about five feet ten inches tall, with a square youthful face with short dark brown hair and had the build of an ox. He was muscular and extremely powerful, but as gentle and playful as a puppy. He watched

Matt approaching the house and said, "Matt, you look madder than usual. You already have Tiffany scared to death to face you after telling Gabriel about you. You won't need to tear her up one side, and down the other, Annie already did. But she's scared to death to see you anyway."

"Oh, I was talking to Billy Jo in the barn. I swear she's about as bright as a sheep. What's happening with Tiffany?" he asked, ill-tempered.

Steven chuckled good-naturedly. "Now, Matt, sheep don't know the difference between a kind ram and mean one, as long as it's a ram. Negative attention is still attention, even if it butts them a lot more than it protects them. Sheep are stupid; they don't know."

Matt grimaced. "I don't know if that's true or not. You'd think even a sheep would learn to stay away from the abusive ram. Anyway, what were you saying about Tiffany?"

Steven pointed to Annie's house as he sipped his cup of coffee. "She's been hiding in her room all day, afraid of you getting here."

Matt sighed silently. "I suppose I better go talk to her then."

"Hey, before you go, I'm going to be going to Branson to pick up a load of iron next week, mind if I camp out at your place for the night?"

"You're more than welcome. I only have a davenport for you, though."

Steven stepped off the porch and came closer to Matt to speak quieter although they were alone, "That's fine. Do you think you can have your friend

I keep hearing about help me pick out a new dress for Nora? I want to get her something nice, and I know nothing about dresses."

Matt smiled and whispered, "I could probably arrange that. She'll need measurements."

"Like with a yardstick or what?"

Matt chuckled for the first time. "I'll make it easy for you, tell Aunt Mary what you want to do, and she'll somehow get the measurements for you."

"Great idea. I'll do that."

"Is there a special reason for the dress?"

Steven shook his head. "No. I was watching her one day and thought, she'd look nice in a new dress. I wanted to do something nice for her."

Matt grinned. "You made her mad, didn't you?"

Steven frowned. "No. I just thought it would be nice. I've saved up enough money to get her something nice, and what she needs is a nice dress."

Matt nodded, impressed by his sincerity. "Yeah, I'm sure Christine will be thrilled to help you for a reason like that."

The door opened, and Albert Bannister stepped out onto the porch carrying a bowl of stew. He closed the door behind him. "Matt, I came by your office to pick up my dog, but no one was there. And I didn't have time to catch up with you before we came out here. I appreciate you keeping my dog there until I find it a home."

"I gave your dog to Chusi two days ago, Albert."

"You did?"

Matt widened his eyes with emphasis. "Yeah, I did. That thing never shut up, to begin with, and it crapped all over my jail and office. I gave it to Chusi for the cost of cleaning it all up."

"Oh," Albert said with a hint of disappointment. "Can he feed it? He seems unable to take care of himself half of the time."

"He'll take better care of that dog than he will himself, I'm pretty sure. He was excited about it. Plus, he cleaned up your dog's crap. I think it had dysentery!"

Steven laughed at the expression of disgust on Matt's face as he said it.

"I'm sorry. I did come by, though."

"I'm sure Chusi would sell it back to you if you want it bad enough."

Albert raised his eyebrows. "Melissa would grab a strap and whip my hide if I spent another cent on that dog."

"What kind of dog was it?" Steven asked.

"I'm going to go see Tiffany. I'll see you, boys, soon," Matt said, leaving his two brothers to discuss the dog.

He went to Annie's house and stepped inside. He saw Rory Jackson in the kitchen making a large pot of something and could smell the fresh bread baking in the oven. "Hi, Rory. Where's everyone at, next door?"

"Matt!" she said with a smile and came forward to hug him. "I'm so glad to see you. Yeah, Annie is over there with the family. I'm just finishing up with some things and then will bake another two loaves of bread." She was a very attractive black lady with long black hair tied back in a loose ponytail that reached the mid-back of her light blue dress. Her face was thin and oval-shaped with large brown eyes and a beautiful smile.

"It smells great. How are you?"

"I'm well. And I hear you're doing quite well yourself."

"Not too bad. The next time you come to Branson, you and Annie will have have to come and stay a few days."

"You know I don't go to Branson too often. But next time she goes, I will."

"Good. I came over here looking for Tiffany. Steven said she was hiding over here."

Rory bit her lip and raised her eyebrows while nodding her head. "She's upstairs. She knows your coming today and is afraid to see you. Go gentle on her. She feels horrible about telling Gabriel about you."

"That's what I hear." He went upstairs and knocked on her bedroom door before opening it. "Tiffany, how are you?" he asked as he entered. She was sitting nervously on her bed.

"Okay," she answered in a shaking voice. She was afraid of being in trouble with the one man she respected the most.

He sat down beside her. He put an arm around her affectionately. Tears were already streaming slowly down her cheek. "I'm not mad at you."

"You should be, I broke my promise to you," her voice revealed her shame.

"Well, maybe I'm just the kind of guy who thinks it might've been a mistake on your part, and you learned not to break a promise again. What do you think?"

She nodded slowly.

"I'm assuming that's a yes?"

She nodded again, keeping her eyes downward, refusing to look at Matt.

"I probably don't need to tell you how bad that could've been. Sometimes you have to consider how many others could be hurt by a confidential bit of information, especially in my line of work. Trust is everything when it comes to me, okay? You don't want me not to trust you. So, from here on out, no more broken promises, lies, or deceptions, right?"

She looked at him with a hurt expression. "I never lied to you."

"I know. I don't ever want you to."

"I'm sorry, Matt. I didn't want you to be disappointed in me." A tear slipped out her eye.

"I'll let it slide this time. Come on, get your eyes dried up, and let's go have some fun, huh?"

"Is Gabriel still missing?"

"No. He's at home and doing just fine."

"Did you talk to him?"

"Yes. He's been at my place, so we talked a lot."

"Is he mad at me?"

"No. No one is mad at you."

"So, you're not mad at me?" she asked, sincerely.

"No, I'm not."

"Promise?"

He smiled. "I promise."

She hugged him tightly.

When she let him go, he asked, "Is everything going okay for you out here? Are you feeling at home yet?"

She smiled. "Yes, it's going well. Thank you for bringing me here. I love your family."

He held up a finger to stop her. "It's our family. Just like you are my family now. Speaking of which, do you think we should go see our family and maybe steal a piece of pie or something?"

She laughed as she wiped her face dry. "Yeah, let's go."

30

"Prairieville was a bit scary because we were out-numbered. I didn't want to take William originally because, well, he's William. But I wouldn't have survived without him, so I'm glad he went," Matt answered a question that Steven had asked him. It was late in the evening, and all of the children had been taken over to Annie's to go to sleep. Annie and all the other women went over to her house to have an evening of woman's talk without the men around. As usual, any wine that was brought over by them was taken over there for the night.

The Ziegler family room was full of all five of the Bannister brothers, Charlie and Mary Fasana, Luther Fasana, Darius Jackson, and Nathan Pearce, all sitting down in a circle of chairs and furniture. Mary usually always preferred to stay and visit with her brothers, nephews and other men that she rarily got to see, rather than go next door to drink with the ladies.

Lee spoke sincerely, "When we were in the cavalry, William was a big part of what made our unit not just fearsome but unique." He smirked. "He could find a way to get in trouble out in the middle of nowhere. Uncle James used to scream at him a lot, but when it came right down to it, he was a warrior and a darn good one. If William had stayed in the military, he had the potential to be a General by now, but he'd still be a private because he'd get bored and liked to play too much."

Adam snickered quietly. "Remember when he put a dead scorpion in Uncle James' pocket?"

"Remember his rattlesnake?" Lee asked and joined with Adam in their laughter at long-ago memories. Lee explained to the others, "Uncle Joel or Luther, someone, had taught him how he could grab a snake by the tail and whip it to break its neck to kill it. Anyway, one day out on patrol, we were camped by a stream way down by the California border, and William ran across a rattlesnake. He broke its neck and didn't tell anyone. That night he coiled it up in cousin Seth's bedroll. They shared a tent, and everything was dead quiet when Seth screamed like a girl." He laughed. "Seth screamed and began shooting this dead snake. We thought we were being attacked, so everyone was scrambling to grab boots and guns and ran out of our tents, not knowing what was going on! William had volunteered to take first watch, and when we came running out of our tents ready to fight, we found William laughing hysterically. Seth had a temper, you know, and could be heard from miles around;

I'm sure when he yelled, 'William!' He came running out of that tent and jumped on William and began hitting him. And William just laughed the whole time. Oh my gosh," he laughed and wiped his eyes.

"How'd James like that?" Charlie asked of his older brother, who was their Colonial in charge of training and leading the Oregon 7th Cavalry Company E during the Snake War in the western states.

"Oh, he didn't!" Lee laughed. "But that's the kind of crap William would do out on patrol. If he weren't Uncle James' nephew, he would have been court-martialed for sure if not shot or hung out there in the brush and his death recorded as killed in action. He was always looking for a laugh. But," he added seriously, "When it came to fighting, he was dependable and efficient. That's why I have him working for me in the hotel."

Luther smiled as he shook his head. "I taught him that out at the quarry when he was a kid. He caught a garter snake and showed him how to break a snake's neck. I never thought he'd try it on a rattler, though."

Adam spoke, "Oh yeah. That wasn't the only time he did that. William had a thousand ideas of how to be a menace. That's why I don't feel bad about teasing him so bad. It's just paying him back for having to camp with him every day for two years of my life."

Albert looked over at Matt and asked, "Is he still courting Dad's wife's daughter?"

Adam's eyebrows lowered curiously. "Who?"

Matt nodded. "It's okay to say his stepdaughter or your stepsister. But yeah. He's coming out with them tomorrow."

"He is? Is he serious about her?" Albert asked skeptically.

"Who are you talking about?" Adam asked. He had never met Rhoda or Maggie.

"Dad's stepdaughter, Maggie. William's been spending a lot of time with her." Matt explained. "She told me just today she calls him Wooley William, now." He finished with raised eyebrows and a slow continuous nod to emphasize it.

Adam laughed with the others.

Steven laughed. "Well, Wooley William is a cute name. Most serious relationships have nicknames. Nora calls me Honorable Sir. And I call her Stove's Calling. So, in the morning, she'll ask, 'how are you Honorable, Sir? And I'll say, 'I'm fine, Stove's Calling.' And she'll know to go cook some breakfast. The same thing for dinner."

Charlie Ziegler scoffed with a smile. "Bull."

Darius Jackson asked with a smile. "I suppose you only call her that when you're hungry?"

Steven nodded. "Hmm, mm."

Mary padded Matt on the arm to get his attention. "The boys were telling me that you were not very friendly with your father at dinner the other night. How are you going to feel about him being here tomorrow?"

"I am fine with it, Aunt Mary. We had a pretty good conversation last night, and yeah, I feel fine about it. You?"

She shrugged. "Everyone changes as they get older, and I'm waiting to see. I'm sure it will be fine. He wasn't my favorite man, but as I said, people can change. I think if God can forgive us for our sins and what we've done to others and remember them no more, then maybe it would be wrong for us to hold those same sins against them, even if they hurt us or someone we loved. I think forgiving someone can be hard to do, but in the end, it is the only way to heal and move on from them. That doesn't mean I have to be his friend or trust him again, but I have forgiven him for what he did to my sister and you kids. I don't feel like I have a right to judge a man thirty years after the fact without giving him a chance to redeem himself, do you?"

Matt laughed slightly. "Three days ago, I would have disagreed wholeheartedly. But Christine… Well, she pointed out how my unforgiveness of him had brought out the ugliness in me and how that might transfer onto others. I didn't want to talk to him, but we did, and I'm thankful for it."

Mary had a warm smile on her aging face. "I like that young lady already."

"Me too."

"Are you courting her yet?"

Matt shook his head. "No. We're just friends and taking our time. There's no hurry."

"I suppose not. She sounds like a very wise young lady."

Matt took a deep breath and said thoughtfully. "She's been a blessing. She really has."

31

Floyd Bannister was quite nervous when he arrived at the Big Z Ranch with Rhoda, Maggie, and William. He stepped out of the coach and sighed nervously, but grateful that William was there with him.

"Come on, Uncle Floyd, let's go grab some of Aunt Mary's good food," William said as he helped Maggie out of the coach.

"I'm coming," he said, looking around the ranch. It was the first time he'd been on the Big Z in many years, even though he had come to Branson a few times to see his grown children. Annie, Steven, and Adam had traveled to Branson to see him the few times he had come east from Portland.

Rhoda sniffed the air, which held the sweet scent of a barnyard from the pig pens, and stalls of calves and horses in the barn not too far away. "I don't know why anyone would want to live way out in the middle of nowhere like this. I suppose that's why I like Portland and my apartment. At least I can down and buy a turkey without plucking it myself. If there's any one thing, I can't stand it's the smell of wet feathers."

"Stop your belly-aching Aunt Rhoda. Come on; I'll introduce you," William replied. He had the great pleasure of irritating her all the way from Branson. She had not held back on her snide remarks and letting him know how she felt about any subject he brought up. Even her insults slid off him like rain on a turtle's shell.

The front door opened, as Charlie and Mary Ziegler came outside with Luther Fasana and others behind them. Floyd watched them walk closer with an anxiety building as he wondered if he would be asked to leave the ranch. After all, it wasn't Charlie nor Mary, who had invited him and his new family to share their Thanksgiving feast. "Hello, Mary," he said softly with a nervous smile.

Mary smiled kindly. "Floyd, it's so good to see you." Her eyes misted over slightly.

Floyd could feel a sense of relief come over him when he saw the welcoming smile of his old sister-in-law. "Mary, you're still beautiful even after all these years," he said as she hugged him quickly. He looked at the two men. "Charlie, Luther, it's good to see you both again," he said a bit uneasily.

Charlie smiled slightly as he shook Floyd's hand. "It's been a long time. Floyd. Well, welcome back to the Big Z."

"Thank you." He reached out to shake Luther's hand. It was swallowed up in the firm grasp of the bigger man's rough hand.

"Floyd, good to see you."

Mary tilted her head slightly to look at the ladies that stood just behind Floyd. "Well, are you going to introduce us to your family."

"Yeah. This is my wife, Rhoda, and our daughter, Maggie. Maggie is my step-daughter, but there's no step in our family, she's my daughter. This is Ruth's sister Mary. Mary's husband Charlie, and Ruth's brother Luther. My former in-laws."

Mary spoke in a welcoming manner, "We're getting too old for that former stuff. We call ourselves family around here. Please, come inside and make yourselves at home. We have a lot of introducing to do." She looked at Maggie pointedly. "I can see why William likes you. You're a very pretty girl."

William's eyes widened uncomfortably and shot a hard glance towards Matt, who was standing back with a growing smirk on his face. He realized all of the Bannister brothers were watching him with the same half-smile. William closed his eyes and shook his head slightly, knowing what was coming ahead.

Maggie blushed. "Thank you. But I think he likes me just to harass my mother."

Mary laughed lightly. "I doubt that. Come on inside so we can visit."

As Mary led the two ladies toward the house, William was stopped by Albert as he tried to walk past him. The other brothers suddenly circled him. Albert asked, "What are you trying to court our sister for? Don't you know that's not normal?" He pushed William into Lee, who pushed him into Steven. Steven quickly pushed him forward to

Adam. Adam grabbed him by his coat collar and pulled him close to him with a serious expression on his face. Adam spoke in a high pitched toddler's voice, "Wittle Wooley William wuvs wittle waggie! Huh, Wittle Wooley William?" All of the brothers began laughing loudly.

"Matt! I swear!" William yelled and turned around, looking at Matt, who was laughing.

Maggie tried to turn around and look back curiously as they reached the porch, but Mary guided her forward with her arm. "Trust me, he's fine. Those Bannister boys are just doing what they always do. Surround him like a pack of wolves and tear into him a bit. It's all in good fun, though. I guess you could say if they didn't harass you a little bit, then they don't like you. Isn't that right, Nathan?" she asked as they passed by him on the porch.

Nathan Pearce laughed quietly as he nodded. "Yeah, that's about right."

Floyd, Rhoda, and Maggie were welcomed inside and introduced to a long list of family and grandchildren. Floyd had met them all before, but for Rhoda and Maggie, it was an endless list of names to remember of who was related and who was friends. The long table was set, and quite a few dishes were set out to start dinner, but it was quickly known that the turkey wasn't quite done. Conversations were happening all around them, and there were too many questions being asked at once to answer. Floyd and Rhoda might've feared feeling out of place and unwelcome, but they were quickly welcomed and treated like family. After an hour or so, they felt more settled in, and Floyd was able to have quieter conversations and tell them about what a wonderful time he had getting to know Gabriel.

As the conversation went to Gabriel, William Fasana, who was sitting on the floor beside Maggie, nudged her shoulder and said quietly, "Let's go for a walk." They stood up.

"Where are you going?" Rhoda asked pointedly.

William answered, "Aunt Rhoda, it's hot in here. We're going out to cool down a bit."

Annie Lenning laughed. "Sure, you are."

"Wittle Wooley Willy Wot. Weal Wot!" Adam said in a high pitched voice again.

"Wat?" Albert asked in the same high pitched voice.

"Wittle Wooley Willy Wot! Weally Wot!"

"Wooley Willy weaving wif wittle Waggie," Lee added with a laugh.

"We'll be back," William laughed lightly with an embarrassed smile. "I apologize for my family, they're a bunch of idiots," he said to Maggie as he paused to step over Adam Bannister's legs to reach the door. Adam was sitting on the floor, smiling up at him. They stepped over Adam and went outside and closing the door behind him.

"Wittle Wooley Willy will we wight wack!" Adam said, nodding his head reassuringly.

"Willy wooks wad. Weally weally wad," Annie chimed in as she looked out the window.

Adam sat up to look out the window and then

looked at the clock before sitting back beside his wife, Hazel.

"Be nice," Hazel said quietly.

"Oh, I am."

Mary asked Matt, "Is Gabriel coming here?"

Matt shrugged. "I invited them. I don't know if they are or not."

Floyd spoke, "Well, I'll be here for a day or two and will go see him before I leave for sure if he doesn't."

Mary said, "I have been waiting and praying since he was a baby that he would know who his family is. I can not wait to hug that boy and not have to hide the fact that I love him."

Charlie scoffed. "Sweetheart, I don't think you've ever hidden that. He just didn't understand it is all."

"Well, now, he will."

Adam began to stand up, and Mary asked, "Where are you going?"

"Outside."

Mary frowned skeptically. "I know that look, Adam. Will you leave William alone, please? He finally found a lady who likes him. Don't you go looking to ruin it for him."

Annie laughed.

Adam chuckled. "I'm just going to help him out."

"No, you're not. Sit back down."

He sat back down by Hazel with a disappointed expression on his face. He looked at his friend Nathan Pearce and said, "I really wanted to go help him out. He needs it, you know." He said towards his Aunt Mary, "He's probably out there right now stroking his revolver telling that young lady she's almost as pretty as his gun. I'm telling you, if you want him married off, you should send the boys and me out there."

Nathan nodded in agreement. "I think he's right. William's not prepared for a moment of romance."

Mary looked at Adam and said, "Wittle Wooley Willy's womance is none of your concern. You've embarrassed him enough today."

Adam and the other's laughed at her feeble attempt to copy Adam. "Fine. We'll let him be...for now"

Gabriel Smith felt odd, leaving his family's Thanksgiving meal at his grandparent's house. There was no doubt it had hurt his parents and grandparents to see him leave their dinner to ride out to the Big Z to share Thanksgiving with Matt's family. He felt a bit awkward himself doing so, but if he ever wanted to meet the other side of his family, he needed to do so. He had enjoyed the time spent with his grandfather, and he also enjoyed working at the Big Z Ranch and everyone on it. He knew he shouldn't feel as awkward as he did, but this time he was going out there as a family member and not an employee. He felt bad, though; he had seen the sadness in his father's eyes, and it broke his heart. He may have been a Bannister by blood, but his love and loyalty were made clear to him when he left his family's Thanksgiving dinner. The father he had always known would always be his father. He loved him too much to be anything other than his father.

He rode to the front of Charlie and Mary's house and was greeted with the door opening and Mary Fasana coming outside with a large smile along with Annie Lenning, Mellissa and Regina Bannister, and a few others. He stepped towards the stairs and was quickly engulfed in Mary's arms.

"Gabriel Smith," she said with her hands on his shoulders, looking at him with tears in her eyes. "I have been waiting for sixteen years for this moment to say; I love you. Welcome to the family, Gabriel."

"Let me in there," Annie said, forcing her way towards Gabriel. She grabbed a fistful of his hair and turned his head to look at her. There was a crinkle in her brow as she scowled. "Now that you're related, I don't have to be nice to you." Her eyebrows raised thoughtfully. "I don't even have to pay you. You've had enough school'n I want you here early tomorrow morning to start planting posts to fence off my garden." She laughed and tousled his hair. "Welcome home, nephew."

For the first time in nearly thirty years, Floyd was surrounded by his six children and grandchildren. He was no longer afraid to face his sons or his old brother and sister-in-laws. He was made welcome, and all of the years of wishing he could be where he was had been a dream he never thought would come true. The turkey was on the table and everyone was settling down to eat. He stood with a glass of buttermilk and watched his daughter, Annie laughing at one of Lee's daughter's, Matt was listening to Luther tell him a story about one thing or another. William Fasana sat next to Maggie with a quiet spirit within him, and she seemed quite content to sit beside him. Mary, who resembled Ruth quite a bit, was showing Gabriel and a few other of his grandchildren a tintype of her father and mother. Albert, always the family man, sat with his wife, Melissa, and their children waiting for the Thanksgiving prayer. Lee, Steven, and Adam spoke in a close huddle with Darius Jackson and Nathan Pearce. Charlie thumb wrestled with the older grandsons, and Regina, Rory, Tiffany, and Rhoda all stood around Nathan Pearce's wife Sarah talking about the baby inside of her. She wasn't showing much, but the topic of a baby was always big news. Rhoda looked up at Floyd and smiled contently.

"Thank you, Jesus," Floyd said to himself as he paused to look around at each face of his family. He thought of Ruth and how she would be glowing with pride if she could see her sons and daughter now. He knew she would love to hold and cuddle every one of their grandchildren. It never took more than family to make Ruth happy. He knew she would be in paradise if she could be there with all the love and family that surrounded him that day. He wished he could hold onto the moment forever. If there was one thing he had learned in his lifetime of errors, it was he never should have let his family go. There was nothing that mattered more than his family; unfortunately, sometimes it takes a lifetime to figure that out.

About the Author

Ken Pratt and his wife, Cathy, have been married for 22 years and are blessed with five children and six grandchildren. They live on the Oregon Coast where they are raising the youngest of their children. Ken Pratt grew up in the small farming community of Dayton, Oregon.

Ken worked to make a living, but his passion has always been writing. Having a busy family, the only "free" time he had to write was late at night getting no more than five hours of sleep a night. He has penned several novels that are being published along with several children stories as well.

READ MORE ABOUT KEN PRATT AT http:// christiankindlenews.com